THE HONEYMOON

GEMMA ROGERS

Boldwood

First published in Great Britain in 2024 by Boldwood Books Ltd.

Copyright © Gemma Rogers, 2024

Cover Images: iStock

A CIP catalogue record for this book is available from the British Library.

Paperback ISBN 978-1-80549-501-7

Large Print ISBN 978-1-80549-502-4

Hardback ISBN 978-1-80549-500-0

Ebook ISBN 978-1-80549-503-1

Kindle ISBN 978-1-80549-504-8

Audio CD ISBN 978-1-80549-495-9

MP3 CD ISBN 978-1-80549-496-6

Digital audio download ISBN 978-1-80549-498-0

This book is printed on certified sustainable paper. Boldwood Books is dedicated to putting sustainability at the heart of our business. For more information please visit https://www.boldwoodbooks.com/about-us/sustainability/

Boldwood Books Ltd, 23 Bowerdean Street, London, SW6 3TN

www.boldwoodbooks.com

For Boycie

1

The last thing I expected to find when I rounded the corner of the beautiful white wooden summer house, which glowed ethereal in the setting sun, was my husband of seven hours and twenty-four minutes, Ryan Carbon, entwined in the arms of another woman.

I'd wanted a break from the loud music, to cool down from the sticky evening and get some fresh air. Bobby, Ryan's best man, who'd been throwing shapes with my sister, Ruby, on the crowded dance floor, had witnessed him stagger out into the grounds of the impressive sixteenth-century Elizabethan manor house. I'd barely seen my husband since our first dance, there'd been too many people queuing up to offer their congratulations, telling me how stunning I looked in my bridal gown and how happy they were for us both. The afternoon had morphed into the evening at such speed my head spun but not as much as it was spinning now at the sight before me.

I glimpsed the two of them through the wall of pretty pink roses climbing the trellises partially concealing their indiscretion, recoiling as I recognised who was entangled with my husband. Ryan's hand glided over Bobby's wife's olive skin, straying up her thigh and under her black dress, the other clasped around her birdlike neck. Short moans of pleasure escaped Liza's full lips and her head lolled back, eyelids fluttering.

I froze on the manicured lawn, not wanting to be seen. The two of them blissfully unaware they had a spectator. Sounds of our wedding reception blared out from the house, guests dancing to 'Come on Eileen', stamping their feet on the dance floor with no idea the groom was already breaking his vows.

A painful eruption began in my chest, a volcano getting ready to blow, hitting me with a grief so profound, it swallowed me whole. My lips parted to speak, but nothing came out. I had no words nor voice for the sight before me.

Ryan nuzzled Liza's neck and I heard the chink of his belt buckle, followed by a giggle. Vomit forced its way up my throat and I gagged, backing away on the grass before taking off my heels and turning to flee. Blinking rapidly, I stumbled back towards the house, trying to exorcise the scene I'd witnessed from my eyes. A few hours ago, we'd promised to love and cherish one another, but after the photos were over, he'd hit the whisky hard. As the whirlwind of greeting guests for the evening reception got underway, being congratulated and making small talk, I'd seen my husband fleetingly as he worked the room, a tumbler in hand. He'd been bought drink after drink and I knew he might not even find his way to the honeymoon suite later. It didn't matter, it was our wedding day, a celebration. Everyone was entitled to let their hair down.

When the disco had started, he'd swung me around the floor for our first dance, slurring promises of a happy ever after to our chosen song, 'Stay With Me' by Sam Smith. It was from the year we'd met – 2014. Ten years together, teenage sweethearts sticking by each other's sides through thick and thin, and he'd just dropped a bomb on it all. Liza was my friend; she and Bobby were our friends and the betrayal sliced into my heart like a knife through butter.

'Kelly, you okay? Did you go for a walk?' My big sister, Ruby, emerged from the door of the function room, the Tythe Barn, her gaze travelling down to the satin heels clutched in my hand. Her chirpy voice broke through my despair, but I only had one thought, I couldn't let her go outside.

'I did, I wanted some fresh air, but now I need the toilet.' I blocked her exit onto the patio. 'I'm just going to go up to the suite.' I smiled weakly, pretending everything was fine despite the tornado in my chest.

Ruby looked stunning in her apple-green bridesmaid dress, a satin gown she'd picked herself when I told her to choose whatever she wanted. The shade was perfect for our pale skin, which barely tanned no matter how long either of us sat in the sun. We had the same small nose which turned up slightly at the end and our eyes were both hazel, although mine sat closer together. However, that was where the similarities ended, she was taller than me and broader, her long hair was highlighted blonde, whereas mine was still a sandy brown which fell in waves to my shoulders.

'Do you need any help with your dress?' she asked, fanning herself from the heat, her maid-of-honour duties taken with the utmost seriousness.

'No, no, I'm fine. Go and relax, have a drink, grab something from the buffet before they take it away.'

'Are you sure you're okay?' Ruby narrowed her eyes, nose twitching like the bloodhound she was.

'I'm tired, it's been a long day.' I clasped her hand in mine, swallowing hard. 'A long, perfect day. I'm just aware we have a flight to catch at six tomorrow morning and Ryan is going to be green around the gills, for sure.' His name stuck in my throat like a bitter pill.

'Don't worry, I'll round him up,' Ruby volunteered, already turning back towards the party, her floor-length gown swishing behind her.

I caught her arm. 'No, don't, Rubes, leave him. His mum is on the case,' I lied. 'Is Dad okay?' I asked, changing the subject despite wanting nothing more than to run away from the horror behind me. I didn't want to be standing here when the two of them emerged from the summer house.

'He's fine, starting to drift a bit now. Mum's called the carers to come and pick him up. He was good for a while though, right, got through the service, and the speeches.'

'Yeah,' I agreed, watching Ruby's eyes dampen. Our dad had multiple sclerosis and had been moved into an assisted-living facility nine months ago, something we were still coming to terms with.

'Go, have a drink for me. I'm dying for a wee and I might get changed.' I followed behind Ruby as she went back into the function room, pausing to put my heels on and darting out of the exit, heading for the stairs.

'Seen Liza, Kel?' Bobby swayed in front of me when I reached the grand staircase, his eyes glazed.

I swallowed the lump in my throat, unable to look at him. Bobby was Liza's husband as well as being Ryan's best friend and business partner. They'd only been married a year, yet his world had been blown apart in the past few minutes too and he didn't even know it.

'No, not for a while,' I managed.

'Ah well, she must be around somewhere,' he turned in a full circle, arms outstretched, his sweat patches on display and worryingly unsteady on his feet. 'You make a beautiful bride, Kel,' he added, grabbing my hand and kissing it, a cheeky grin spreading across his face, showcasing his dimples. His curly mop of brown hair fell into his eyes.

'Thanks, Bob,' I replied, the onset of tears pricking the corners of my eyes. I slid my hand out of his damp palm and took the stairs as quickly as I could manage in my heavy ivory gown.

By the time I reached the honeymoon suite, my throat was thick with misery and I fumbled for the key in the satin bag hanging from my wrist. The tears came even before I had a chance to close the door to the room. Our enormous four-poster bed with crisp white sheets covered in red rose petals made me sob harder. Was it a one-off? Had Ryan got so drunk he'd made a pass at Liza or had they both been lying to me and Bobby for months?

I sat on the edge of the bed and put my head in my hands. Life as I knew it crumbled around me. Ryan and I owned a house together in Crawley a few miles away, he ran a business with Bobby, what was he thinking? Clearly he wasn't thinking at all, not with his brain anyway. Part of me wished I hadn't stumbled upon them and was unaware that Ryan's vow of 'forsaking all others' had been a lie.

My breath hitched as panic rose in my chest, the sudden onset of dread combined with the inability to breathe. The more I tried to calm down, the worse it got, until finally it peaked. I laid back, exhausted, gulping in lungfuls of air as my heart rate slowly resumed its natural rhythm.

Bastard, the lying, cheating bastard. How could he do that to me? What about the sanctity of marriage, the money we'd spent on our perfect day and all the presents we'd received? Sitting up, I kicked off my heels and tore at my dress like a wild animal, ripping the lace sleeves and yanking the corset undone as best I could, desperate to get it off me. It was a lie, everything the dress symbolised was bullshit.

Standing in the specially chosen bridal underwear, silk French knickers, strapless bra and cornflower blue garter, I stared at my reflection in the mirror. Mascara smeared my red blotchy face and my elegant pinned-up hairstyle was now a bedraggled mess. I wasn't going to let him get away with it. I should storm out there, rip that bitch's hair from her scalp, scratch his eyes out and throw my shiny gold band at him, but it wasn't me. I hated confrontation, I needed to think and space to do so, but how was I going to escape my own wedding reception? It wasn't as if I wouldn't be missed.

I looked around the grand bedroom for inspiration, glancing over at my pink suitcase, packed and ready for our flight to Crete. The honeymoon I'd been dreaming of, but now Ryan had ruined everything.

Although it didn't have to be?

It was already ten to ten, just two hours of the reception left and we were due to check-in at Gatwick airport at four tomorrow morning. A taxi was coming to pick us up at quarter to four from Gravetye Manor, the place we'd chosen for our combined wedding and reception, only five miles from the airport. The bridal suite had been thrown in as part of the package, although at the time we'd joked about how little sleep we were likely to get.

I'd looked forward to the honeymoon even more than the wedding. We hadn't had a holiday in years and Ryan had booked a luxury beachfront hotel for ten days. Perhaps Crete was far enough away from Ryan for me to get my head straight and figure out what I was going to do.

I wiped away the smeared mascara and forced a brush through my hair before putting on the comfy outfit I'd chosen to fly in, already laid out over the chair for the morning. Everything else I'd packed away already, oblivious to what lay ahead. Ryan's backpack had been left beside his suitcase and I riffled through it, digging out our passports, printed tickets and euros. In a moment of inspiration, I shoved Ryan's passport beneath the mattress of the bed, as close to the middle as I could reach, and put the rest of the items in my bag. Finally I rolled up the layers of white satin, torn lace and netting and hid my wedding dress in the empty wardrobe.

Checking I had everything I needed, I dialled the taxi company.

'Hi, I already have a pick-up booked for three forty-five tomorrow morning for Kelly Carbon, but my plans are changing. Do you have a car available now to take me from Gravetye Manor to Gatwick, North Terminal please?'

2

Metro Cars told me they would be outside in fifteen minutes and I was pleasantly surprised they had availability on a busy Saturday night. I bit my lip, trying to figure out how I was going to get out of the hotel unseen. The bride walking through the grand reception with a suitcase was hardly inconspicuous and there was bound to be guests outside the front of the manor house, hidden away in an attempt to find somewhere discreet to smoke.

Leafing through Ryan's backpack again, I pulled out his favourite England baseball cap and put it on, although it made my scalp sweat in the mid-July heat. Tucking my wayward hair into the cap, it wasn't much of a disguise, but at least it was something.

Smoothing out the bed cover from where I'd laid and checking our room looked untouched, I threw my bag over my shoulder and dragged my suitcase into the hallway. Hopefully Ryan would be so drunk when he came back to the room, he wouldn't notice it was missing or even that I was missing. Knowing him, he'd likely fall into bed and be unconscious in seconds whether I was there or not, unless he was spending the night with Liza. I gritted my teeth at the thought. He'd likely done some consummating this evening, but not with his wife.

The stairs I climbed before were to my right but those ended on the ground floor right outside the Tythe Barn where the reception was taking place. It was bound to be a hive of people in the hallways, either using the bathroom or collecting their coats and getting ready to leave. I wheeled the suitcase along the carpeted hallway in the opposite direction, pleased to find another set of stairs at the end. The suitcase was hard to lug down the steps – Ryan had carried them both up – but I took it slowly. When I finally reached the bottom, someone had to be smiling down on me because there was a fire exit door.

I couldn't hear anyone over the sounds of the disco, but the corridor was empty. I just hoped the door wasn't alarmed.

'Screw it,' I muttered to myself, pushing the lever. The door sprang open with no siren wailing to alert my presence and I stepped out in the humid night air at the rear of the manor house into a small car park. Staying away from the lights, I wheeled my case alongside the bushes at the edge of the car park towards the entrance from the road, flagging down the taxi as it arrived.

'Kelly Carbon, going to Gatwick Airport?'

'Yes, I'm Kelly.' My married name stuck in my throat, I couldn't bring myself to say it again. It had been hard enough to say it to the call handler when booking the taxi. To think I'd been so looking forward to using my new name, my new signature.

Tears blurred my vision and I stood there while my taxi driver jumped out of the Skoda estate, leaving it running, and lifted my case into the boot. I scanned the car park for any wayward guests but there was still a couple of hours of the reception left and thankfully everyone was in full party mode inside. The driver opened my door and I ducked inside. He climbed back in and did a U-turn, but I didn't exhale until we were on the dual carriageway heading for the airport.

'Business or pleasure?' he asked, one hand on the wheel, the other rubbing his salt-and-pepper beard.

I leaned back into the leather seats, my head whirring and in no mood for small talk. 'Pleasure,' I replied, staring out of the window at the lights whizzing past, blurring into fine lines in the darkness. I twisted the wedding ring which burned on my finger, remembering the shots the photographer had taken of our entwined hands after the service, rings on display. Glad at the time I'd had the French manicure. I considered taking it off, but I was flying out for my honeymoon, it would be good to keep up appearances as much as I wanted to throw the ring out of the moving car. Although the fact my groom wasn't with me was a massive giveaway that something was wrong.

I'd sobered up quickly from the champagne I'd drank, yet a headache threatened at my temples. I checked my phone as though I was holding a stick of dynamite, waiting for it to go off any second. As soon as Ruby hadn't seen me for a while, she'd come looking and when she couldn't find me, she'd call. I dropped her a quick text.

> Still in the room. Have a banging headache so just going to take a quick nap. If I don't see you, thank you for everything today, big sis. Love you. X

My throat was choked with emotion. I was sure she'd think it was weird I hadn't said goodbye to Mum and Dad, so I sent them a similar text. Despite it looking odd not seeing my parents off in person, how could I face my family and friends after what Ryan had done? He'd humiliated me on my wedding day. The shame of it clung to my skin like grease, despite it not being my fault. It took one second for him to ruin everything and I had no idea why.

Had Ryan fallen out of love with me? We'd been together a long time, but surely he would have said something before we shelled out ten grand on a wedding, and that was doing it on a shoestring! Wasn't I enough?

I swiped my tears and pulled Ryan's cap low as the driver hummed along to Magic FM.

My phone pinged, a message from Ruby.

> Okay, get a couple of hours in. Ryan is still dancing. I'll send him up later. Text if you need anything. Love you. X

Of course Ryan was dancing, he was having the best day ever, unaware I'd caught him cheating.

I shifted in my seat, anger surging through me. What was I going to do once I got to the airport, a ridiculous eight hours before my flight departed? Hopefully there would be a bed available at one of the hotels in the terminal, although I was too wired to sleep. I had my credit card, which had been cleared before our honeymoon in case we wanted to do a few trips whilst we were there. There was a catamaran cruise to Dia Island Ryan had been desperate to go on. Recalling him excitedly showing me the images on his phone made my heart wrench. We could have been so happy; we *were* happy, and now I'd fled my wedding reception. Unable to deal with what I'd seen, to confront Ryan.

Ruby would say it was typical of me. She said I ran away from my problems instead of facing them, which I couldn't deny was true, but I hated confrontation and always chose to retreat to sort through my jumbled thoughts. I needed to work out the logistics of what it meant to dismantle our lives, because that's what I was going to do, wasn't it? I couldn't stay, not now. Ryan didn't randomly cheat on me with a stranger, it wasn't a drunken fumble in a nightclub. He'd cheated on me with his business partner's wife, our friends, whom we saw most weeks in some capacity. Takeaways at ours, game nights at theirs, Friday drinks in the pub after a hard week at work. In fact, Liza was the closest thing I had to a best mate, which made it sting even more. How long had it been going on for? How long had I been taken for a fool – and not just me, but Bobby too?

Anger bubbled in my veins. I was going through the whole range of emotions, unable to stick with one for more than a few minutes. *Shock, you're in shock*, I told myself as, before I knew it, the taxi driver pulled into the lay-by at departures and was switching on the overhead light.

'That'll be fourteen pounds please,' he said, looking back over his shoulder.

I tapped my phone on his card reader and fumbled in my purse for some change, handing over a five-pound note, worth the tip for the silent car ride.

He hopped out of the taxi and retrieved my suitcase, wishing me a good flight, and I blindly followed the stream of excited holidaymakers up the travellator towards check-in. Obviously the travel agent desk wasn't yet open for my flight, so I followed signs for the Hilton hotel to see if I could get a room. I might not sleep, but I wanted a bed to curl up in and a duvet to pull over my head and shut out the world, for a few hours at least.

It cost one hundred and sixty pounds for a standard double room with no breakfast and I handed over my card willingly, accepting the room key and directions to number 93 with a nod. I requested a wake-up call at three thirty. When I reached my room, I hung the do not disturb card on the door and retreated inside.

The room was small but clean and I was pleased to find it had a bath. Turning the taps on full blast, I undressed and got in as soon as it was ready, pulling my knees to my chest, hoping the heat of the water would soothe my shattered heart.

My phone pinged again, another message from Ruby. Still nothing from my husband.

> Ryan is looking for you, I told him you're sleeping. He's having one more drink then coming to bed. X

I laughed, *one more drink.* He always *said* he was going to have one more drink but once he got started, he didn't know when to stop. At least he didn't know I'd gone yet, that I was five miles away, at an airport hotel. What would Ryan do when he realised I'd left the manor and how long would it take him to work out why.

I closed my eyes and laid back in the steaming hot water, a chill from the air conditioning making me sink lower into the heat. He was going to be so mad. When would he come looking?

3

With the adrenaline leaving my system, I got out of the bath, my eyes red and swollen, barely a stitch of bridal make-up remained. A wave of tiredness washed over me. I had to get a couple of hours sleep before check-in opened, but the compulsion to check my phone meant I couldn't relax. It was like waiting for a bomb to go off, for Ryan or Ruby to realise I wasn't in my room at all and had disappeared. Finally I gave in and switched it off, promising myself I wouldn't turn it back on again until I was on the plane and no one could talk me out of going on my honeymoon alone.

With the phone face down on the bedside table, I climbed beneath the soft white sheets, pulling the plush duvet to my ears, and closed my eyes, trying to block out the image of Ryan and Liza nestled inside the summer house, his hand up her dress. It was like a horror movie which kept replaying on loop, one I couldn't look away from. All the questions I had about their affair pulsated in my head until I wanted to scream, sure sleep would never come and denying me respite from my nightmare.

* * *

The shrill tone of the wake-up call jolted me upright, my eyes so puffy I struggled to peel them open while listening to the automated message coming through the receiver I'd manhandled off the bedside table. Dragging myself out of bed, I got dressed in the same clothes I'd worn last night, not bothering with any make-up. I felt dreadful and looked as bad. My hair was just long enough to tie in a short ponytail and I stuck the cap back on, which made me feel anonymous, if nothing else.

Check-out at reception was swift, and a few minutes later, I was back in the grey terminal queuing with other holidaymakers for the easyJet desk. My eyes darted around at the blur of faces, those in the queue and milling around. There were people everywhere and anxiety scaled my back like snaking vines. What if Ryan was here? What if he'd found his passport and made his way to the airport? I wanted to switch my phone on, mind in overdrive, fretting at not knowing what was happening, but maybe it was better that way.

I was now a lone traveller, heading out for a much-needed break to figure out how I was going to move forward after my life had imploded. It was a narrative I'd created for myself as I shuffled forward in the queue, a new persona, although I knew I wouldn't be able to relax until the wheels of the plane had left the tarmac. Not until I was sure Ryan had not made the flight.

Half of me wanted him to show up, to beg my forgiveness, because what did it say about him otherwise? He'd committed the ultimate betrayal and yet hadn't even realised his wife had gone AWOL on our wedding night. It just showed what I meant to him. Yet I prayed he wouldn't make it to the airport, I hated any kind of public scene and there was no way I was going to Crete if Ryan was too. The thought of being trapped with him for ten nights would be torture despite the exotic location. Ryan would make it his mission to talk me round, promising it would never happen again, that we had too much of a good thing to throw it away, but I wasn't going to fall for his bullshit.

He'd abused my trust, sleeping with Liza on our wedding day. What kind of man did that when, hours before, we'd pledged to love each other forever. One who only thought of himself, an egotistic narcissist who acted without fear of the consequences. Perhaps he was vain enough to think there wouldn't be any, that he'd get away with it. I never would have imagined he'd cheat on me, in all our years together he'd never given me any reason to doubt him, which was why it was such a sucker punch. In fact, if I hadn't seen it with my own eyes, I wouldn't have believed it.

Was it the drink? Ryan enjoyed a drink, perhaps a little too much. He had a work hard, play hard attitude and spent hours in the pub after his weekly five-a-side matches or sometimes at the end of a hard day's graft. Alcohol made him argumentative at times and although he wasn't physically imposing, I avoided upsetting him as I didn't want his nasty streak to come out. Sometimes he'd sulk, but other times, if he didn't get his way, especially if he'd had a drink, he got angry and that's when he scared me. I was glad not to be around when he eventually woke up this morning and reality hit. I kicked myself for hiding his passport and not bringing it with me to toss into a bin, but I wasn't thinking clearly, too desperate to get away.

With any luck, he was still sleeping off last night's binge, unaware his passport and wife were missing, having no clue he'd been caught out. It was a possibility. If he'd come back to the room and fallen asleep without bothering to try to find me, assuming I was still partying somewhere, it was likely he'd wake up hours later having missed our flight altogether. Would he, as drunk as he was, have remembered to set an alarm? I doubted anyone else would be up to check. Hardly any of our guests were staying at the hotel as so many lived locally and we hadn't thought to request a wake-up call.

'Good morning.' The bright-eyed lady manning the easyJet desk took my passport and ticket when I reached the front of the queue.

'Morning,' I replied, trying to muster a smile as I lifted my suitcase onto the scales for it to be weighed. It occurred to me as the destination label was printed and wrapped around the handle that I'd never travelled alone before. Any previous holidays were with my family and then Ryan once we'd got together. Thankfully, I was too exhausted and emotionally wrung out to be anxious. All I could focus on was getting through security and finding a shady corner and a large coffee to get me through the next few hours.

'All done, please make your way to security.'

I thanked the lady, watching my suitcase zoom away, and swiftly followed a family of four who had been at the next desk, trailing them up the escalator towards security. Before I got in the queue, I checked my bag at one of the tables to see if I had anything I needed to take out, but there was only my phone, AirPods, lip gloss and Kindle.

'Please remove your cap,' one of the security guards instructed before I stepped towards the scanner.

I mumbled an apology and put it in the plastic tray along with my bag and electronics before he waved me through. There was no beep as I passed through the metal arch and I continued on to collect my things once they'd been X-rayed.

I breathed a little sigh of relief at having got this far without Ryan catching up with me. There was an hour and a half before my flight, and they'd probably start boarding in an hour. Enough time to get a coffee and a pastry. My stomach growled as I yearned for food, having barely eaten at the reception, too busy socialising while Ryan had been busy elsewhere. The thought sat in my throat like an undigested morsel making me gag.

I hurried through duty-free, somewhere I would have liked to have taken my time, smelling all the perfumes and buying top-brand cosmetics I could have got cheaper online, but not today. Right now, I just wanted to find somewhere to hide.

It was the middle of July and the airport was busy, parents having taken their kids out of school early to start their summer holidays. After queuing upstairs for a large Americano and a chocolate twist, I found a free seat in the corner of a row of four, next to a mum and her two boys. A perfect spot where my back was against the wall and I could keep an eye on who was approaching, paying particular attention to tall, slender, dark-haired men with beards.

The pastry was warm and delicious, every mouthful worth being covered in tiny flakes. My eyes stung from lack of sleep and were still puffy from crying, but I wasn't going to waste any more tears on my husband, not today anyway.

It was kind of exciting to be running away and my stomach fizzed with the anticipation of a solo all-inclusive trip. I knew I'd have to face everyone eventually, but ten days laying by a pool would give me enough time to prepare myself for what I'd have to do, the conversations I'd need to have. I'd ring Ruby when I landed, she would be sleeping now, and she could pass on the news to Mum. Ryan would have to lay low as Ruby would be on the warpath as soon as she heard what he'd done. The two of them hadn't always gotten along, at times their personalities clashed, but they'd tolerated each other for my sake.

I was sixteen when I met Ryan hanging out at the local snooker club in Crawley, which was the only place any of us could get served at the time. He was two years older, tall and athletic, with chestnut-coloured doe-like eyes. Back then, he had long straight hair tied back in a ponytail, which I'd adored. I was captivated by the way he leaned his long body across the table, pocketing the balls expertly, a telltale sign of misspent youth. My group of friends were not nearly as good, but one night he'd challenged Alfie, one of our group, to a game. Ryan had thrashed him of course, but it was all in good spirits. Afterwards, he bought me a Jack Daniel's and Coke and we got chatting at the bar. He walked me home that night to make sure I got back safely, kissing me on the cheek at the garden gate and asking to meet again.

It was like my life had finally started when I met Ryan, having been a shy teenager who'd never had a boyfriend, and we quickly became inseparable. I had just finished my GCSEs and was enrolled in a dog grooming and canine behaviour course at Plumpton College. Ryan had an apprenticeship with a local plumbing company and we dated while we lived at home. When he turned twenty, we rented a grotty one-bedroom flat and got engaged, despite everyone telling me I was too young to marry.

In the last six years, both of us had taken the leap and started our own businesses, mine a local dog walking service, while Ryan and Bobby, who he'd met as an apprentice, had launched their own plumbing company. Money was tight to begin with, but we both built our client base and saved like mad to buy a two-bed terraced house in Crawley we could call our own. It was only then we looked at getting married.

In the ten years we'd been together I'd never once suspected Ryan of cheating, that was other men, not him. We were solid, a perfect match, childhood sweethearts, and it had been us against the world. Bobby and Liza had been together for five years, married for one and Ryan had never shown any interest in her, past being his best mate and business partner's wife. When had that changed?

4

When the digital board changed and displayed a gate for the easyJet flight to Heraklion, I headed back down the escalator, searching for number 147. I wrapped my arms around myself as I walked, my body cold from lack of sleep and the stress of the last few hours. I'd made good on my promise not to check my phone, but the uncertainty of whether Ryan was going to pop up at any second set my nerves on edge. I knew he'd be mad and I imagined him tearing the hotel room apart, searching for his passport. Perhaps he suspected I'd taken it with me? It gave me a surge of pleasure as I visualised his panic. Surely he would put two and two together when he realised I was gone.

Looking back, I should have confronted the cheating shitbag at the time, but I was in shock and didn't want to believe what I was seeing, choosing to flee rather than fight and cause a scene at my own wedding. Even now I couldn't find any words – other than expletives – for what they'd done behind my back, unable to contain themselves even on our wedding day. It was beyond reproach.

When I reached the gate, I waited until boarding began,

fidgeting nervously and biting at my cuticles, unable to relax as I systematically checked every face of the surrounding holiday-makers due to get on the same plane, all the time praying Ryan wasn't going to miraculously appear. Boarding was announced a short time later and I got in the queue, handing over my ticket and passport for the second time.

'Um, my husband has been delayed,' I coughed, my voice came out squeaky. The last thing I wanted was to delay take-off if they waited for their missing passenger. Better to pre-empt and tell them he wasn't coming.

'I'm afraid we're unable to hold the plane, Miss Quinn,' the stewardess replied, glancing again at my passport. It was nice to hear my maiden name, the one my passport displayed and my ticket was booked in.

A large man behind me tutted and my cheeks flamed.

'No, no, I just didn't want you to delay it because,' I cleared my throat, projecting my voice, 'he's not going to make it.'

'Okay, thank you for letting us know. His name is?' She ran her finger down the passenger list.

'Ryan Carbon.'

'Thank you,' she said, making a note on the list. 'Please make your way onboard.'

I followed the other passengers, walking quickly to close the gap along the tunnel to the plane entrance. My heart pounded in my chest as I stepped onboard, there was no going back now. Was I going to do this, go on my honeymoon by myself?

'Good morning,' a male steward welcomed me, and I smiled, moving along the aircraft to find my seat, which I knew was towards the back.

My ticket stated 29B, Ryan had begged for the window seat, sorely disappointed he hadn't been able to secure the seats with extra legroom, so he was 29A. Satisfaction hit as I slid into the seat that should have been his and looked out across the tarmac. The flight was only four hours, but I'd have plenty of room as the middle seat was going to be unoccupied unless they backfilled it. I hoped not.

Passengers continued to board, putting their hand luggage in the overhead compartments and creating jams in the aisles. I steeled myself to switch my phone on. I only had a small window of opportunity while we were on the tarmac before I'd have to put it on airplane mode. As soon as it switched on and I typed in my pin, it beeped so many times that the passenger who was in the aisle seat, a man in his fifties in a Hawaiian shirt, stared at me, a bemused grin on his face.

'Sorry,' I mumbled, switching it to silent. I swallowed the lump in my throat as message alerts and voicemail notifications kept the phone vibrating. Ignoring the notifications, I tapped a quick message to Ruby to let her know I was fine and would be in touch in a few hours, saying as little as possible to not cause alarm. I'd likely be in Crete before she woke up and I could tell her everything then.

When I opened the first message that had come through, the phone began buzzing continuously in my hand and Ryan's profile picture, his bearded grin while holding a pint of lager, filled the screen. I jumped so hard, I nearly dropped the phone, sliding the bar across the screen and accidentally answering the call as I fumbled not to drop it.

'Kelly, Kelly?' Ryan's irritation echoed as he shouted down the phone.

'Ladies and gentlemen, welcome aboard flight 180 to Heraklion. We will shortly be departing.'

'Shit,' I hissed, ending the call as the captain introduced himself, switching the phone to airplane mode so no more calls could come through.

'Please could you ensure your bags are placed in the overhead compartments or beneath the seat in front of you for take-off. Electronics must be turned off or switched to airplane mode, and please can you fasten your seatbelts and prepare for the safety briefing.'

How much had Ryan heard? Did he know I was on the flight? The tannoy was loud, he must have heard something, or did I manage to end the call in time?

Sweat beaded beneath the peak of Ryan's cap and I pulled it off my head, releasing my ponytail and trying to flatten my wayward hair. My hands shook and nausea swept over me.

'Afraid of flying?' The man in the Hawaiian shirt watched as the blood drained from my face.

'Uh-huh,' I managed because it was easier than having to explain that I was terrified of my husband discovering I was on my way to our honeymoon destination without him.

He leaned across the empty seat as though he was about to disclose a secret. 'I promise you, it's the safest form of transport,' he said softly.

I took a deep breath and leaned back into the seat, closing my eyes and exhaling.

I wasn't afraid of flying; in fact, I loved the buzz of take-off and landing. Ryan thought I was weird, but it was a rush. No, the nerves now were nothing to do with the flight. My phone was slippery in my clammy palm and I slotted it between my thighs, waiting for the panic attack to pass before I read the influx of messages. Outside, the engines fired up and the plane jolted forwards.

I opened my eyes and looked out at the sun already ascending the sky, surrounded by a gorgeous pink hue. I'd done it, I was on my way to Crete, Ryan had missed the flight.

Had I made a mistake? Should I be going alone?

It serves him right, the voice in my head countered, anger inflating my chest like a balloon. He'd brought it on himself. He should be the one clearing up the mess at home while I supped cocktails and laid for hours in the sun. It should be him facing my family and explaining why I'd flown out without him. That's if he lived long enough once Bobby found out about the affair. The Bobby I knew was placid, took everything in his stride but there had always been something lurking behind those doe-like eyes. Liza only pushed him so far knowing when to back away before he'd reached his limit but this revelation would send him careening off the edge.

As the plane accelerated along the runway, the nose lifting and the jolt of the tail going with it, I breathed a sigh of relief. The seat next to me was still empty. Ryan had been left behind and I had ten days to sort my head out before I returned home to get my marriage annulled.

'Wasn't so bad, was it?'

I looked over at my fellow passenger who had dug a copy of the latest Peter James novel out of his backpack and opened it to his bookmark.

'No, no it wasn't.' I smiled, putting my AirPods in and opening a playlist of spa music I'd downloaded specifically to help me sleep while we were in flight, knowing Ryan and I would be tired and hungover after the celebrations. But I knew I wouldn't be able to sleep until I'd read through all the messages I'd received. I had five from Ryan and three from Ruby. Eight missed calls between them and two voicemail messages.

I couldn't listen to the voicemails because there was no service, so I started with Ryan's drunken messages, which got more desperate as I read through them.

Whre ar yo?

Rub is loking for yu?

I sory baby I lov yu

Ansr Phone!

The last one made the blood swim faster in my veins. It was sent at five o'clock this morning, so he must have set an alarm after all. He'd obviously sobered up since the previous messages and was livid.

What the fuck have you done with my passport?

5

I spent the first two hours of the flight staring out of the window, a sickening feeling in the depths of my stomach. The refreshment trolley came around and I bought a bottle of water, my headache now in full swing. I needed to sleep, but the realisation of what I'd done and Ryan's reaction weighed heavy. Ruby's texts had both been a variation of asking where I was and requesting I call her. I hoped my response would make her stop worrying.

I kept reminding myself I hadn't done anything wrong. Ryan had betrayed me, on our wedding day. What would he do, would he jump on the next plane when he found his passport? And if he did turn up, would he be infuriated at my desertion or would he drop to his knees and beg my forgiveness?

Eventually, my mind gave up with the questions and I fell asleep until a flight attendant put her hand on my shoulder to gently rouse me.

'We're starting our descent, please can you put your seat belt on,' she said with a grateful smile.

I nodded, wiping the saliva from the corner of my mouth and looking out at the bright sunshine and blue ocean beneath us.

Just the sight lifted my spirits and I knew I'd made the right decision. I needed this holiday, now more than ever. The next ten days were going to be about me.

Our landing was smooth and as passengers descended the steps, the heat hit everyone smack in the face before we squeezed onto the bus to take us safely across the concourse to the terminal entrance. I queued with the crowd at passport control, waiting in line for our passports to be stamped and being waved through quickly. My shoulders loosening with every step towards baggage reclaim as I listened to the excited chatter of the surrounding holidaymakers. Luckily, my bright pink suitcase was one of the first onto the baggage carousel and I made my way to arrivals, where I found a man in a suit and tie holding a placard with Mr & Mrs Carbon written in thick black pen.

'Hi, I'm Mrs Carbon, but I'm afraid it's just me, my husband has been delayed at work.' The lie now rolled off the tongue.

'Of course, mam, please follow me.' Without waiting to be asked, he took hold of my suitcase and wheeled it towards the exit.

'Oh no, that's awful, will your husband be delayed long?' A rosy-faced woman with a West Country accent fell in step with me as we moved through the glass doors, having overheard my conversation.

'No, a couple of days maybe,' I replied, hoping I was wrong. Would Ryan be headed to the airport already, booking a seat on the next available flight or would he wait to call me first?

'Enjoy the peace.' She giggled, giving me a wave and directing her husband towards the queue of coaches waiting to transfer holidaymakers to their hotels.

Outside the airport, the sun was so bright, I dug in my bag for my sunglasses and took great delight in tossing Ryan's favourite hat into a nearby bin as I passed, trying to keep up with the chauffeur as he weaved through parked cars. A spring in my step as the heat blazed upon my back, absorbing the smell of boiling tarmac beneath my feet. Excitement bubbled in my veins at the island waiting to be explored. The ride was a luxurious black Mercedes with leather seats and air conditioning that gave instant relief the moment the engine was turned on.

'Elouda Bay Beach Hotel,' he said, checking his paperwork.

'Yes please,' I managed, shifting in my seat.

The area was desolate leading away from the airport. We drove past many partly built dwellings of naked cinder blocks set amongst sparse vegetation, as though construction had ceased midway through the build.

The nap on the plane had perked me up and with my head no longer foggy, I called my voicemail to listen to Ryan ranting that he couldn't find me. He was so drunk when he'd made the first call, he didn't make much sense, but there was no mention of Liza or the fact he was a cheating bastard. No apology in the more sober second call either, just demanding to know where I'd disappeared to and where the hell was his passport. I deleted them both before tapping out a text to Ruby.

> Please don't worry. I'm fine, have landed safely in Crete. Don't tell Ryan you've heard from me. K. X

Within seconds, I received a message back.

> I've been so worried, what happened? Ryan is going crazy!

I bit my lip as a wave of guilt hit me. It was obvious Ryan hadn't come clean. No doubt painting me as the mad woman who'd jetted off without him.

I'll call you later, but keep away from Ryan. K. X

I knew as soon as Ruby found out what he'd done she'd likely tear him to pieces, Liza too, and even though I was the victim I didn't want to be the catalyst for destroying her and Bobby's marriage. I loved Bobby to bits; he'd been Ryan's best man and I still couldn't fathom how he'd betrayed him as well.

The car journey was long, although I tried my best to relax into the comfortable seat and enjoy the scenery, thankful that the driver didn't try to make small talk. Eventually, we arrived outside an impressive white building with gold pillars and sliding glass doors at the entrance. My hotel looked much grander than the photos we'd seen online and for a second I was overwhelmed. I'd never been anywhere so luxurious; it was going to be heavenly.

I thanked the driver, slipping him some euros despite having paid for the car already, and headed up the marble steps to check in, keen to get to my room and relax after my journey.

A waiter stood at the entrance, holding out a flute of champagne which I received gratefully, the bubbles fizzing in my nose.

'Welcome to Elouda Bay. Please may I have your passport?' the lady said with a flourish when I reached the reception desk.

I dutifully slid it across the counter and stood awkwardly while she checked my reservation.

'Congratulations on your recent nuptials, Mrs Carbon,' she said, reading from her screen.

I squirmed, biting my lip.

'Thank you,' I managed.

'Is your husband not with you, mam?' she asked.

'He's been delayed at work,' I explained, awarding her a thin-lipped smile.

'That's a shame, hopefully he'll arrive soon,' she said, making a note on our booking and handing me a room key.

I tried to take in her instructions on opening hours of the various restaurants, the spa and entertainment, but my head swam.

'Arlo will take you to your room,' she gestured to a young man with slicked-back hair in a white cotton shirt and beige trousers waiting by the entrance, who wheeled my case back outside to where a buggy waited.

He zoomed around the complex, pointing out where everything was in heavily accented English as we passed and said I was in one of the speciality apartments with a small pool at the far end of the development.

Finally alone inside the cool marble room, I revelled in my luxurious surroundings. The kitchenette had a fully stocked fridge of soft drinks, beers and a bottle of champagne adorned with a red bow. Also inside was a wrapped plate of cold meats, cheese, butter and two baguettes. In the lounge area, a large fruit basket had been left on the coffee table between two sofas and a huge TV fitted onto the wall. I carried on exploring, heading into the bathroom next, which had a walk-in shower and whirlpool bath, before finally checking out the bedroom. A pang hit me when I saw that our huge bed had been decorated with a layer of rose petals and individually wrapped chocolates, our towels shaped to form kissing swans.

Moving swiftly on, I returned to the lounge area, where patio doors opened onto a small decking area with two sun loungers and a plunge pool. I raised my head to the sky, soaking in the rays and the warmth, which soothed my soul. Ryan didn't know what he was missing.

Within ten minutes, I'd logged on to the Wi-Fi, retrieved my bikini, sprayed on sun cream and laid by the pool, enjoying the privacy of the high walls which separated me from the neighbouring apartments. As my skin began to soak up the heat, the tension I'd been holding in my shoulders dissolved. I closed my eyes and snoozed, grateful for the reprieve of the misery of the past twelve hours. Even if I only left my room to eat and didn't speak to another person for the next ten days, it would still be an amazing holiday. The sun made everything better, although I knew dread would creep in as soon as the clock ticked closer to flying home.

Hunger pains eventually made me get up and I opened the fridge to get some food which would tide me over until dinner. I teared into my makeshift sandwich ravenously, freezing mid chew when my phone rang. Even the sound sent ripples of fear through me. I didn't want to speak to Ryan, it was too soon, and I was too distressed to listen to him rant down the phone or offer his weak excuses, but when I checked who was calling, I was relieved to see it was Ruby and quickly answered.

'Kel, what's happened? Everyone is frantic?' she puffed. I imagined her pacing the tiny front room in her rented flat, wearing out the carpet.

'Where's Ryan?' I asked.

'No idea. I haven't seen him since we left the hotel this morning. He said he couldn't find his passport and you'd disappeared!'

'I caught him with Liza last night in the summer house, just before I saw you. I should have said something, but I was in shock.' I began to sob. The dam had broken and bitterness flooded out of me in an unstoppable tide.

'Liza?' Ruby exclaimed, the shock in her voice making me move the phone inches away from my ear. 'Oh, Kel!' Her voice dropped as she listened to me cry. I knew if I was there, she would be rubbing my back and stroking my hair, doing whatever she could to console me. 'What a bastard,' she spat finally when I'd composed myself.

'I don't know what possessed me, but I just grabbed my suitcase and fled.'

'Did you take his passport?'

'No... I hid it.'

Ruby burst into laughter and I smiled down the phone,
wiping my nose.

'Do you want me to come out there, I'd have to check if I
could get the time off work, but I could ask?'

I contemplated having my big sister around for support, the
idea was nice, but her boss was a stickler for booking holidays in
advance and it was about time I stood on my own two feet.

'No, I'll be fine. I'll keep in touch though, I promise.'

'You better had!'

'Listen, don't say anything about Liza yet. I have no idea if he
even realises I saw them. I'll sort it out when I get back, but can
you cover for me with Mum? I don't want her worrying while I'm
away, not with what's going on with Dad.'

'It's one hell of a whopper,' she laughed, referring to all the
lies she'd told for me when we were younger and used to sneak
out of the house, taking turns covering for one another. 'God,
Kel, what are you going to do? I can't believe he cheated on your
fucking wedding night... and with *her!*'

'I know. I can't either, but I can't stay with him now, can I?'
Already, doubt had crept in, the thought of moving on without
the man who had been in my life for ten years left me feeling
emotionally crippled. Living alone, sleeping alone, an empty
house to come home to after work, I couldn't face the prospect of
it, but at the same time how could we move on from what he'd
done?

'He doesn't deserve you,' she seethed, adding, 'poor Bobby.'

'I know. Ryan keeps calling and texting.' More messages had
popped up on the screen.

'Block him,' Ruby replied simply, 'it'll give you the space you need to get your head straight and if he doesn't realise what he's done, I'll tell him the next time I see him.'

I cringed at the thought, knowing Ryan was likely to get a slap in the face from my big sister at the very least, not that he didn't deserve it. Not only was my marriage now a wreck, but our friendship group had also been shattered. I'd lost my closest female friend and what would happen when Bobby found out? Their partnership, the plumbing business would be broken beyond repair. How could the two of them have been so selfish?

6

In part, it was like a weight had been lifted, telling Ruby what Ryan had done. Speaking the words out loud made it real and the raw emotion of it hit me like a truck all over again, as though I was back standing on that lawn watching them writhe in the summer house, tainting the picturesque scene with their sordidness, but I had to face it. My short-lived marriage was over.

Ryan had sent more venomous messages about his passport, asking, *what the fuck was I playing at*. I took Ruby's advice and blocked him, but within half an hour, he'd messaged me through every medium possible – Instagram, Twitter, Facebook and WhatsApp, until I blocked him there too. There was a possibility he'd phone the hotel, so I called reception and asked them not to put any calls through to the apartment.

It was so out of character for me to pull a stunt like this, he must have realised I'd found out. I was tempted to post a photo of myself by the pool with the hashtag *#holidayforone* but decided it wouldn't do me any favours. Despite my anger, I didn't want to antagonise him. Plus I wasn't about to air my dirty laundry, to be greedily consumed by all the guests who'd attended my wedding less than twenty-four hours ago. The fact he'd cheated was humiliating enough.

With Ryan thousands of miles away and now unable to contact me, I spent the remainder of the afternoon in and out of my own private pool, eating the rest of the bread and drinking lots of water, relishing the peace. When my skin glowed red and my freckles had multiplied, I showered and got dressed for dinner, looking forward to having a cocktail in hand to watch the glorious sunset, determined to make the most of the honeymoon I'd worked hard for.

I'd arranged for my dog walking schedule to be taken over by Michelle of Paws & Pups, another local dog walker who I was friendly with. She wasn't like some I knew who took their dogs for walks around concrete car parks, Michelle cared for all her dogs like they were her own, the same as I did. We often recommended each other if we didn't have enough space to take more dogs on, and she was saving for a new kitchen, so was happy to help me out whilst I was away.

With all my four-legged friends taken care of and Ruby around if Mum or Dad needed anything, I had the opportunity to relax. Organising the wedding had been stressful enough, trying to stick to the budget we'd given ourselves yet wanting to have the nicest day possible. Ruby and I had handmade all the wedding favours and she'd done my hair and make-up on the day. My dress, although beautiful, was on sale, as was Ryan's suit. We got one of his colleagues, Steve, who ran a side hustle DJing, to give us mates rates for the reception, so the biggest outlay was the venue and flowers. Gravetye Manor had been my first choice of venue. I'd fallen in love with the place as soon as we'd turned into the vast gravel drive for our appointment with the events coordinator. Everything about it resembled a set from *Bridgerton* and I'd spent hours visualising our perfect day since the tour; the reception in the Tythe Barn, the immaculate lawns and patio area for mingling. I'd wanted the perfect day and it had been, until Ryan tarnished it forever.

Trying to remember the directions to the restaurant, I bumped into the woman I'd met at the airport. She'd clearly been in the sun all afternoon; her face was tomato red and she was sweating in the humidity.

'Oh hey!' She smiled warmly as she recognised me. 'Isn't this place just amazing.' We fell into step, her husband a few strides ahead talking on his phone.

'It is!' I agreed, glancing around at the manicured lawns and shaped foliage alongside the paved walkways. Everything was a variation of gold, white and beige, beautifully clean and well maintained. Elouda Beach was every bit the five-star adults-only resort it claimed to be. I couldn't take any credit, Ryan had chosen and booked it when I'd said I'd dreamt of visiting Crete.

'Are you going for dinner?' She pointed towards the main building where we were both heading.

'Yes, if I'm going in the right direction.' I laughed.

'Just follow the crowd, you're welcome to join us, honey, if you don't want to eat alone.' She dabbed at her shiny forehead with the sleeve of her chiffon top. I guessed she was in her late forties, or maybe early fifties, her husband a similar age.

'No, I'm fine, thank you. I bought a book,' I tapped my bag, 'but I'll be in the bar later,' I offered, making the effort to be gracious, despite having little interest in making small talk. The plan was to have a few cocktails and fall into that giant bed and sleep my troubles away. Maybe tomorrow I'd venture out to the main pool and people watch while I worked on trying to get a tan.

'Hopefully I'll see you later. Do you think your husband will be held up for long?' Her eyebrows dipped in a sympathetic expression, the corners of her mouth downturned.

'A few days maybe,' I said noncommittally.

We entered the large airy restaurant together, splitting up to find seats. I took a table for two in the corner, laying down my sunglasses and phone to claim the space before helping myself to a glass of lemonade from the self-service machine. In the centre of the restaurant was an oval-shaped counter with various trays of hot food underneath heat lamps and chefs milling around waiting to replenish the trays once they were empty. One of the chefs was cooking burritos, my favourite, and I approached him with a smile, my plate outstretched.

Despite all the bread I'd eaten in the room, I was hungry and took my dinner back to the table to dig in. The restaurant quickly filled with couples and I was the only one sitting alone. A twinge of self-consciousness made me bow my head and concentrate on my phone. Surely people still travelled on their own. It hadn't been a concern when I was coming with Ryan, but I stuck out like a sore thumb in the couples-only setting.

Michelle from Paws & Pups had tagged me in some photographs on Instagram and I clicked on them, inhaling sharply at the images of me in my beautiful wedding dress, gazing at Ryan amongst the disco lights as we came together for our first dance, his hands wrapped around my waist, beaming like he was the luckiest man in the world.

I pushed my plate away, unable to face any more, and swiped to the next image, another of us dancing but Liza could be seen in the background, her arms folded across her chest, the only one of the crowd not smiling. I'd thought it was odd she'd worn a long black dress to a summer wedding, thinking perhaps she was making a statement, but looking at that photo it was obvious. It had to have been going on before, there was no other explanation why she would be glaring at our happy moment. I gritted my teeth, that bitch, she was as much to blame as Ryan. The reminder of their betrayal was like a knife in the chest.

What doesn't kill you makes you stronger. I remembered Mum's mantra after Dad became so ill with multiple sclerosis she could no longer care for him at home. Ruby and I both contributed to the exorbitant care home fees to help Mum out. She was nearing sixty and still had two jobs, trying to cover the costs. Without our help, Dad wouldn't get the round-the-clock care he had access to now. My business was successful, but I wasn't raking it in. Ryan paid for most of our contribution and a lump grew in my throat. How would I do it alone? But what choice did I have, I couldn't stay with him now, not after what he'd done, not when it seemed like it had been going on for a while right under my nose.

Ryan had been distant for months, but I had too, so focused on the wedding, my business and Dad; I'd neglected to see what may have been obvious. Yet how he could have stooped so low was beyond me. Once I was back home, I'd arrange to get the marriage annulled and we'd have to sell our house to pay back the loans for the wedding and my van.

With such a massive life-change looming over me, I got palpitations. There'd be little left to start again, so I'd have no choice but to move back in with Mum until I got myself straight. It was overwhelming and not something I wanted to think too much about.

Having only eaten half of my burrito, despite it being delicious, my appetite faded and I got up to leave. The sun was beginning to dip and I wanted to find the bar and get myself a stiff drink.

7

The pool shimmered in the setting the sun, the water calm and still. It was a gorgeous inviting blue that made me want to dip my feet in, but I carried on around to the nearby bar, which looked more like a shack with a roof made of straw. Pulling up a wicker stool, I put my bag on the bar and the man behind the counter beamed at me, ready to take my order.

'May I have a piña colada please?' I asked, perusing the cocktail menu but going for my usual staple. Across the other side of the pool by the main building was a larger bar and seating area, where a band began to play, the lead singer murdering a song by Keane.

'I know,' the barman laughed when he saw me wince as the man on the microphone belted out a note off key.

'I feel sorry for you, you're stuck here listening to it.'

He grinned, handing me my drink. 'I need support, right.' When I met his eyes, he winked at me and I blushed, only now fully appreciating how handsome he was. Tall with a slim build, he had glossy black hair swept back from his face and enviably long eyelashes. His skin was a dark caramel colour and the tight beige trousers of his uniform showed off the curve of his behind when he turned to use the optics.

'Thank you.' I put ten euros of Ryan's money in the tip jar, slightly giddy.

The creamy cocktail was delicious and I relaxed into the music now the band had moved on to another cover, one more suited to the lead singer's range. Ruby messaged, checking in to see if I was okay, and I took a photo of my drink with its tiny orange umbrella and sent it to her in reply.

The bar slowly filled with couples who had finished eating and were looking for refreshment before the main entertainment started in the amphitheatre. Their voices drowned out the band and I soaked up the ambience, trying to enjoy the moment, but it wasn't easy to block out thoughts of Ryan. I imagined us at one of the tables, surrounded by empty glasses, laughing like hyenas, drunk on sun and sangria. Had I made a mistake coming here alone?

'Can I get anything for your husband?' the barman asked, delivering another cocktail minutes after I'd finished the first. I caught him looking at my wedding band and searching the crowd as if he might miraculously appear.

'He's not here,' I raised my voice over the noise.

He nodded, giving a small shrug before turning away to serve another customer. Strangely, a trickle of disappointment made its way down my back and I averted my gaze.

The sun set over the pool and I watched it inch lower, alcohol warming my blood. I scratched at a mosquito bite. I'd neglected to put any repellent on my skin before I came out and I'd pay for that tomorrow.

'Try this one.' The barman was back, coveting my attention. 'It's a pineapple daiquiri.' He smiled, placing another drink before me and wiping the bar with a damp cloth.

'Looks delicious,' I said, taking a sip and growing bold. 'What's your name?'

'Nico,' he replied.

I planted a palm on my chest. 'I'm Kelly.'

He leaned over to shake my hand.

'So where is your husband?' he asked, putting his elbows on the bar, leaning closer still.

'We're not together any more.'

I watched his smile widen. 'His loss.'

'Hey, Nico,' a customer called for him at the other end of the bar.

'Excuse me,' he said and I waved him away, hoping he didn't notice my palpitations.

By the time ten o'clock had rolled around, my backside was numb and my legs like jelly as I got up to stand. I'd consumed way too much alcohol on a partly filled stomach, the measures far larger than they were back home, and my surroundings swayed like they were being blown in the wind. I blinked rapidly, trying to focus, my bag slipping from my shoulder.

Nico shouted at another barman, holding his fingers up, indicating he was taking five minutes, and was by my side in a split second. 'Too many cocktails?' His eyes were wolfish.

I grinned as I let him walk me around the pool, pointing in the direction of my apartment, the blurry lights along the path guiding our late-evening stroll. Finding it impossible to ignore the thrill of anticipation that pounded in my chest.

Was it this easy to take someone home for the night? Was it even what I wanted? I'd never slept with another man, only Ryan, the knowledge at the forefront of my mind as Nico's hand gripped my waist, rocketing my pulse skyward.

'Why do you still wear it?' Nico asked, gesturing to the band on my left hand.

'Because I got married yesterday?'

He frowned, tilting his head to one side. 'And you already broke up?'

'Yep, that tends to happen if the groom sleeps with someone else on your wedding day,' I hiccupped, trying to mask my devastation with a wry laugh. It sounded empty.

'Jesus,' Nico said, running his hand through his slick hair.

I bit my lip as we reached the entrance to my apartment.

'This is me.' A lump formed in my throat. I'd decided to go with it; whatever was about to happen, I was going to embrace it. After all, what did I have to lose.

'Then I wish you goodnight, Kelly.' Nico took my hand to kiss it before giving a little bow.

I watched as he walked away, a bizarre combination of relief and disappointment washing over me. My face reddened at the shame of rejection and I wrenched the ring from my finger and shoved it in my bag before unlocking the door.

The apartment was dark, curtains had been drawn, towels and petals moved from the sheets and the bed turned down, with tiny heart chocolates left on each pillow. I pushed them to the floor, crying until no more tears would come, beating at my pillow with the unspent rage I had towards Ryan and what he'd reduced me to.

* * *

I woke with a dry mouth and a throbbing headache just after eight, dehydration from too much alcohol. My cotton dress from the night before was bunched around my waist from tossing and turning in my sleep. Sounds from next door already out by their pool drifted through the patio doors and I winced as I pulled the curtain back, bright sunlight hitting me square in the face. My stomach growled, wanting food. I needed to eat, something to soak up the alcohol from last night. I dug out the charger and adapter and plugged in my battery-depleted phone, leaving it while I unpacked the rest of my suitcase and took a quick shower.

Breakfast was in the same restaurant and I didn't hesitate to load my plate with eggs, bacon, sausage and beans, washed down with two large cups of black coffee and an iced water. I wasn't as self-conscious as I had been the day before. Who cared I was alone? No one, it seemed, as not one person gave me a second glance.

As soon as the food hit my stomach, I began to feel human again despite my embarrassment returning as I remembered Nico walking me back to my room. How stupid I'd been to assume he'd found me attractive. I'm sure he had a line of girls queuing up for him. What would a one-night stand do for me anyway? In the moment, it seemed like a cry for attention, to find someone who wanted me, for a short time at least, because my husband no longer did. I was glad Nico hadn't taken advantage of my drunken state. I would have woken up regretting it, feeling wretched, despite having no loyalty to Ryan or my sham of a marriage. That had evaporated the second I saw him with Liza.

Returning to the room to get a bag ready with a towel and sun cream, I changed into my turquoise bikini and remembered my phone was still charging. My stomach plummeted when I saw I had four missed calls from Ruby. Suddenly queasy from my large breakfast, I dialled her number, waiting for the long tone to connect. Was it Ryan, or had something happened with Dad?

'Rubes, it's me,' I blurted as soon as the call connected.

She didn't bother with pleasantries, getting straight to the point. 'Ryan's found his passport, Gravetye Manor called him yesterday afternoon when they made up the suite.' Her words came out in a rush and I gasped, sinking onto the edge of the bed. 'He just called me and told me to give you a message seeing as you've blocked him everywhere.' Ruby's voice cracked and I looked at my watch. It was only nine o'clock in Crete, which would be seven o'clock UK time on a Monday morning.

'What?' I asked.

'He told me to tell you, sorry for the delay, but he'll be with you soon.'

8

Shit. Ryan was going to fly out to Crete. I'd known it was a possibility but had hoped he'd find a rock to crawl under instead. Now it had been confirmed, nausea made my stomach roll.

'Did he tell you anything else?'

'No, I told him it was a bad idea, but he just laughed.' Ruby's voice was clipped, her irritation at Ryan's flippancy obvious.

'Did he mention Liza?'

'No and I didn't say anything either, I wanted to get off the phone so I could call you.'

'Do you have any idea when his flight is? Has he even booked one?'

'No clue,' she paused, 'but, Kel, he's coming.'

As I got off the phone, fear lodged in my chest. I wasn't ready to confront Ryan, I hadn't even contemplated what I was going to say. Now he was flying out to force my hand. Even though I knew he had no right to be angry considering what he'd done, he would be livid I'd gone off without him. He'd have felt humiliated and when Ryan was mad, he scared me.

Taking my phone and my bag, I left the room and headed to

the pool, desperate for some air. I'd decided not to hide away. I had nothing to be ashamed of, why should I, just because I was alone. However, when I got poolside most of the sun loungers were already taken, not by people, but their towels. I managed to find one free by a palm tree and claimed it. I hadn't wanted to stay in the room where the walls were closing in on me, knowing Ryan was a mere four hours away. What if he'd already booked a flight? What if he was at Gatwick Airport right now, boarding a plane, and would be here by the afternoon?

I sat on the lounger, trying to breathe deeply and expel the anxiety that had built in my chest. No longer was I relaxed. Surrounded by hundreds of strangers, my eyes searched their faces, looking for my husband, despite knowing he couldn't possibly be here, not yet. But I felt sick at the thought of coming face to face with him.

What if I melted and forgave him. He had an annoying ability to talk me round, get me onboard to his way of thinking, worming himself out of sticky situations... But not this time. I couldn't, I wouldn't. There was no explanation he could come up with that would make me stay. Not after what he'd done.

'Excuse me, miss, I just wanted to let you know about the activities we have today.'

I shielded my eyes from the sun despite my sunglasses and looked up at the hotel representative welding leaflets.

'Oh hello.' A slim black man with a bald head covered in tiny beads of sweat stood before me, shifting to the left to keep the sun out of my eyes. He had an infectious smile and I reciprocated with one of my own, taking a leaflet.

'We have aqua aerobics in the pool at eleven, water polo at one and there's a circus show on the main stage tonight. Tomorrow, there is a day trip to the local market with lunch included, if you are interested.' He gestured towards the leaflet in my hand. 'You can book a spot at reception; the coach will pick up at nine tomorrow morning.' He flashed me a wide pearly white smile, before moving on to a neighbouring couple and reciting his spiel again.

It wouldn't be a bad idea to leave the hotel for the day. If Ryan couldn't get a flight today, would he be waitlisted? Would he sit at the airport until he got a seat? I squeezed my eyes shut before snapping them open and grabbing my phone. On the internet, I searched the easyJet website for flights from Gatwick to Heraklion. It looked as though there were no seats available this morning and I prayed he hadn't already booked a spot on it after retrieving his passport yesterday.

I propped myself up, grabbed my Kindle and tried to concentrate on Victoria Hislop's *The Island*, based on a Cretan island, Spinalonga. It was my favourite book; I'd yearned to visit Crete since the first time I read it and countless times since, but now I couldn't relax into it. Regretfully, I put it down and had a swim around the pool, eventually coming to rest at the side. With my head laid upon my arms and body weightless in the water, I began to unwind. As the sun warmed my back and the cool water swished around my legs, it felt like paradise, and it would have been without couples around me chatting and canoodling, their romantic displays amplifying my solitude. Watching their happiness stung and it seemed I was the only one with a dark cloud hanging over my head in an otherwise unblemished Mediterranean sky.

Around lunchtime, the smell of chicken being barbecued wafted along from the lunch hut, making me drool. I sat on the sun lounger to dry off and checked my phone. Mum had sent me a long text message; I was guessing because she had got it out of Ruby what Ryan had done. I skimmed it, not wanting to get too emotional surrounded by strangers, and sent a heart emoji back, with just four words.

> Don't worry, I'm okay.

Ruby had sent a photo through that was taking ages to download on the hotel's Wi-Fi, so I slipped on my sarong and made my way around to queue for a chicken wrap.

'Hey, woman with no husband,' a familiar voice came from behind me.

I turned to find Nico strolling past.

'Kelly,' I reminded him, glad I had my sunglasses on to hide my mortification.

'Ah, that's it. The wedding band is gone, I see.' He grinned, looking at the hand holding my phone. I felt naked and exposed despite the sarong covering my bikini.

'It is.'

Should I put it back on before Ryan arrived? No, as far as I was concerned, we weren't married any more.

'Are you working already?' I asked, noting his freshly ironed uniform.

'Yep, just starting my shift. You coming to the bar later?'

'Maybe.' I shuffled forward in the queue, almost at the front, my ears growing hot.

'I'll have a piña colada waiting for you.' Nico winked and I cringed inwardly. No doubt he was being nice because I'd tipped. I'd forever be known as the drunk woman he had to escort back to her apartment because she could barely walk. It was humiliating, but at least I hadn't thrown myself at him.

I ordered a chicken wrap, which was handed over in grease-proof paper with a serviette, and took it back to my sun lounger to see what Ruby had sent me, almost spitting out my first bite when the photo finally downloaded. Ruby had taken a screen-shot of Ryan's Facebook post, a photo of a pint on a dark wood table with the caption: *At Gatwick, getting ready to start my honeymoon.* I baulked at the image, although there was no mention of a flight time, quickly tapping a message back to Ruby asking her to keep me posted. She'd clearly been stalking his social media, trying to find out when he was travelling. Forewarned was forearmed and I guessed I should have thought about that when I'd blocked him everywhere.

Determined to make the most of what relaxation time I had left before Ryan's imminent arrival I forced my anxiety down and focused on my surroundings. Concentrating on the here and now helped to centre my thoughts and I read a few pages of my book before my mind wandered to what I would wear later when I went to the bar. It was silly, but the flirtation with Nico, the necessary distraction, had lifted my spirits and my self-esteem. Even if it wasn't real, I was glad to be thinking about anything other than the impending arrival of my husband and what that would bring with it. I'd have to make sure I stayed sober so as not to make a fool of myself as I had last night.

On the way back to the room, I stopped off at reception and impulsively booked a spot on the trip to the market for the following day. Even if Ryan turned up, I didn't have to spend time with him, as much as was possible considering we were sharing a room. Perhaps it would be like ripping off a plaster, easier once we both knew where we stood. Although I feared if he was flying out to Crete he wasn't going to let me go without a fight.

Later, I bumped into the red-faced lady again on the way to the restaurant for dinner, finally introducing myself properly. Her name was Janice and she was a teaching assistant, married to Greg, who worked as a custody sergeant at their local police station. When she invited me to dine with them again, I didn't

feel like I could refuse and the three of us sat awkwardly at a
table for four. I sat opposite Greg whose leg constantly jiggled.
Once he'd had a drink, he warmed up, regaling stories of prob-
lematic prisoners, including one who was so drunk, they
watched on camera as, alone in his cell, he delivered a full stand-
up routine in a fake Irish accent.

Janice was the sort of woman whose laugh was loud and
unabashed despite gaining curious looks from the other diners. I
found it refreshing and endearing rather than annoying and
surprised myself by genuinely laughing with her. Her and Greg
were on holiday celebrating their twentieth wedding anniversary,
yet she was warm and friendly, making me instantly comfortable
despite being the gooseberry.

'So, tell me, Kelly, what on earth is holding up your
husband?' She rested her knife and fork across her plate, eyes
locked onto mine, giving me nowhere to hide.

I slid my left hand off the table and rested it in my lap, not
wanting Janice to notice the absence of my wedding band. I
briefly considered telling her everything, but shame prevented
me from sharing my sorrows.

She grimaced at my lack of answer, reaching over and patting
my arm knowingly, as if by saying nothing, I'd said it all.

Greg, who'd watched our exchange, cleared his throat and
glugged the rest of his beer. 'Right,' he said, slapping his thigh,
'who fancies a cocktail? I know you do, wife of mine.' He beamed
at Janice, all at once reminding me of everything I'd lost. It could
have been Ryan and I in twenty years, knowing what the other
one wanted before they'd even uttered a word. An intimacy that
wasn't forced or rehearsed, but now I didn't know what my future
held and the thought scared me to death.

9

Janice and Greg had suggested a drink in the bar directly in front of the live music and tonight on the small stage was a jazz singer and a saxophonist. They were an amazing pairing, playing songs I'd forgotten existed, and it was a marked improvement from yesterday's warbler.

'I much prefer this to the main amphitheatre, hurts my backside sitting on that stone,' Janice admitted, supping from a dirty martini.

'I was at the bar over there last night,' I pointed across the pool, my stomach fluttered knowing Nico was inside, 'so I could hear the music, but this is much more comfortable.'

I leaned back in a cushioned wicker chair and enjoyed the setting sun over the crisp white buildings beyond. Citronella permeated the air; each table had a candle lit and thankfully I'd remembered the mosquito spray when I'd spritzed perfume on before I left. There would be plenty of time to make good on my promise of a cocktail at Nico's bar.

'It's a lovely hotel, isn't it, and those sunbeds. I've never been anywhere before that has cushioned sunbeds. I mean, it's all right for you at your age, but as you get older...' Greg's words drifted off as I spied Nico the other side of the pool carrying a plastic crate full of glasses around the back of the bar.

'There's a circus act tonight,' I said as he disappeared out of view.

'Most of the entertainment is a little in your face for me. I think tomorrow we'll venture out and soak up the local sights.' Janice patted my knee. 'Come with us.'

'No, no, I don't want to intrude. I'm going to go to the market tomorrow. I've booked myself on the trip the rep was touting, so I'll probably be shattered.'

'I think we're going to go on that shopping trip later on in the week, aren't we, Jan?' Greg asked and Janice nodded, finishing her drink already, whereas I was only halfway through my first cocktail.

The evening went quickly as we chatted and listened to the music, clapping after every song. In company, I found I wasn't searching for Ryan's face in the crowd and the distraction was just what I needed. Greg chivalrously insisted on going to the bar each time our drinks needed refilling, and when the music finally came to a close, they bid me goodnight. I remained in my seat to finish my fourth cocktail as fleeting thoughts of mum's favourite movie, *Shirley Valentine*, came to mind. It was a British film about a middle-aged housewife who leaves her servient life behind for a new start in Greece and I briefly contemplated what it would be like to live in paradise. With alcohol thrumming in my veins and a feeling I couldn't describe, I was propelled across the bridge to find Nico.

When I got there, the circus entertainment had just finished, so the bar was heaving, but Nico caught my eye loitering at the corner and shot me a wink. Within minutes, he'd slid a drink across to me, bumping me up the queue.

'Don't go anywhere,' he said, pointing at me before returning to the bunch of thirsty customers. He looked just as gorgeous as he had last night, the buzz of attraction I felt was so alien to me yet impossible to ignore.

I watched as him and his colleagues whizzed around the bar, sweat dripping from their foreheads and the backs of their white shirts saturated. It was humid and sticky under the bright lights. Even once I got to the bottom of my glass, the line was never-ending. I wouldn't be able to talk to Nico, he was too busy. It was pointless and I felt foolish, like a groupie waiting at the side of the stage for their favourite band to finish playing, desperate for the slightest bit of interaction. With Ryan's imminent arrival I wanted to be someone else for a couple of hours but perhaps I was making a mistake.

While he was serving, I slipped away in the direction of my room, but I only made it as far as the wooden bridge when a hand caught mine, our fingers intertwining.

'Leaving so soon?' Nico's eyes darted to my lips.

'I have to be up early,' I said in way of an apology, trying to ignore the tingling sensation that raced through my body at his touch.

He looked over his shoulder and pulled me the rest of the way across the bridge, into a shadowy path between apartment blocks. My heart raced as he cupped my face and kissed me, his lips soft and salty with sweat. My body slackened, the wall holding me up as Nico pressed himself against me, shirt damp against my chest and shrubs scratching at bare ankles. My head felt light, like the breeze would carry me away, my resolve with it as I surrendered, all doubt fading away.

'I have to get back.' He rested his forehead against mine, his breath hot on my lips.

'Okay,' I managed, my voice barely audible.

'Tomorrow,' he said, as though we'd agreed, before releasing me and jogging over the bridge, back to his shift at the bar.

I straightened, pushing off the wall with legs like jelly, my fingertips tracing my lips where Nico's had been seconds before. A surreal feeling engulfed me as I stumbled back to my room as if it had all been a dream. Nico was gorgeous, there was no denying it, and a desire stirred inside me which had laid dormant for years. Despite it being a stupid infatuation that wouldn't go anywhere. How could it? I was married, on holiday and making out with a bartender, such a cliché. Still, the fuzziness I had was something to be cherished, however fleeting.

Inside my room, I locked the door and reality crept in as my mind returned to Ryan and his impending arrival. What if he turned up in the middle of the night? Would reception hand him over a key? I guessed they'd have no choice. As far as they were concerned, there was no reason not to, the room was in joint names. I'd had no messages from Ruby throughout the evening, so she couldn't have any information to pass on, but I was dying to know if Ryan was still waiting at Gatwick airport for an available seat or if he was already here, making his way to Elouda Bay.

Such thoughts were not conducive to sleep, but there was no way I could stop him getting in, I couldn't barricade the door. A simple swipe of a keycard would gain him access and I wasn't prepared for the showdown that would follow. Should I call reception and tell them not to give him a key? But if they turned him away, it would add fuel to the already raging fire. I laid in bed, my mind erratic, imagining every movement I heard outside was my husband's arrival.

Eventually, I drifted off to sleep, waking at seven to an empty apartment. I sent Ruby a message to let her know Ryan hadn't arrived yet, asking if she'd seen or heard anything, but knowing

Crete was two hours in front, I wouldn't get a reply for a while and I was happy to be blissfully ignorant for as long as I could.

I showered, putting on shorts and a T-shirt, and packed my bag, ready for a day at the market. I needed a distraction and had euros to spend, looking forward to giving haggling a go if I saw anything I liked for Ruby, Mum or Dad. Checking my social media, I saw Michelle had tagged me in an Instagram post from yesterday, walking my regulars. She had taken Freddie, Max and Boycie, two Yorkshire terriers and a French bulldog, to Paddock Hurst woods, one of my usual haunts, and I hearted the cute photo, glad they were being well looked after in my absence.

When I'd started the dog walking business, I had no idea it would take off straight away, but there were so many people needing their dogs cared for while they were at work. I took on as many as I could safely manage, until my books were full, walking miles on three scheduled walks a day. I'd always wanted to work with animals and dogs were so much easier than people, they loved unconditionally. Their happiness rubbed off on me and I loved my job, especially in the summer months. The winters were cold and wet, but I'd invested in fleece lined leggings and waterproofs, becoming used to being soggy all day. It beat the hell out of being stuck in an office with people you didn't get on with day in, day out.

I sent Michelle a message with a selfie I'd taken yesterday, while I had a quick breakfast of Danish pastries, fresh fruit and coffee, thanking her again for taking the dogs on while I was away. I didn't see Janice and Greg at the buffet and guessed they were having a lie-in. I'd wanted to thank them for their kindness yesterday, but I could do that later. Finishing my coffee, I headed to reception.

'I don't suppose my husband has checked in?' I asked a man behind the counter, who looked at me strangely as soon as the question was out of my mouth. 'He was delayed at work, we didn't arrive together,' I clarified, adding, 'Ryan Carbon, room 207.'

He tapped at his computer and shook his head. 'No, I'm afraid not, mam.'

I walked outside as though I'd been given a reprieve as the heat hit me, a stark comparison from the cool reception. A crowd had gathered on the steps and I overheard them talking about the market, so I waited on the fringe of the group for the coach to arrive.

A few minutes later, one turned into the hotel and pulled up out front, the driver getting off and ushering us onboard. Staring out of my window as we pulled away, a taxi passed us and I tensed, craning my neck to see who would get out. Just as our coach indicated left and we slowly swung out of the complex, my stomach plummeted, catching a glimpse of Ryan's scowl as he waited for his suitcase to be unloaded from the boot of the car.

10

'He's here,' I whispered into the phone as a groggy Ruby answered.

'Wait, what?' she mumbled. 'Shit, I overslept.' Noises of her scrabbling out of bed came down the line and I heard another fleeting voice in the background but dismissed it as her radio.

'He's just arrived, but I'm going out on a day trip, he hasn't seen me yet.'

'Oh shit, what are you going to do?'

'There's not much I can do, Ruby. How can I face him?' I felt the sting of tears as the coach rumbled along a narrow hilly road interspersed with hotels.

'You've done nothing wrong, Kel, he cheated, he should be on his knees begging for forgiveness.'

I sniffed and Ruby sighed, her voice softening.

'Listen, enjoy your day, think about what you want to say to him when you get back.'

I imagined Ryan in my room, touching my things and acid burned in my stomach. Why did he have to come out to Crete?

Why couldn't he have sloped off and hidden under a rock back home? It was like he had no shame or regret for his actions.

'I've got to get ready for work, but call me later.'

'Is Mum okay?' I asked, despite knowing I was making her even later. Her voice was a comfort I needed thousands of miles away from home. Perhaps I should have asked her to fly out after all.

'Yeah, she's waiting for you to call her, obviously.' I'd deliberately not called Mum, unsure what I would say. I couldn't face her and I couldn't face Ryan either. The thought of talking to either of them made me light-headed. Mum would feel the betrayal as keenly as I had, she adored Ryan, plus with so much going on with dad I didn't want to add to her worries. She had enough on her plate already.

Ruby ended the call, declaring she had to go, and within minutes we'd arrived in the hustle and bustle of the market. Stalls ran the length of the paved street as far as the eye could see. Gorgeous scarves, bags, bracelets and rugs, as well as souvenirs, invited holidaymakers to part with their money. Our guide instructed we were to be picked up from the same spot and each of us was given a voucher for a Greek restaurant at the bottom of the hill. I filed off the coach on autopilot, my stomach in knots. How was I supposed to enjoy the excursion knowing Ryan was waiting back at the hotel? I imagined him roaming the pool and the sunbeds, searching the complex, desperate to find me.

'Mam, would you like a rug?' I shook my head at the stallholder with a variety of colourful rugs over his arm and followed the group down the hill.

Wanting to gather myself, I decided to head to the restaurant early, using my voucher for a coffee and a wrapped baguette I put in my bag for later. I watched our group make their way along the market, stopping to haggle at the stalls.

'This is ridiculous,' I berated myself, anger stirring. Why was I letting Ryan ruin my day? I knew he was here and there was nothing I could do about it. Sooner or later, I'd have to face him and tell him our marriage was over. But I had another three hours before we were being collected, so I left the coffee shop to go shopping, determined to make the most of my time before I had to confront my cheating husband.

I bought some baklava, haggled over a beautiful shawl with an intricate dragonfly print and selected a couple of bracelets for Ruby and Michelle. There was a long queue of tourists with their children waiting to get their hair braided by a local woman who had every colour hair wrap you could imagine. I soaked up the atmosphere, the sounds of the bustling crowd and smells from the food vendors, paying no mind to the niggling thoughts of Ryan until my phone rang.

It was a local number, which I ignored, waiting for the voice-mail I knew would come, and listening to Ryan's gruff voice asking where I was. He'd called from the room because his mobile number had been blocked. It was a charge he could pay for as I wasn't going to foot the bill. He sounded irritated, telling me he was going to wait in the bar. What bar? The thought of him striking up a conversation with Nico made the vein in my neck twitch. After our kiss what would he think when my husband appeared today? Would he think I'd been lying? By the time I got back, he'd have been at the bar for a while, drunk and argumentative, and I envisioned the hotel staff calling security if he caused a scene.

When the coach arrived to collect us, I was glad to be out of the relentless heat despite the dread that washed over me as soon as the coach moved towards the hotel, knowing what I was heading into. It arrived a little after half past two and the talk of the passengers was that no one was going to be able to find a sunbed so late in the day. I waited until last to get off, dropping some change in the tip bowl for the driver. With legs like lead, I made my way through the hotel, immediately spotting Ryan propping up Nico's bar. He was red-faced, likely having neglected to put any sun cream on, gesticulating to the bartender. I couldn't tell if it was Nico as I was too far away, but as I approached, inwardly I cringed when I saw he was working.

'There you are! There's my girl.' Ryan jumped off his stool, his face alight as I made my way around a pillar. He bounded towards me wearing a white vest with low-slung cargo shorts, shins shiny with sweat and a new baseball hat he must have bought at the airport. Like nothing had happened, he pulled me into an embrace I didn't reciprocate, his beard scratching my neck. My body instantly went rigid and over his shoulder, I saw Nico frowning at us. I couldn't meet his eye, my cheeks flushing with embarrassment.

Extracting myself from Ryan's grip, I gestured towards a table and suggested we sit.

'It's bloody lovely here, isn't it?' he said, taking a gulp of his beer and looking around.

I swallowed, taking in the sight of my already half-cut husband, his sweaty brow and red face I used to find so handsome. The smile which was always so infectious left me cold, despite the heat of the afternoon.

'Why did you come?' I asked.

'What do you mean, it's our honeymoon. Why on earth did you leave without me?' He was slurring slightly. How much had he had to drink? Had he been at the bar all day?

Ryan rested his clammy hand on mine but I slid it out beneath, his touch making my throat tighten.

'Why did I leave without you?' I replied, incredulous. 'I left because I saw you with your tongue down Liza's throat,' I snapped, gritting my teeth.

Ryan didn't even have the grace to look apologetic. 'Oh, it was nothing, she'd had too much drink, that's all. She threw herself at me when I went to get some air.'

'And you let her down gently, did you?' I scoffed, just as Nico delivered a fresh beer and a piña colada to our table.

'Everything okay?' he asked, immediately sensing the tension between us.

'Everything's fine, mate,' Ryan spat, shoving his empty glass across the table for him to take.

I bit my lip and waited for Nico to leave, wishing the ground would swallow me whole.

'You're overreacting,' Ryan soothed, putting his hand on my knee.

Bile rose in my throat, but I swallowed it down with a mouthful of cocktail.

'Why aren't you wearing your ring?' he asked, his eyebrows knitting together.

'Because we're over, Ryan. How can we not be? You cheated, on our wedding day.' I couldn't believe I had to spell it out for him.

'Don't be ridiculous, you didn't see what you thought you saw. Look, I'm sorry. She jumped on me when I went outside; she's always had a bit of a thing for me.'

I shook my head, eyes blurry with tears. 'How long has it been going on for?' It was the only question I wanted an answer to, the only one that mattered.

'It hasn't. It's not. God, Kel, chill out. I told you, it was nothing.'

Ryan's words rung in my ears. Was I going mad? Was I sure of what I saw, or was I overreacting? Was he gaslighting me?

I closed my eyes, remembering the scene. Ryan's hand up Liza's dress, the chime of his belt being undone. No, I knew what I saw and it wasn't nothing like he was trying to claim. Ryan was a lying, cheating bastard and I hated him for putting me through the wringer and not only that, he was trying to wriggle out of it. I got up like I'd been poked with a cattle prod, shaking the table, and Ryan's beer slopped over the side of the glass.

'Jesus.' The liquid ran off the table and spilled onto his shorts.

Without another word, I walked away, Ryan's voice carried behind me as he spoke to the neighbouring table.

'She'll be all right, once she calms down.'

11

'Is there really nothing you can do?' I asked the male receptionist, my credit card already out on the desk, ready to be swiped.

'I'm sorry, mam, we're fully booked.'

'There's no rooms at all?' I pleaded, not willing to believe that in a hotel of this size there wasn't a cupboard I could hide out in.

'I'm sorry.' The short stumpy man with perspiration on his top lip grimaced.

I sighed, the idea of sharing a room with Ryan for another week filled me with dread.

As I walked back to the room, my mum called. I debated whether to answer but I couldn't put off speaking to her any longer. She just wanted to know I was all right.

'Hiya, love, how are you?'

'I've been better,' I replied. 'How's dad?'

'He's fine, we're going out for afternoon tea soon.' She paused. 'I've not said anything to him, but I've been worried about you.'

I cringed inwardly; I should have called them both. 'It's complicated but... I'm leaving Ryan. Don't say anything to Dad.' The tears cascaded down my face as I swiped my key card and entered the apartment, scowling at Ryan's messy suitcase open on the bed, his clothes strewn around haphazardly, mirroring our bedroom at home.

'Oh, Kelly, I'm so sorry. Ruby said he'd been a shit!'

'More than a shit! I'll explain properly when I'm back home, but I'm fine. He's turned up today and I'm thinking about flying home early.' The idea popped into my head.

'Well, let me know if you need anything – money for a plane ticket, a place to stay. Whatever you need.'

Warmth flooded my chest and I longed for a hug, the comfort only a parent can give, but Mum had enough on her plate with Dad. His multiple sclerosis had advanced from his initial prognosis of relapsing MS to secondary progressive and he now struggled to walk as his left side was so weak. He often had problems remembering things and communicating. Occasionally, on particularly bad days, he was unable to hold his bowels. It was such a stark contrast to the capable dad Ruby and I had grown up with that it was painful to witness his decline.

Mum became clinically depressed trying to look after him, until we found an assisted living centre where carers were on site at all times. It gave Mum some respite, but she saw Dad every day, taking him out with the help of a carer, and always there to prepare his evening meal. It hadn't been an easy decision to move him, but it meant Mum could carry on working and stay in the marital home we grew up in. It had been tough on her and I hated adding to her load.

'Thanks, Mum, I'll keep in touch, I promise. Tell Ruby I'm okay and give Dad a kiss for me.'

I hung up and paced the apartment, not sure what to do with myself before stripping off and slipping into the private pool, letting the cool water cleanse my mind. Should I fly home, cut short the honeymoon I'd worked so hard for, or was that giving in? Ryan would stay, I knew he would. He'd drink the bar dry and enjoy every minute of the free food, booze and sun, making sure he got his money's worth.

He was so nonchalant about his betrayal, downplaying it like it was nothing, unable to comprehend I was mortified and humiliated. Even if Liza had thrown herself at him, he was hardly fighting her off when I saw them.

A headache brewed at my temples while my stomach groaned in hunger, so I retrieved the soggy baguette from my bag and lay on a lounger in the sun to dry off.

'Are you going to get ready for dinner?'

I must have dozed off after I'd eaten as when I opened my eyes, Ryan was stood over me, swaying, the sun had moved round and I was now in the shade.

'Come on, you need to eat. We can talk properly. I booked us into the Mexican restaurant for six, it's just gone five.' He slurred his words slightly, if anyone needed to eat it was him, to soak up the amount of alcohol he'd consumed on his first day here.

I sighed, getting up, ravenous at the mention of food. Perhaps once I'd made it clear over dinner we were over, we could discuss what we were going to do when we got home like adults. Would we sell the house? Would I move out or would he? Practical things which needed to be determined, no matter how painful.

'Don't suppose you want me to join you?' he smirked as I entered the bathroom and set the shower running.

'Fuck off, Ryan,' I snapped, slamming the door and locking it.

We got to the Mexican restaurant at six, Ryan in navy shorts and a linen shirt. I had on a strappy black dress to counteract the redness of my skin. Ryan stood twisting his wedding band around his finger as we waited to be seated. Mine was still in the bottom of my bag.

'So listen, we can move past this, babe,' he hiccupped.

'Nothing happened, I promise, and we've got our whole lives ahead of us. We've just got married.' Ryan clasped my hand across the table for four, almost knocking off our cutlery as a waitress brought us a bottle of red wine.

'I can't move past it, Ryan, not when you're still lying to me.'

'I'm not lying, she was hammered, she came onto me. That's what you saw. Nothing else happened,' he implored, his eyes glassy.

'It looked like you were into it,' I shot back, draining half my glass as soon as it was poured. I needed something to get me through the evening.

'I wasn't, I was really drunk, that's all.'

'Oh that's your excuse, is it? What if it had been me and Bobby, you wouldn't be so nonchalant then! It was supposed to be the best day of my life,' I added, my voice breaking, 'but it was the worst.'

'I'm sorry I ruined it. I love you, Kel, this can't be it for us, not after all these years. Come on, we're good together.'

I looked into Ryan's eyes, wanting to believe him. He was all I'd ever known, but my heart had been ripped in two and I wasn't sure if I'd ever be able to trust him again.

'We were, but you've broken us,' I said, swiping a tear away, not wanting to ruin my make-up. 'We need to talk about what's going to happen when we get home. We'll have to get the marriage annulled.'

Ryan leaned back in his seat, eyes darkening. 'You can't be serious?'

The service was slow and the waitress hadn't been back to take our order yet. I nibbled on a breadstick, Ryan's expression leaving me mute.

'We're not doing that,' Ryan said, shaking his head and rearranging his cutlery.

'Are you ready to order?' A dark-haired waitress finally returned to our table with a small notepad and looked at us expectantly.

'I'll have the chicken fajitas please,' I requested, mustering a smile.

'The same for me please.' Ryan handed the waitress our menus and she walked away. I took another large gulp of wine, which was going straight to my head on an empty stomach.

'How can I trust you, Ryan? We'd just exchanged our bloody wedding vows to each other, which hours later you trashed.'

'You know you can fucking trust me.' Ryan leant across the table, frustration emanating from his every pore. He must have assumed a few empty promises would be enough to smooth everything between us, but he was wrong.

I shrunk back at his shift of mood, my gaze straying over Ryan's shoulder towards the door, jaw instantly dropping. Blinking rapidly, convinced my eyes were deceiving me, I gawped as I registered Bobby and Liza strolling towards us, holding hands with massive smiles on their faces.

'Surprise!'

12

I was struck dumb, unable to comprehend what was happening. Like when you were a child at school and couldn't reconcile it when you saw your teacher in the supermarket, out of their usual habitat. The pair of them shouldn't be here, in Crete, they were supposed to be back home, in Crawley. Had Bobby and Liza flown out to join our honeymoon?

'Hey, guys,' Ryan's voice was flat and he awarded them a weak smile as they sat either side of us at the table.

Bobby's grin was wide, clearly not reading the room, either that or relishing the awkwardness.

Stunned, I stared open-mouthed at him, then at Liza, who tossed her long glossy black hair, yet to succumb to the humidity, over her shoulder.

I gripped the table, knuckles white, she looked stunning in a fuchsia pink bandeau dress, and the green-eyed monster I'd been trying to bury erupted. Liza's smile receded when she saw my hate-filled face, she was sharper than Bobby, I'd give her that. My eyes met Ryan's and he shifted awkwardly in his seat, trying to avoid scrutiny. He knew they were coming!

'You've got to be fucking kidding me!' I bolted up from the table, shooting daggers at Liza and Ryan before stalking out of the restaurant, blood pumping in my ears.

'Kel, wait,' Ryan called behind me, his chair scraping on the tiled floor.

'I cannot fucking believe you,' I said through gritted teeth when he caught my arm a few steps outside the entrance, whirling around to give him the full force of my rage.

'It was supposed to be a surprise, we'd have a few days on our own and then...'

'You thought you'd fly your whore out to join us, a nice little threesome honeymoon?' I shouted over him, trying to resist the urge to slap him across his cheek. I was a volcano exploding, spouting lava that desecrated everything in its wake. Holiday-makers stopped to stare, but I was too incensed to care. 'I'm flying home!' I spat, turning away, but Ryan grabbed my upper arm again, his nails like knives on my sunburn.

He drew me closer, eyes black like a shark about to strike. 'No, you're fucking not. Remember who pays for your dad's care home.'

My mouth dropped open and I hunched over like I'd been shot, the wine I'd consumed rushing up and out of my mouth spilling onto the path at our feet.

Ryan tutted and shook his head, releasing me, his lip curling in disgust. 'Go and clean up. You're embarrassing yourself.' He looked me up and down like I was something he'd trod in and went back inside the restaurant.

I wiped my hand across my mouth, bile burning the back of my throat. My dream honeymoon had turned into a nightmare.

Through raging tears, I rushed to the nearest toilet to splash water on my face and left the hotel, walking with zero direction, wanting to put as much distance between me and my lowlife husband as possible. I took off my sandals when I reached the beach, gritty sand beneath my toes. It was still busy despite the fading light. Children played with buckets and spades, some still jumping over the white foam which flowed onto the shore. I envied their carefree lives, having fun in this idyllic setting which had been tainted for me with Ryan's arrival.

I sat with my toes in the water, chest compressed, like a lead weight had been strapped to it. Had that been a threat? Ryan and I paid a third of the total, twelve hundred pounds every month and I couldn't afford the amount by myself, he knew that. Dog walking was what I loved, but it wasn't lucrative. Ryan had been the one to suggest the assisted living centre; the plumbing business was doing well and he could see how concerned Ruby and I were about Mum struggling to cope with Dad's deterioration. It had been *his* idea, a solution that would support everyone and, with a little persuasion, Dad had moved into the home. That was nine months ago and he'd settled well. As a result, Mum was much calmer and less stressed and we realised how vital the extra care had been.

Was Ryan now going to dangle Dad's care home fees in front of me like a carrot, to make me stay? How had the man I loved become so manipulative? It wasn't the Ryan I knew, not the one I'd met when I was sixteen. What had changed and, more importantly, how had I missed it?

I remained on the beach when the surrounding families packed up and left, watching the sun sink into the sea. Couples came for a romantic moonlight stroll across the sand as I wept, wishing more than anything I hadn't got on the plane, because now I was trapped in a foreign country with my cheating husband and his mistress.

Wiping away my tears, I checked my phone for available flights home, the earliest bookable one was on Thursday – the day after tomorrow – and the price was extortionate. Despite wanting to run away, again, I couldn't bring myself to book it, not with Ryan's threat ringing in my ears. I had to talk to him first, find a way forward that wouldn't affect my dad, but it didn't exist, did it? If we were separating I'd be on my own, he was my family, my responsibility, not Ryan's. With a dark cloud over my head I picked up my sandals and made my way off the sand and back onto the road towards the hotel, smacking straight into Nico as I reached the entrance to the complex.

'Hi!' He looked over my shoulder, obviously expecting Ryan to be following behind.

'He's in there somewhere.' I pointed towards the hotel.

'Are you okay? You look terrible!'

I laughed at his blunt but fair assessment of my tear-streaked face.

'Why aren't you working?' I asked, dodging his question, not quite ready to spill my guts yet.

'I've just finished, day off tomorrow, back at the bar Thursday.'

'Do you want to get a drink with me?' I blurted, surprised at my forwardness. I chewed my lip, praying he'd say yes. I didn't want to go back to Ryan and I certainly didn't want to see Liza.

A slow smile spread across his face and he slung his arm around my shoulder, manoeuvring me on the pavement. 'I know just the place.'

We walked in the opposite direction from the beach toward a parade of shops until Nico pointed to a bar with a neon sign outside depicting pitchers of beer clinking together. The thought of being wedged inside a bar with hundreds of sweaty partygoers where you couldn't hear yourself think wasn't my idea of fun. What was I doing?

'It'll be quiet, it's a Tuesday.' Seeing the look on my face, he pushed the door open.

Nico wasn't wrong, inside it was dark and dingy and a lone man sat at the bar bent over a pint of beer. He looked like he'd had a similar day to me.

'Take a seat.' Nico pointed towards a table before going to the bar and coming back with two whiskies. 'You look like you need this for, how do you say, medicine...'

'Medicinal purposes,' I chuckled and took a sip, shuddering. It was strong and tasted awful, but I persevered regardless.

'So, you were telling the truth about your husband?' Nico leaned back in his seat and put his hands behind his head.

My eyes wandered to the smattering of dark chest hair escaping out of the unbuttoned collar of his shirt, catapulting me back to last night when he'd kissed me.

'The affair?' he continued, bringing me back on course. Maybe he hadn't believed me at first, and I couldn't blame him. Who came out on honeymoon without their significant other?

'Yes, but it seems he flew out here anyway, along with the woman he had an affair with.'

Nico's eyes widened, his jaw slack. 'Really?'

'Really,' I said, nodding before giving Nico a quick description of what I'd stumbled upon the evening of my wedding.

'The guy's an asshole, he showed me a photo of you when he was at the bar, asking where you were. He said "I'm in her bad books" while he sits drinking and laughing.'

I shrugged, not sure how to answer. I couldn't defend Ryan, not now.

'He doesn't deserve you.' His voice was so low, almost a growl, eyes boring into me, their intensity pushing me back into my seat.

'You don't know me,' I reminded Nico.

'I am a good judge of character.' He smiled and I had to resist the urge to jump over the table and climb onto his lap.

'Chips.' The spell was broken by the barman delivering an enormous bowl of chips smothered in melted cheese. My stomach growled appreciatively, and I dove straight in.

'Hungry?' Nico laughed at my appetite.

'I haven't eaten in hours,' I mumbled, cupping my hand over my stuffed mouth.

We stayed in the bar for three hours, moving on from whisky to red wine until the room was spinning despite the carb fest I'd indulged in. Customers trickled in, the sound of people chatting and laughing surrounded us. The hollowness from earlier went away as I listened to Nico tell me about his family. His parents owned a car rental company near the airport and his two sisters both worked at hotels in Heraklion. His father wanted him to run the family business, but he was young, twenty-five, and still wanted to travel. He had plans to backpack around Europe, staying in hostels, and said he'd always wanted to visit England, although I wasn't sure if it was a line. Although, at that moment I didn't care.

In turn, I told him about my family back home, the dog walking business and my dreams of opening a grooming parlour. I described where I lived in Crawley and how London was only a short train ride away before telling him about my love for reading and hours spent watching period dramas. He laughed as I confessed how much I hated reality television and middle-of-the-road music. It was surreal talking about my life, purposefully not mentioning Ryan, but that was a void I'd need to fill with other things when I got home.

'How about a stroll on the beach?' Nico suggested, the dimple on his stubbled chin making him look like a naughty schoolboy.

'Is that where you take all your ladies?' I asked, raising an eyebrow. My boldness fuelled by alcohol and the fizz of desire.

'Only the special ones.'

13

The main thing I liked about Nico was he had no pretence. He didn't pretend I was the only girl he'd pursued out of the thousands of holidaymakers who came through Elouda Bay each year. There were no grand romantic gestures, or cheap tricks to get me into bed. He was just a nice guy, out to have a good time, so when he offered to show me his place, which was a tiny flat above a convenience store, I agreed, in part wanting to delay having to face Ryan for as long as possible. I was a little drunk, but when he kissed me, the tension crackled between us and I kissed him back hungrily. When he lowered the straps on my dress while gently caressing my neck, I unbuttoned his shirt and ran my fingertips across his hairy chest.

We fell into bed, our bodies wrapped around each other, and Nico replaced any thoughts I had about Ryan with pleasure. It was strange having another man's hands on my skin when there had only ever been Ryan, but it felt right, natural even. Ruby teased me about all the missed opportunities I'd had settling down so young, but I wasn't interested. A one-night stand was something I'd never even contemplated, yet being in a different country, it didn't feel real. There was no guilt or shame attached to it and it was good to forget about everything.

* * *

'Morning, princess,' Nico said as I sat and groaned, covering my naked body with the faded blue sheet.

'What time is it?' My mouth was like sandpaper, head throbbing like someone was playing the cymbals inside my skull.

'Eight. Do you want some water?' Nico's amused expression at my morning fog made me laugh.

'Yes please.' Nico got up and walked naked to the kitchen, completely unabashed, his toned backside on full display.

I turned my head away when he returned, cheeks flaming. In the cold light of day a twinge of guilt sobered me immediately. Two wrongs didn't make a right.

'*Now* you're blushing?' He was incredulous, climbing back into bed and handing me a glass of cold water, which I gulped down.

'Oh God, I don't want to go back,' I whined. It had been good to get away from everything last night but I couldn't hide indefinitely, I had to face Ryan which was bad enough, without adding Bobby and Liza into the mix.

'So don't, spend the day here with me.' He patted the bed where his invitation lay and as appealing as it was, I knew I had to go back to reality.

'I wish I could, but I need to go.' I reached for my dress and slipped it over my head while searching the floor for my underwear.

'Give me your phone.' Nico held his hand out and I pulled it from my bag, unlocked it and tossed it over to him. 'Wow, ten missed calls.' He tapped the screen for a minute before handing it back to me.

I groaned, Ryan had called multiple times from the apartment last night. I unblocked his number as there was little point hiding from him now he was here.

'I've put my number in, if you need a place to hide you know where to find me.'

'Thank you, and thanks for last night, the drinks and...' I blushed. 'I had a nice time.' As clichéd as it sounded, I felt like a new woman; one who was still attractive, desirable even and it had boosted my confidence no end.

'Me too.' Nico took my hand and kissed it before flopping back onto his pillow.

'I'll see you later,' I said, quickly checking myself in Nico's bathroom mirror before I headed out into the bright morning sun with a spring in my step. Last night had been amazing and I had no regrets about what we'd done, but I had to return to reality.

Back at Elouda Bay, holidaymakers hurried around the pool, placing towels on the remaining sunbeds, claiming their spots for the day. Couples were already heading out for breakfast and I kept my head low, as if everyone knew I was doing the walk of shame back to the apartment, where my husband was waiting. I let myself in, but the place was empty. Had Ryan already gone to breakfast? The bed was rumpled and the sheets pulled back so he'd slept here last night.

I took a long shower before heading to the main pool, snaring one of the few remaining sunbeds. I didn't want to walk in on Ryan having a cosy breakfast with Liza and Bobby. In fact, the longer I could avoid them the better. Lathering myself in sun cream, I put on my shades and snoozed in the sun, enjoying the ache of my muscles from sex with Nico last night. It felt good to have a secret and I sent Nico a message thanking him for a great time.

I knew Ryan would go mental if he found out, not that I'd ever tell him, although I knew he'd make his own assumptions about my whereabouts. A tiny trickle of guilt hit me, what if Ryan *had* been telling the truth and Liza threw herself at him? That the night of our wedding was the first and only time they'd been together? Maybe they hadn't even done the deed.

I shook the thought from my head, remembering the photo of her glaring at us on the dance floor. Even if she had come onto him, he'd hardly rebuffed her advances.

Across the pool, my stomach lurched as I spotted Liza in a tiny yellow string bikini climbing onto a lounger between Bobby and Ryan, who were sat talking. Ryan held his phone to his ear and a second later my mobile vibrated.

'I'm across the pool.' I raised my hand to catch his eye.

'Where have you been, I've been worried!'

I watched as Bobby sat up, shielding his eyes from the sun as he searched the row of sunbeds to find me. Liza didn't even twitch.

'I'm fine. We need to talk.'

'I saved you a sunbed.' Ryan gestured to the one next to him covered with a white hotel towel.

'Not with them,' I scoffed. The audacity of my husband was unbelievable.

'Fine, I'll come over.' He begrudgingly got to his feet and made his way around the pool. The sunbeds either side of me were vacant, although covered with towels, perhaps their owners were still at breakfast or had gone to the beach. Either way, I was glad Ryan and I would have some privacy for our awkward conversation.

'Where were you?' Ryan sat on the adjacent sunbed and I

swung my legs round to face him. His grey swimming shorts bunched up around his thighs and he took off his sunglasses, revealing bloodshot eyes. He must have got hammered after I left.

'I didn't want to be around you last night.' I looked across the pool at Liza and Bobby, both flat out on their sunbeds. 'Why did you invite them, Ryan?'

'I told you; it was supposed to be a surprise. I thought we'd have a good time, the four of us together. They only flew out for four nights, they're going home on Saturday and we'll have another three days to ourselves.'

'And was that decided before or after you slept with your best mate's wife?'

Ryan scowled at my flippancy. 'I didn't sleep with her, for God's sake. Look, Kel, we're here now, let's just have a good week, yeah?' He opened his arms, trying to pacify me, but I remained steely.

'You are joking?' I laughed, but Ryan shook his head. 'It was our wedding day, Ryan, and you couldn't keep your hands off another woman!' I tried to drill the point into his thick skull, but he rolled his eyes as though I was overreacting.

'It was nothing!' He enunciated each word like I was a child.

'Does Bobby know?'

Ryan's face darkened and he raised it skyward in frustration. 'We're going around in circles.'

'We need to talk about what happens when we get back, selling the house, who's moving where, all that stuff?'

'Whoa, whoa, whoa.' Ryan's eyes bulged. 'We're not breaking up.'

'You don't get to decide that. It's over.' I sighed as he hung his head.

'You're blowing this way out of proportion.'

'I know what I saw, Ryan, and we're done. I can't move on from this. When we get back, we'll put the house up for sale.' My resolve remaining firm despite waiting for him to bring my dad's care home fees into the conversation again.

Ryan's jaw clenched and he raised his hand to scratch his beard, already growing out the trim he'd had for the wedding. 'We can't.'

I frowned. 'Why not?'

'Because I took out a loan against the house to support the business. Costs have gone up, suppliers had to be paid and Bobby's inheritance has run out. We were hit with a huge tax bill and I had no way to pay it.' He rubbed the back of his neck as though his stress had accumulated there. 'If we sell, the equity will probably only be enough to pay off the loan, plus what we borrowed for your new van.'

I breathed deeply, trying to process what Ryan was telling me. He'd been lying to me for months. Another bombshell to digest.

'I don't understand, I thought the business was doing well?'

'It was, until the tax bill came in, now we're just keeping afloat. Everything is hanging in the balance, so if you tell Bobby what you *think* you saw, he'll walk, and the business will collapse. I won't be able to complete the jobs we've got coming up without him. We'll lose the house, it'll bankrupt us.'

My throat was dry, time seemed to shift around me. All the years, all the savings, us ploughing money into the mortgage, had it all been for nothing?

'What about the wedding?' I asked, as he'd taken care of most of the bills.

'Another loan. We're drowning, Kel.'

Why hadn't he confided in me? We could have cut back, postponed the wedding, prioritised what we had to pay. I would have done an extra walk every day if need be, I had enough interest for it. Then it hit me, Ryan's words repeating in my head, *a loan against the house.*

'How did you get a loan out against the house? I haven't signed anything.'

Ryan looked at his trainers, the awkward silence broken by the couple next to us arriving, hovering to use the sunbed he was perched on. I put on my sarong and we walked away from the beds to a patch of grass beneath a palm tree as it dawned on me what Ryan had done.

'So, let me get this right, you forged my signature and now we're up to our eyes in debt?'

At least my husband had the good grace to look sheepish.

'You do realise that's illegal, you could go to prison,' I added.

'Are you threatening me? Because it's your word against mine.' Ryan's voice was bitter, but he softened at my wide-eyed reaction, the hurt written across my face. 'Listen, Kel, we can get through it. You wanted the wedding and the honeymoon, we couldn't really afford it, but I didn't want to let you down.' Ryan kicked at the grass with the toe of his trainer, creating a divot.

'You let me down the moment you lied,' I shot back, pacing in a circle around the tree.

'If you leave, you'll have nothing but debt. We stick together and carry on. Things will turn around,' Ryan grabbed my wrist and I recoiled, 'but if you tell Bobby, we're fucked.' He looked scared, something I hadn't seen before, and I sensed I wasn't getting the full picture. 'Right now, we're managing, your dad's care home fees included, but I don't know how long for.'

'The care home was your idea, Ryan!'

'I know, but I thought your mum was going to sell up and downsize, I thought she was going to take over the fees eventually. I didn't know it was going to be for this long.'

I blew air out through my cheeks. He had a point but perhaps he should have mentioned that when he agreed we'd contribute.

'How much are we talking?' I asked, bracing myself.

'Altogether... about forty grand.'

I swallowed hard, feeling sick at the dizzying figure. 'Jesus Christ.'

'So come over, yeah, be nice, let's enjoy the next few days.' His face softened and he released his grip, rubbing the top of my arm. It took all my willpower not to shrink away from his touch. I didn't even know who he was any more.

'You want me to pretend?' I sneered.

'If that's what you have to do then, yeah, because if you don't, it's all going to go to shit.'

14

My heart sank as I picked up my towel and bag, reluctantly following Ryan back over to where Liza and Bobby were laying. The last thing I wanted to do was interact with Liza, but what choice did I have? Reeling from the huge amount of debt Ryan had got us into, the only way to claw ourselves out of it was to keep the plumbing business afloat. If Ryan was going to lie and make out we'd jointly signed the paperwork, then how could I prove otherwise? I could pretend things were fine, for a few days at least, but I wasn't about to let Liza off the hook. The bitch jumped my husband on my wedding day.

'Hey, Kelly.' Bobby sat up, waving awkwardly as I approached.

'Hiya, Bobby.' My voice was flat as I laid my towel over the spare lounger, chucking the white hotel one back on Ryan's bed.

'Nice of you to join us,' Liza chipped in, propped up on her elbows, dark sunglasses shielding her eyes. I hoped she could feel my hatred burning through them.

'Well, it was a surprise seeing the pair of you on our honeymoon, that's for sure.' The words stuck in my throat. I couldn't do it; I couldn't play nice when I wanted to drown her. 'And, Liza, I've not seen you since my wedding day, in the grounds I think, the summer house maybe,' I added, resting a finger on my chin in mock contemplation.

'I'm sorry if you feel like we've barged in on your honeymoon,' she replied without a note of sincerity in her voice, ignoring my jibe.

Liza was normally so warm and friendly, but now it was like we were a pair of cats prowling around each other, our hackles up, preparing for a scrap.

'I guess you're here now,' I replied flatly, laying down and seeing Bobby grimace at Ryan in my peripheral vision.

'Obviously if Ryan hadn't been held up at work, you would have had the first three days together on your own.' She stuck out her bottom lip and it took all the willpower I had not to scratch at her contoured face. Who wore make-up in thirty-degree heat?

'Yeah well, shit happens,' Ryan interjected, his tone buoyant, trying to lighten the mood.

'I still can't believe that guy demanded it was you and not me, I could have fixed his leak!' Bobby said, scratching his head.

So that was the lie he'd told Bobby as to why he'd been delayed, nothing to do with being caught cheating and his wife hiding his passport. Behind my sunglasses, I rolled my eyes and tried to get lost in my book. The tension simmered for a while. Liza made a show of getting Bobby to lather her back with sun cream, loosening her bikini top so her breasts were barely covered. All for Ryan's benefit, no doubt, or was it a power play for me? How low was she prepared to sink? I had no idea what she hoped to achieve, and if the atmosphere was frosty between us, it wasn't much better between Ryan and her either. I hoped he was feeling as awkward and uncomfortable as I was because the next few days were going to be hellish.

I tried to breathe through my anger and be as zen as I could, thinking about Nico when I couldn't concentrate on the plot of my book despite knowing it inside out. Replaying last night's events in my head and trying to transport myself back there got me through.

After an hour, I had a swim in the pool, distancing myself from Bobby and Liza, who were canoodling by the waterfall under the watchful eye of Ryan. He swam over to me and tried to put his arm around me in a show of affection, but I shrugged him off.

'Kel!'

'I don't want you touching me,' I spat.

'They'll notice something's off.'

'You're damn right something's off!' I swam away to the centre of the pool, where a tiled platform was filled with picturesque shrubs. It was suffocating being around them, having to bite my tongue whenever Liza opened her mouth, convinced she was deliberately trying to provoke me. Was she enjoying this? Did she want Ryan for herself or did she plan to lead them both a merry dance? Did she plan to have her cake and eat it too? I couldn't believe our friendship meant so little to her that she had no qualms about taking my man for herself. Perhaps we weren't as close as I'd thought, maybe getting closer to Ryan had been her plan since we'd met. The thought left a bad taste in my mouth, I'd been well and truly hoodwinked.

After lunch, Bobby persuaded Ryan to go to the swim-up bar for a beer, leaving Liza and I alone. She appeared to be sleeping, laying on her back. I could tell Ryan didn't want to go and leave the two of us alone, giving me a pointed look before they left. I smiled sweetly at him, already looking forward to being able to get some things off my chest as soon as our husbands were out of earshot.

'So, how long have you been screwing my husband?' I asked as soon as they walked away.

Liza sat up, glaring at me. 'What?' To her credit, she acted like she didn't know what I was talking about.

'Don't play dumb, I saw you, on my fucking wedding day, Liza. You were supposed to be my best friend. How could you?' My neck mottled with rage, everything I'd buried since she'd walked in the door of the restaurant spilling out.

'I don't know what you're on about.' Liza was calm, she'd anticipated my confrontation and decided how she was going to play it. Unfortunately, her incredulity just enraged me further.

'And why him – of all the men, why did it have to be my husband? Was he the first man not to pay you any attention so you had to pursue him?' I said, trying to understand what on earth could have possessed her. Ryan was good-looking sure, but so was Bobby. What did Ryan have that Bobby didn't and what was it that was worth risking her marriage for?

'Do you really think if I was sleeping with Ryan, I'd let Bobby drag me out here to join you on your honeymoon?' she purred.

'I bet you couldn't wait,' I shot back.

'It was Bobby's idea, not mine. I prefer not to holiday with other couples.' Was it true? Did Bobby talk Ryan into inviting them? I didn't think so, not when Liza was so hostile, it had to be about Ryan. Attack was always the best course of defence for her.

'Unless you're having an affair with one of them! Did you think about Bobby, or me, at all?'

She pursed her lips, not answering and a wicked smile crept across my face.

'Because I cannot wait to tell him as soon as we get back home.'

I scooped up my bag and towel and headed back to the apartment, I'd had about as much of Liza as I could stomach. The bitch was lying to my damn face and didn't seem to have a care in the world.

Taking the opportunity of finally being alone, I called Ruby outside by the pool, but it went to voicemail.

'Liza and Bobby are here!' I whispered into the phone. 'It's so messed up, but I have to stay. I'll call you tomorrow.' Events of today played on loop in my mind and as much as I wanted to switch off I couldn't, I just wanted to run away and not have to deal with it all.

Ryan came back an hour later, deep lines etched into his forehead.

'You need to try harder; Bobby knows you're pissed.'

'Well, they did just invade our honeymoon, so let's roll with me being a little upset about that, okay,' I snapped.

'I'm serious, Kel,' Ryan grabbed my upper arms and although I tried to shake myself free, he wouldn't let go.

'I don't fucking care. You broke my heart, Ryan, you both did, and now I'm supposed to just carry on like it never happened. Get the hell off me.' I shoved him away and when he bowled back up to me, I slapped his face, the sting in my palm radiating through my wrist.

Without a second's warning, Ryan slapped me back, hard across the cheek, leaving my ears ringing. I gasped, staggering backwards.

'Grow the fuck up, Kel. We're stuck, get it.'

'No, Ryan, you're stuck,' I sobbed. 'You've created this mess, this shitshow. You forged legal documents and brought your bit on the side on our honeymoon. Why? Wasn't I enough?' I clutched my throbbing cheek, adding, 'I don't care about the money.'

He jabbed a finger at me. 'I care, so put your big-girl pants on and get on with it. When we get home, we can talk, I'll move into the spare room if you want, we can have a break, but we're *not* getting divorced and we're *not* selling the house.'

Ryan stormed into the bathroom and slammed the door so hard the apartment shook, leaving me to curl up on the bed and cry. How had life gone from being perfect to such a nightmare in a matter of days?

I looked again on my phone at the flight out tomorrow and the temptation to book it was overwhelming. Ryan had never struck me before, although I had hit him first. It was an explosion of the anger contained all day released with one slap. But Ryan's knee-jerk reaction had caught me off guard, he was wound tightly like a spring, poised to snap at any moment and I had to be more careful. I knew Ryan had a temper, but I'd never seen him so unhinged. It was like he'd been backed into a corner, frustration mounting until he couldn't contain it. How far would he go to get me to maintain the charade that everything was fine and what would he do if I didn't comply?

All I wanted was to get away and the pull of racing to the airport and jumping on the first plane home was tough to ignore. If I stayed, every minute would be spent with them and I wasn't sure I could bear it. My mask would slip, I knew it would. Because all I was filled with now was hate. Hate for my cheating husband, hate for Liza the home-wrecking slut and hate for Bobby's stupidity that he couldn't see what was going on right in front of his face.

Although, I couldn't blame him; before my wedding day, I'd been just as clueless, or maybe I hadn't wanted to see it. Ryan had been stressed, like I was, quick to fly off the handle at the slightest thing, but I put it down to wedding jitters.

I breathed deeply, wiping away my tears, cheek smarting from Ryan's palm. What had happened to the man I couldn't wait to marry, the one I dreamt of raising a family with? Ten years was a long time and yet he'd changed, and I hadn't seen it. He'd turned into a lying, manipulating cheat who hadn't even flinched when hitting a woman. Where was his remorse? The slap was one thing, but the deceit was another. How had he managed to conceal forty grand's worth of debt from me? He had to be in it deep, over his head, and I worried about his state of mind. The Ryan I loved had gone and I didn't know the man who had replaced him.

Yet we were stuck together, for the next seven days at least, sharing a room. I didn't know how I'd survive it. I'd be counting down the minutes until we flew home, where I could find solace in my family. I couldn't turn to my best friend; she was at the heart of all this and I hadn't even begun to process that loss. Out here I was alone, sharing an apartment with a man I was fearful of. If he'd hit me once, then it was likely he'd do it again.

15

I made an effort to look flawless for dinner, covering up my red cheek with a layer of make-up. It was more of a pissing contest than anything else. Liza was stunning, her heritage a mix of Malaysian and English. She had her mother's olive skin and dark poker-straight hair paired with her father's almond shaped eyes and full lips. Her limbs were long and slender, her waist tiny something I hadn't overly noticed until all of a sudden we were in competition.

The warmth Liza used to radiate had disappeared, her thermostat broken, and since her arrival, she was stony-faced, all hard lines and angles. Attack had always been the best form of defence for her. Liza was rarely wrong and Bobby would roll over, even if she was, so she was used to getting her way. As soon as Bobby had introduced us, six years ago now, I knew we'd be friends, which was why the betrayal was doubly painful. She used to make me laugh so much, her cutting observations and no-nonsense attitude had me in stitches, but now I seethed whenever she opened her mouth. How many times had her pretty mouth been planted on my husband's?

To make a point I wasn't the dowdy wife my husband had cheated on, I wore a two-piece matching top and ruffle skirt which showcased my midriff, but all I could think when I looked in the mirror was how it was a shame Nico wasn't working to see me in it.

'You look fantastic,' Ryan whistled as I put large, hooped earrings in, his mood significantly improved from earlier.

'Thanks,' I replied, trying to keep the sarcasm from my voice. As if I'd got all dressed up for him.

'I'm sorry about earlier, I didn't mean to lose my temper.' Ryan's apology was a little too late, he'd crossed a line, we both knew it, but I managed a nod in response, keen not to rile him up anymore and get through the next few days without too much trauma.

'Ready?' he asked, opening the apartment door.

I checked my hair in the mirror a final time, I'd scrunched my dark waves which seemed to match the carnival style outfit, and grabbed my bag.

As we left the apartment, Ryan took my hand and my shoulders tensed immediately, skin crawling. I didn't want my husband anywhere near me, but my cheek was still tender and I wasn't about to provoke him again. If keeping up appearances would pacify him for now, then I'd bear it.

'I'm starving,' Ryan said when we met Bobby and Liza by the water fountain outside the main restaurant, where I managed to free myself from Ryan's grip. Bobby gawped at my outfit, his eyes out on stalks, and inwardly I glowed with satisfaction. At least I could still turn a head.

'I think it's Chinese-themed tonight.' Liza nudged him. She wore an off-the-shoulder yellow dress which clung to her frame right down to her calves.

'You look lovely.' She beamed at my compliment. 'Like a

beautiful canary,' I added as we made our way inside. One point to me.

We sat and the boys went to fill their plates while we waited, keeping hold of the table as the restaurant was busy.

'Look, Kelly, I have no interest in your man,' Liza simpered, 'so let's just make the best of this, okay?'

'No interest? That's not what it looked like at our wedding; you were plenty interested when his hand was up your dress and his flies were down.'

Liza laughed, a tinkling sound which jarred my ears. 'Oh please.'

'Do you know what, you're welcome to him because I'm done with you both. As soon as we get off this island, I never want to see either of you again.'

Before Liza could respond, the boys were back, their plates brimming with meat, rice and spring rolls, laughing heartily at some inside joke.

'Shall we go and get ours?' I said in a saccharine voice to Liza. Maybe I could play this game after all, I might be able to have a little fun.

'Sure,' she replied a little stiffly.

We moved around the central island, looking at the various dishes on offer. I chose sweet and sour chicken, noodles and a couple of spring rolls, being sure to bump into Liza while she was spooning beef in black bean sauce onto her plate.

'Shit,' she scowled as I melted back into the throng of hungry holidaymakers before returning to the table. Smirking as she came back, a dark stain across her middle.

'I'll have to change after dinner,' she scowled, dabbing at it with her napkin.

'Don't worry, babe, you brought plenty of clothes with you, no biggie,' Bobby tried to pacify her as I clamped my lips together to stop a giggle bursting out.

We ate and I concentrated on my food while the others chatted about plans for the following day. Ryan was trying to sell the catamaran trip he'd been talking about before, although Liza wasn't keen.

'Do you have to snorkel?' She wrinkled her nose.

'No, you can swim in the sea if you want, they take you to a secluded beach for a barbecue lunch, but you don't have to go in the water at all if you don't want to.'

Liza beamed at Ryan and my throat tightened as I watched him blush.

'I'm up for it,' Bobby chipped in, munching on a prawn cracker. 'This grub is lovely!'

'The food here is great,' I agreed, enjoying the meal far more than the company.

On the way out of the restaurant, we bumped into Janice and Greg.

'He's arrived, that's fantastic.' Janice clapped her hands together at the sight of Ryan beside me, while he looked momentarily confused at this strange woman grinning at him.

'Janice and Greg let me tag along with them while I waited for you,' I explained, smiling tightly. 'Would you like to join us?' I asked. 'We're going to the bigger bar near reception, I think there's a singer tonight, isn't there?' My voice was cheery, knowing full well Ryan would be annoyed at my inviting strangers to join our group for the evening. If it meant I wouldn't have to talk to Liza, it was a bonus for me. Plus it was nice to get my own back. Bobby and Liza had imposed on our honeymoon, it wouldn't do any harm for him to see how it felt.

'That would be lovely,' Janice said, falling in step with us and relaying her and Greg's trip to the market today.

We grabbed a table for four, pulling up two more chairs, and the three men went to the bar for drinks.

'Sorry, I haven't introduced you, this is Liza, Bobby's wife. They flew out to join us on our honeymoon,' I said, my eyebrows raised.

'Oh,' Janice's mouth slowly lifted into a polite yet perplexed smile.

'It was a surprise.' My voice dripped with sarcasm.

'We all get on so well,' Liza said through gritted teeth. 'Actually, I'll just pop back and change my dress. I had a bit of an accident at dinner.'

'Liza's so clumsy,' I said with a flourish, watching as she smiled tightly before walking away.

'That's a bit off, isn't it, turning up on your honeymoon,' Janice leaned towards me, whispering.

'I can't say I'm thrilled,' I admitted.

Greg, Ryan and Bobby returned before I had the chance to say anything else, already discussing the Euros and England crashing out, leaving Janice and I to talk amongst ourselves.

Liza, when she returned in a floral dress, sat stoney-faced, unable to hear our conversation over the men's spirited debate, which had moved on to who had the better home team. It felt good to exclude her and I relished the bored expression on her pretty little face.

'Right, I'll get the drinks in. Who's for a margarita?' Janice asked, standing and putting a hand on her husband's shoulder as he started to get to his feet. 'Sit, I'll get them for a change.'

'I'll help.' I stood, taking orders. Ryan and Bobby wanted a beer.

'Can I have a virgin mojito please?' Liza asked, directing her request at Janice rather than me.

'Virgin?' I exclaimed, frowning. 'That'll be a first!' Unable to hide my snarkiness. When had Liza turned down the chance of a cocktail? It was unheard of; she drank like a fish back home.

'Yeah, Liza's not drinking at the moment.' Bobby gazed at his wife, a shadow passing his face.

'Not at the moment,' she agreed and I watched in horror as her hand went straight to her stomach, rubbing the colourful fabric. She looked pointedly at Bobby, a smile spreading across her face as though she couldn't contain it.

I glanced immediately at Ryan, whose eyes were like saucers, sweat beaded beneath his hairline and he choked on the remainder of his pint.

'You're not?' he said, the colour draining from his face.

'I am,' Liza grinned, reaching over to hold Bobby's hand. 'We're pregnant,' she announced as Janice and Greg whooped, oblivious to the horrified expressions on mine and Ryan's faces.

16

I composed myself quickly.

'Congratulations.' I cleared my throat. 'How far along are you?'

'Three months,' Bobby answered, releasing Liza's hand.

'It's been so difficult keeping it a secret,' Liza giggled.

My throat tightened, but Ryan looked like he was going to be sick. I stared at him, oblivious to the fact he'd just given himself away. No man who'd allegedly only cheated once, and was even denying it happened altogether, looked that terrified.

'Shall we?' Janice gestured to the bar.

'Sure.' The world seemed to sway, my legs like jelly.

'You don't seem overly happy for them?' Janice said once we were side by side at the bar waiting to be served.

'It's complicated,' I replied, not wanting to go into it, but realising I needed to come up with something. 'Ryan and I have been trying for ages, but it's not happened for us yet,' I lied, ignoring the twinge of guilt.

'Oh, don't worry, love, your time will come.' Janice rubbed my arm soothingly. Thankfully, her attention was taken reciting our order as my brain whirled.

So Ryan had been cheating and for at least three months it seemed, by the look on his face. Could Liza's baby be his? Poor Bobby, what had he got himself into? He had to know the truth. I couldn't stand by and let him unwittingly raise another man's child, not without making sure it was his. If there had been any doubt in my mind Ryan and I were finished, it had evaporated. He was a lying, cheating bastard who may have knocked up his best mate's wife. How anyone could stoop so low was beyond me.

Back at the table, Bobby was talking about how they were already looking to move to a bigger house. They'd been scoping out the suitability of primary schools and it was heartbreaking to watch him glow with pride at becoming a dad when there was a possibility the child wasn't his. He was too nice for his own good and I wasn't about to let Liza treat him like a doormat. He had to know the truth about everything, but now wasn't the time. I had no idea they'd even been trying to have a baby, Liza hadn't mentioned it and I hadn't heard it through Ryan. Perhaps it had been a happy accident, in Bobby's eyes anyway.

Ryan and I had discussed having children, but he'd wanted to wait until the plumbing business was more established and regular income was guaranteed. Having my own business meant I had no paid holiday or maternity leave to fall back on, so we had decided to make sure we were secure financially before we took the plunge. It was the sensible thing to do but it didn't reduce my desire to have a family. I'd been waiting impatiently for the time to be right.

Now I knew I'd dodged a bullet. The rug had been well and truly pulled out from beneath my feet the past few days, but it could have been much worse if we'd had kids. I had no qualms about walking away from Ryan with nothing, even if it meant shouldering some of the debt he'd racked up without me knowing. Better that than stay with a man I hated for the sake of money. I'd get by with Mum's support, she'd let me move back in and I could start again. Even if Ryan's business wasn't doing well, mine was growing. Perhaps Michelle and I could merge our businesses together, combine our client lists, even set up franchises in other areas? The sky was the limit and I wasn't going to let Ryan hold me back.

'You okay, Kel?' Bobby asked me later, sliding into the seat next to me while Ryan went to the toilet. Liza was chatting to Greg and Janice about baby names, although I noticed her back stiffen when Bobby switched seats.

'Yeah I'm good, Bobby, I'm really pleased for you both.'

'Thanks. I am sorry we gate-crashed your honeymoon. It seemed like a great idea at the time when Ryan suggested it.'

'When did he suggest it?' I asked, keen to get the details.

'Ages ago, I don't know, about six months, whenever he booked it.'

I nodded. So either the affair had been going on for that long or Ryan had totally misunderstood the brief for a romantic honeymoon and wanted Bobby and Liza to fly out and join us so we could have a week of partying. I wasn't sure which was worse, his deceit or stupidity.

'How is the business doing?' I asked, changing the subject.

'It's okay, materials have gone up, and what with the cost of living, everyone wants cheap labour. Our profit margins have shrunk, but we'll make it out the other side. Just got to keep plugging away.'

'Did you know Ryan had taken a loan out against the house?' I asked, trying to keep my expression neutral.

Bobby grimaced. 'I knew he'd borrowed money. Sorry, Kel, I

didn't know it was against the house. It's a blip, all businesses have peaks and troughs, as you know yourself.'

'I do,' I admitted, remembering struggling in the early days and barely making anything above petrol and insurance costs. At the time, I was practically walking dogs for free.

Ryan came back, hovering by my side until Bobby moved back to his seat.

'How about we hit the nightclub tonight, there's one onsite, isn't there?' Bobby suggested.

'I'm not sure,' Liza pouted.

'Come on, it'll be good to have a dance and let our hair down. I'll get some shots in,' Ryan said, heading over to the bar.

'It's time for us to bow out, I'm afraid. Have a lovely evening. Nice to meet you all and congratulations on the baby.' Janice got to her feet and I bid her and Greg goodnight before Ryan returned with a tray of six shots of tequila, two each for the three of us.

'I might have an early night,' Liza said, stifling a yawn.

'Come on, babe, we can go for a quick dance, then I'll take you back, I promise.' They were famous last words as whenever Bobby and Ryan started drinking, they always found it difficult to stop.

I necked a shot, keeping my thoughts to myself. I was happy to prolong having to return to the apartment with Ryan, even if it meant spending more time with Liza.

'Attagirl.' Ryan kissed me on the cheek before I could move out of the way, his lips wet. He made me want to gag and I drank the second shot quickly.

'Is that a grey hair in your beard?' I asked, squinting at his chin and inwardly howling as he patted where I was pointing, eyes wide with horror. I had to get my kicks where I could.

* * *

The nightclub was in the basement, beneath reception. Loud music boomed as we descended the steps into a hive of holiday-makers throwing themselves around the dance floor. Flip-flops and sandals had been discarded and I cringed at the thought of my bare feet touching the sticky tiles. The décor was interesting, black walls covered in green glitter which sparkled in the strobe lights. It was like a witch's den.

'Oh my God,' Liza groaned, and I momentarily pitied her having to deal with this sober, at least I'd had a few cocktails and shots to prepare myself.

We found a tall table in the corner and hovered around it until the introduction of a popular song came on and Ryan bounded into the centre of the dance floor, limbs flailing, well on his way to being drunk. Bobby went to the bar to get more shots, leaving Liza and I alone.

'Are you going to tell him then, or am I?' I shouted over the music.

'Tell who what?' She sighed as though I was a pesky fly buzzing around her.

'Tell Bobby his baby might actually be Ryan's.'

'Don't be ridiculous, it's Bobby's. Nothing happened with Ryan.'

'Okay, you're sticking with that then,' I said, rearranging the strap of my top as she scowled at me. 'Because,' I continued, 'the look on Ryan's face, well, I'd be worried if I was you.' I licked my lips and watched Ryan dance amongst the crowd, lifting his chin to the ceiling with his eyes closed like he was at a rave.

'Here you go, babe, tonic water.' Bobby arrived with a drink for Liza and another shot for us, clinking my glass before we both downed it. My head was already starting to feel woozy, but I enjoyed the out-of-body experience. It wasn't me all this shit was happening to but someone else. In that second I wanted to shake off my inhibitions and be anyone else but the victim of my own story so when a club classic I recognised came on I didn't hesitate.

Making my way onto the dance floor, arms in the air, I swayed my hips in time to the music, ignoring Ryan's attempts to get me to move with him. Closing my eyes, I spun around, letting the thud of the bass flow through my body. When I opened them again, Bobby and Liza looked to be arguing. A second later, she stalked towards the exit, bag in hand. Bobby ran his hand through his curls and turned in the opposite direction towards the bar. Across the dance floor I glanced over at Ryan, the only person amongst the throng not dancing. His eyes travelled across the room, watching Liza leave before swiftly heading after her. With a quick look towards the bar where Bobby had headed, I followed Ryan.

17

'Why didn't you tell me?' Ryan seethed, holding Liza by the hand at the top of stairs.

I remained in the shadows below, straining to hear their conversation over the music, disgust rippling through me.

'Because it's not yours, Ryan,' she snapped.

'How can you be so sure?'

The crowd behind me whooped at the intro of another club classic and their voices were drowned out. I couldn't hear their exchange any more but I wasn't sure I wanted to. I knew the truth now.

I slipped back to Bobby, who had returned to the table.

'Liza's got a headache, she's gone to bed,' he grumbled, fingering his wedding band.

'I'm pretty beat too, I'm going to head back.'

I watched his face fall.

'Don't worry, Ryan has a pass to stay out with you as long as he likes!' The longer the better as far as I was concerned. I didn't think it was possible to hate my husband any more than I already did, but tonight's bombshell was proving hard to digest.

At least Bobby's spirits had lifted, knowing he wouldn't have to drink alone, and he looked around for his mate.

'I think he's gone to the toilet. See you tomorrow, Bob,' I said, leaning in to give him a kiss on the cheek. The poor bugger was going to have his heart ripped out soon enough. He didn't deserve this, neither of us did. The rug had been well and truly pulled out from beneath our feet. We'd both been living in our own happy, blissfully ignorant bubbles until a few days ago and not telling Bobby what I knew was eating me up inside.

When I climbed the stairs, Ryan and Liza had both disappeared and I made my way back to the apartment, music still ringing in my ears, seething as I tried to process the fact my husband could have fathered a child. The seats on the available flight tomorrow were looking more attractive by the hour.

* * *

When I woke, Ryan was snoring on the sofa, still fully clothed, and I was grateful he hadn't tried to get into bed with me whatever hour he got back.

He must have heard me moving around and getting dressed as he leapt up, making me jump.

'Shit, we've got that boat trip today. What time is it?'

'Half eight,' I said, watching him run around the room like a headless chicken.

Apparently, Ryan had booked the trip at reception last night when they'd left the club drunk, convincing Bobby it would be fun. More money spent we couldn't afford. I'd been looking forward to a day on the beach, my AirPods in, blocking them out as much as possible. Now it seemed I was going to be stuck on a boat in closer proximity than I cared for but after last night's revelation I didn't want to miss a second Ryan and Liza spent together, otherwise I might have been tempted to feign illness.

'Can you get a bag together – sun cream, towels and stuff?'

I sighed, doing as I was asked like a dutiful wife. There were six nights and seven days until we'd be back on British soil, before Ryan and I could go our separate ways, and I was counting every minute. The flight home today that had been available was likely now full and the price had been extortionate. Knowing now how little money Ryan and I had, there seemed no point in adding to the amount I'd have to pay back.

'Bit of a surprise about Liza last night, wasn't it?' I couldn't resist twisting the knife, especially as I knew Ryan was wondering if the baby was his. It seemed his extramarital affair hadn't panned out the way he'd thought it would. There had been more consequences and our marriage wouldn't be the only casualty. I dreaded to think what Bobby would do to Ryan when he found out. They were pals, but Bobby was definitely the leader of their small pack.

'It's not mine,' he said, avoiding my eye.

'Of course it's not,' I smirked, my voice laced with sarcasm. 'Although you better take a crash course in changing nappies, just in case.'

He ignored me, tapping at his phone to call Bobby and check they were up and would meet us in reception shortly. It seemed Bobby wasn't anywhere near as hungover as Ryan and we found him and Liza in the foyer, munching on almond croissants, waiting for the coach.

Liza wore a large sun hat and playsuit, the straps of her orange bikini, which looked remarkably similar to mine, poking out. She looked about as happy about our day trip as I was. Her nose wrinkled; glare hidden beneath large dark sunglasses.

'Here you go, guys,' Bobby handed Ryan and I a croissant

each. Ryan tore through his, he looked a little green around the gills, whereas Bobby was as fresh as a daisy, bouncing around like an excited schoolboy.

'Looks like you two had fun last night,' I said.

'One shot too many for him though.' Bobby laughed, slapping Ryan on the back.

'Stop, I've got a banging headache.'

'This stupid boat trip was your idea, Ryan,' Liza sniped.

'It'll be good, I promise,' he said, watching as Liza rubbed her stomach, she seemed unable to stop touching it now the news was out.

The bus arrived and drove us to the harbour, where we boarded a large catamaran with three other couples I recognised from around the pool. We chatted as we got onboard, names were exchanged and instantly forgotten, and I got caught up in the enthusiasm for the trip to Dia island. Anything would be better than being stuck around the pool all day with them again.

The boat was bigger than I'd expected, with padded seating areas at the side and a viewing deck up some stairs. Crates of snorkelling gear were stowed below where there was a small lounge area and restroom. The white vessel gleamed in the azure water, sparkling in the sun, and the captain and staff onboard were welcoming, already handing out bottles of water and snacks as soon as we set sail.

The sun beat down and the view was glorious as we stripped to our swimming costumes and applied sun cream.

'Oh.' Liza stared at me as she stepped out of her playsuit revealing her bikini beneath. Both of us were wearing the exact same orange bikini with diamanté straps.

'Zara?' I asked, as that's where I'd bought mine.

'Mmmm,' she agreed, looking far from pleased.

I experienced a twinge of envy as she was taller and wore it better, but where she was soft and supple, I was toned from the hours walking and controlling the dogs. Our bodies were polar opposites, perhaps Ryan had fancied a change.

Now undressed, I could see the slight curve of Liza's stomach. I couldn't help but stare. *My husband's baby could be in there.*

'Want a photo?' she snapped, her hand on her hip.

'Only to throw darts at,' I retorted.

She stalked off and Bobby frowned at me.

'What is going on with you two? Are you still mad at us for coming?'

The look of horror on Ryan's face as Bobby confronted me was a picture.

'She's a bit envious that's all, you know, the baby,' he said before I could answer.

I snorted, ready to let rip when the captain announced we were anchoring and I turned my head to see the white sands of Dia.

'Ladies and gentlemen, we have the option of paddleboarding, snorkelling or you can go for a swim or head over to the island and explore.'

Without hesitating, a couple of the girls squealed and jumped into the water, splashing around. I followed, sliding into the cool water, drifting into a slow breaststroke towards the shore. Within a minute, I could touch the bottom, the soles of my feet disappearing beneath pure golden sand, and I squeezed the water from my hair. There were a few wooden padded loungers on the beach with umbrellas and I climbed on one, lying face down to watch the activity around the catamaran. It was lovely to be away from them but still able to observe from a distance.

As the heat from the sun dried my skin, I watched Ryan and Bobby somersault off the edge of the boat like children, climbing back onboard to do it again. Liza shrieked from the deck as she got splashed, laughing like a hyena at the poses the boys were doing to impress her. I laid my head on my arms and breathed deeply, hoping to have a snooze until lunchtime when the staff onboard were going to do a barbecue.

Just as I was drifting off with thoughts of Nico stroking my back and whispering in my ear, a blood-curdling scream and a splash rang out from the boat.

18

I looked up to see Liza flailing in the sea and Bobby leaning over the side of the boat to haul her out as Ryan watched on. His face was hard to distinguish from such a distance, but he crouched low, rubbing at his beard. From what I could make out, one of them had pushed Liza overboard and she wasn't particularly happy about it. Shame she didn't drown. The thought was fleeting, although guilt gnawed at me regardless, she was with child after all, whoevers it was.

I returned to my slumber once the spectacle was over, resuming my fantasy of Nico and a romantic trip for two to Spinalonga island, hoping I'd get a chance to sneak away and see him at the bar later. I was a little disappointed he hadn't responded to my message, but he knew Ryan was here and probably didn't want to cause any problems. Or possibly he'd had his one-night stand and was already scoping out the next woman on his list. The thought smarted a little, but I banished it, I could hardly complain, I was married and on my honeymoon despite the sham it had turned out to be.

'Wakey wakey, they're serving lunch.' A dripping Ryan tapped my shoulder and I lifted my head, my burnt skin tender to the touch, despite the factor thirty I'd applied.

'Okay.' I got to my feet and waded into the water to swim back to the catamaran, enjoying the instant cooling of my flesh. Ryan swam ahead, looking back at me as though he wanted to say something but decided against it.

Once onboard, I dried off and applied some more sun cream as the smell of barbecued chicken wafted around us. I grabbed a plate and helped myself to a Greek salad and some of the cooked meat, joining Bobby, Liza and Ryan at the seating area.

'Nice nap?' Bobby asked, raising a bottle of beer to his lips.

'Just what I needed.' I feigned a smile. 'What have you been up to?'

'Throwing me overboard,' Liza huffed and I stifled a laugh, trying to resist the urge to throw out a catty comment, knowing Ryan was watching me like a hawk.

'You've got matching bikinis, that's sweet.' Bobby pointed at the two of us.

'It wasn't intentional,' I admitted, accepting a glass of fizz from one of the roaming crew members.

'Yeah, but I wear it better,' Liza grinned, trying to sound like she was joking, although the jibe was fully received.

'Not for long.' I laughed, glancing at her stomach, enjoying her scowl.

'You both look great,' Ryan chipped in, trying to make peace. *Slimy git.* 'What are we doing after lunch, fancy a bit of paddle-boarding?' he suggested.

'Snorkelling,' Bobby announced as though he'd made the decision for all of us already. Liza stuck her bottom lip out like a child but didn't object.

We waited for a while for our food to go down, listening to the captain give us an overview of the history of Dia island. He talked animatedly, telling us that according to Greek mythology a giant lizard had tried to destroy the island of Crete. However, Zeus turned it into stone with a thunderbolt, thus creating the island and its lizard shape.

'I didn't think the price included listening to Captain Birdseye drone on for half an hour,' Ryan grumbled a little too loudly.

I glared at him, inwardly cringing at his rudeness, while Liza giggled. He grinned at her approval and got up to take her plate back to the table, like she was his wife. I held mine out to him when he returned and he took it grudgingly, rolling his eyes. I chewed the inside of my cheek, counting the days again in my head until I would be free of him.

Bobby seemed oblivious as Ryan helped Liza on with her snorkel, explaining how to use it, but I didn't fail to notice the charged looks that passed between them. It wasn't over and I couldn't believe his nerve. Were they a pair of star-crossed lovers destined to be together no matter the odds or was he bewitched by her sensual curves and flirtatious manner? With each new day, I found another reason to hate the man I once loved, for everything he'd put me through and was still putting me through.

'If you two are quite finished, perhaps we can get in the water now,' I barked, unable to stop myself.

They looked up abashed and slithered apart. Bobby was already dangling his legs over the edge of the boat, watching the other couples attempt to stand on their paddleboards. I had no idea if he'd heard me.

'Let's see what we can see,' he said, masking up and plopping into the blue.

I followed behind, determined to enjoy what I could of the

expensive day trip, which added more to our growing debt. It weighed around my neck like Jacob Marley's chain, knowing Ryan had gone behind my back and borrowed against our house. Despite all the years pouring money into it, I was to come out with nothing. It was too much to process and I needed time to unpack the emotions all of these life-shattering revelations had produced.

We swam a little way from the boat as instructed, where the sand and silt churned as we kicked, making the water murky. I looked around for signs of life, seeing a few brightly coloured fish darting around. Were there sharks in these waters? Having seen *Jaws* at too young an age, I was perpetually nervous about swimming in any sea, even if I knew the water was too cold for them.

I struggled to master the snorkel at first, but eventually got the hang of it, raising my face out of the water to see where the others were. Bobby and Liza were further away, Ryan was closer, his feet splashing the surface, scaring the fish.

I swam away from his commotion, concentrating on the seabed below and some of the rock formations, where I followed a school of fish, so fast I could barely keep up. It was magical, being alone in the water, the noise from above blocked out. As I kicked, something pulled at my ankle, making me sink beneath the surface. Water filled the snorkel and I began to choke, kicking to free my foot. I turned around, sure I saw an arm amongst the silt which had swirled and muddied in my panicked thrashing. Arms flailing to get my head above water, I accidentally dislodged my mask, which flooded, blinding my vision.

You're going to drown! Reaching down to my ankle, my fingers found rope looped around it as my lungs screamed in protest. Blind with saltwater stinging my eyes, I wrestled with the cord and finally wrenched it off, bursting to the surface, coughing and spluttering.

I was just out of my depth, toes barely a foot from the seabed, but in my panic, I struggled to tread water, sinking again. Tearing off my mask, I screamed before a hand clamped under my armpit, propelling me upwards.

'I've got you.' Bobby lifted his mask onto his forehead.

'You grabbed me,' I said, pushing him away and swimming as fast as I could back to the boat, my discarded mask sinking to the seabed.

'Yeah, to hold you up,' Bobby shouted before swimming to the seabed to retrieve it.

With my heart racing and teeth beginning to chatter, I hauled myself onto the boat, limbs weak with the short burst of exertion and shock.

'You tried to drown me!' I spluttered as Bobby resurfaced at the stern, throwing my mask onto the deck.

'No I didn't! Your foot was caught in an old net,' he said, climbing out, forehead crumpled in confusion.

I turned my face away, fighting back tears, sure I'd felt a hand around my ankle.

'Here you go.' Bobby tossed me my towel and I wrapped it around my shoulders, trying to get my breathing back to normal. I wanted to go back to the hotel, away from Bobby, but on the boat I couldn't escape. He sat across from me, drinking from a water bottle, his narrow eyes unwavering.

'I didn't do anything, Kel,' he said eventually as I repositioned the diamanté strap of my bikini, unease creeping over me. 'Ryan was closer to you than I was.'

I took in Bobby's expression, his static eyes, thin lips pressed together, fingers interlaced so tightly his knuckles were white. There was a chance he was telling the truth and my ankle had just got caught in a discarded net, but my gut told me otherwise. I was sure I'd felt a hand grip my ankle, but was it Bobby's or

Ryan's? He was still in the water, head down, seemingly oblivious to what had happened.

I wrapped my towel tighter around me, glancing at my orange bikini, the exact same one as Liza's. What if I hadn't been the intended victim at all?

19

'That was amazing!' Ryan climbed onto the boat, grabbing his towel to wipe his face.

I was still shivering in mine, moving out of the shade of the canopy towards the edge of the boat, keen to absorb the warmth of the sun.

Ryan frowned at the lack of response from either of us. 'What happened?'

'Kelly got tangled in an old fishing net,' Bobby answered before I could speak.

'Are you okay?' Ryan asked, taking a step towards me.

'I am now.' My voice was like acid and I turned away from the pair of them. 'What time do we sail back?' I asked one of the crew who was checking the rudder.

'In about an hour, miss,' he added kindly. 'Can I get you anything?'

'No, thank you.'

I found a quiet spot, ignoring Ryan and Bobby talking about my *accident*, and checked my phone, a bubble of excitement rising in my chest when I found I'd had a message from Nico earlier in the day.

> See you at the bar tonight?

I quickly replied.

> Definitely. I need a drink after the day I've had. X

Perhaps our one-night stand might extend to a week. Pretending things were fine between me and Ryan wasn't as easy as I'd thought and Bobby had to have sensed it. The prickliness between Liza and I was proving hard to disguise too and there was only so long he'd believe I was pissed off about them infringing on our honeymoon. In fact, I was surprised Bobby wasn't asking more questions already, seeing as tensions were so obviously strained. Perhaps he knew more than he was letting on and that's why he had grabbed me in the water, or had I just panicked and it had been a net after all? My head was all over the place, everything was getting too much, being here with them and with so much on my mind.

I'd had a missed call from Ruby but didn't want to call her out in the open with Ryan in earshot so messaged her to say I was okay but couldn't wait to fly home.

Once I'd had a drink and warmed up, Liza came back aboard, buzzing from her swim.

'Oh my God, that was so good. I saw loads of little fishes,' she trilled, her voice grating. I watched as she bent over right in front of Ryan, brushing silt from her feet. Bobby scowled and pulled her out of the way, while Liza pretended not to know what she'd done. She'd always been a flirt and enjoyed the male attention her striking looks received, but usually Bobby took it in his stride.

Had he noticed something between them like I had since they'd arrived?

'Pathetic,' I muttered under my breath. Ryan could have been right, had she thrown herself at him at the wedding, seduced him to the point where he couldn't resist? It was a possibility. Although I knew now for a fact it wasn't just on our wedding day, it had started months before.

After we suffered a full monologue of every single fish Liza had seen, the shape and the colour, finally the anchor lifted and we set sail back to Elouda Bay. I couldn't wait to get back to dry land and get away from all of them for a while.

'See you at dinner tonight,' Bobby called after me as I was first off the coach when we reached the hotel.

I waved my hand in the air without bothering to turn around.

'Hey, hey,' Ryan jogged after me, catching my hand, 'why are you rushing off?'

'Because I've had about enough of today. I want a shower and some alone time.' I didn't stop walking as Ryan tried to keep up with me, eventually giving up right by the bar, where he queued for a beer. At least he'd taken the hint.

I took a shower, keen to wash the sand from my skin and put on a clean bikini, sitting outside to apply sun cream before laying down on a lounger. I loved the privacy and peacefulness of our small pool with its high white walls. I checked the time – four o'clock in Crete, so two o'clock in the afternoon back in the UK and a good time to call Ruby.

'How's it going?' she answered, whispering at first, and I imagined her walking into an empty office in the solicitors where she worked as a legal secretary.

'I can't wait to come home, I've got so much to tell you,' I said, relaying Ryan's arrival and then Bobby and Liza turning up. It all came rushing out in an explosion of emotion as I described the debt Ryan had got us into and how I was being forced to pretend everything was fine.

'Oh my God, why can't you tell Bobby about Ryan and Liza and blow it all out in the open?'

'I will, but not here. Ryan begged me not to. The plumbing business is just about keeping afloat and if I tell Bobby what I saw in the summer house, it'll sink without a trace. Plus he'll go mental, he'll probably kill Ryan. I want to come home,' I sobbed, not divulging I believed Bobby or maybe Ryan had tried to drown me a few hours ago. I didn't want to give Ruby sleepless nights worrying about my safety when she was thousands of miles away.

'It's their business, let them sort it out between them,' Ruby said, taking control as she always did.

'He's borrowed against our house. Even when we split up and sell, we'll still owe money. Dad's care home fees are hanging in the balance.'

The line went silent for a second.

'Oh, Kel, what are you going to do?'

'I don't know, I can't think straight here, I'm counting the days until I can come home and stay with Mum. Don't tell her about the debt, I don't want her to worry, but I can't bear to be around him anymore, and that's not even all of it!'

'There's more?' Ruby's voice became shrill.

'Liza's pregnant and I'm sure from Ryan's face when she announced it there's a chance it could be his.'

'Fuck!'

I didn't tell Ruby about Nico, there was too much going on without adding him into the mix, plus I knew my sister wouldn't approve. She'd think I was doing it out of revenge and acting recklessly. I guessed it was reckless, but Nico was a small glimmer of hope in the darkness, a possibility, however unlikely, that there was life after Ryan. Not necessarily with him, Nico couldn't be anything more than a fleeting holiday romance, but it was good to know Ryan hadn't broken me beyond repair.

After I'd said goodbye to Ruby, I slipped back inside to fetch a drink, guzzling from a bottle of water from the fridge when there was a knock at the door.

'Bobby?' I took a step back, surprised to see him at the threshold, his brow furrowed.

'Kel, can I come in, I want to apologise about the misunderstanding earlier.' He walked inside as the hairs on the back of my neck stood to attention. In my bikini, I was too exposed. It was different to being outside by the pool surrounded by others just as scantily clad. Why hadn't I grabbed something to cover myself? 'You know I'd never do anything to hurt you.'

'It's fine, forget it,' I said, mustering a smile as my pulse quickened, all too aware we were alone.

'It's been a funny couple of days, hasn't it?' Bobby cocked his head as I stood awkwardly in the kitchenette, the only exit to the apartment blocked.

What was I thinking? Bobby was our friend, Ryan's business partner whom we'd known for years. Before this week, I knew him to be an adorable, cheeky mop-haired gentleman who had been a good influence on Ryan, not the opposite. I sighed.

'It has. I'm sorry, Bobby, there's just a lot going on right now.'

'I know.' He stared at me, eyes penetrating.

Did he know?

I swallowed as he took a step closer, his hand reaching out to touch my upper arm, pulling me into a hug. My body stiffened as he pressed against me, enveloping me into his bulk. My head tucked beneath his chin as he breathed in the scent of my freshly washed hair. His hands rested on the bare skin of my back as I stood rigid, eager to get away.

'You weren't supposed to get caught up in this mess.'

'What mess?' I whispered into his chest, dread seeping into my lungs.

Finally, he released me, leaning in and kissing me full on the mouth. I recoiled and he chuckled wryly.

'See you tonight.' Without any explanation, Bobby turned and left as I shuddered beneath the air-conditioning vent from something other than the icy air hitting my skin. What the hell had just happened?

20

Bobby's visit had unsettled me, leaving me with new questions and an inkling there was more going on than I was privy to. Did he know about Ryan and Liza? I couldn't imagine he'd stand for it and not say anything. What mess was he talking about? The pair of them joining us on our honeymoon? And what was the kiss all about? It wasn't exactly a sumptuous kiss but hardly a peck on the cheek either. Was he getting his own back on Ryan?

My head swirled with ludicrous theories, so I threw on a sundress and sandals, a walk should clear my head. Outside, the sun beat down and sounds of laughter and splashing carried over from the pool. I spotted Liza and Bobby beneath an umbrella having what looked like a heated discussion, but Ryan was nowhere to be seen. Until I reached the bar, recognising the curve of Nico's back and his side profile immediately. Ryan was sat on a wicker stool, pint in hand, digging into a bowl of chips while talking animatedly to Nico. I watched for a minute, trying to gauge what their conversation was about, but Nico wasn't giving anything away.

'Hello, stranger, how are you?' Janice tapped me on the shoulder, a crisp white towel draped across her arm.

'I'm good thanks. How are you and Greg doing?'

'Well, it's paradise, isn't it, can't complain. Greg has dropped off and I've just heard they have a sale on at the spa, thought I'd see if they had a slot free for a massage.'

'Oh that sounds lovely.' I was already imagining someone working out all the knots of tension from my shoulders.

'Come with me, we can only but try, eh.'

The receptionist had mentioned the spa when she'd checked me in on the first day, but I'd barely listened, in fact I wasn't even sure where it was but it sounded like a welcome reprieve right now. I followed Janice and told her about the catamaran trip to Dia island. Her and Greg hadn't left the complex since the trip to the market, except to go to the beach she said.

'Actually, I lie, we had dinner at a seafood restaurant down the road. It was glorious,' she added.

I wrinkled my nose, seafood wasn't something I enjoyed, the smell turned my stomach.

The spa was situated, like the nightclub, beneath the main reception on the other side. 'This place is like a Tardis,' I said, taking in the twenty-metre indoor pool, jacuzzi and sauna through the glass double doors.

We waited at the spa reception desk and were told there was availability for a half-price thirty-minute head, back and shoulder massage if we were happy to share the double room with two massage beds. Janice and I looked at each other and nodded at the lady behind the desk.

Ten minutes later, both of us were lying face down, side by side on a comfortable bed with a towel draped across our lower halves.

'This is the life, isn't it?' Janice sighed blissfully.

'It is,' I agreed as the female masseuse got to work on my lower back. It was worth every cent of the thirty euros. My masseuse was tall and slender, but she had power in her hands and I sunk into the bed while Janice talked.

'I can't believe it's Thursday already; we've only got a couple of days left as we fly home late on Saturday, but it's been a glorious week. Not a cloud in the sky. We'll definitely be back again, it's such a luxurious hotel.'

'Mmmm,' I agreed, my eyelids fluttering.

'How's the infiltrators?'

It took me a second to understand Janice was referring to Liza and Bobby. I groaned.

'I thought as much, I reckon your Ryan feels the same way, especially with her. Although perhaps he should keep his hands to himself, seeing as she's with child.'

I lifted my heavy head, frowning over at Janice. 'What?'

'I saw them having a heated exchange by the pool about an hour ago. He pushed her and she nearly fell. I was going to say something, but Greg told me not to get involved.'

It must have been when Bobby visited the apartment. What were they arguing about?

'Ryan's got a bit of a temper, and she likes to rile him up,' I offered, still making excuses for him.

'Well, I hope he doesn't behave like that with you, pet.'

We lapsed back into silence, although the ability to relax after what Janice had said escaped me. When the massage was over, Janice and I got up from the beds, turning away from each other and slowly dressing.

'I feel drunk.' Janice giggled as she wobbled on one leg to put on her cotton shorts.

'Thanks for letting me tag along, I can't tell you how much I needed this today.'

'Any time, hon. We must swap numbers before you go. Whereabouts do you live? I'm in Bristol.'

'Crawley,' I replied.

'Where's that?'

'Sussex, near Gatwick airport.'

'Well, I come to London occasionally to visit my sister; we'll have to meet up,' she said genuinely, but in all likelihood it was doubtful. Most of the people you meet on holiday you never see again.

'That sounds like a plan.'

'Right, I best get back to Greg. We'll see you at dinner, no doubt. Take care.' Janice climbed the stairs, almost bumping straight into Liza descending.

'Oh, this is where you are, is it?' she sneered once Janice was out of earshot.

'What do you want, Liza?' I sighed, far too zen from my massage to get into an argument.

'I'm going to treat myself to a pedicure, there's half price off treatments.'

I continued up the stairs, moving past her before turning back. 'Liza, do you know the plumbing business is struggling?'

She turned to look back at me, shrugging.

'Ryan said there's been some problems since Bobby's inheritance ran out.'

'What inheritance?' Liza grimaced. She clearly had no idea what I was talking about. Maybe Ryan was lying about the inheritance too.

'Never mind,' I said, quickly adding, 'I hear you and Ryan had a little spat earlier. Let me guess, was it about paternity payments?' I smirked, unable to help myself.

Liza glared at me, tight-lipped, and I carried on up the stairs.

The bright sun hit my eyes as I emerged from reception,

making me squint. It was almost dinner time, yet the pool was still busy.

Ryan wasn't at the bar, so I strolled over, pulling up a stool.

'*Señorita*,' Nico greeted, immediately fixing me a drink and calling to the other barman that he was going on break. His face was shiny, shirt damp, and he drank from a large glass of cola with ice, Adam's apple bobbing as he swallowed.

'How are you?'

'Hot! You?'

'I've just had a massage, it was lovely.'

'Your husband was here earlier.'

'Lucky you.' I was unable to keep the sarcasm from my tone.

'He's an imbecile.' Nico gave a shake of the head and I laughed.

'What time do you finish?'

'Eleven, will you come?' I flushed, surprised by Nico's question. Perhaps it hadn't been a one-night stand after all.

'I'll be here,' I said, taking a sip from my piña colada as my stomach fluttered. I didn't know how, but I'd make it work, even if I had to sneak away. Ryan would be drunk by then, especially if he'd started drinking early but I'd have to be careful.

It was hard being so close to Nico and not touching him and he must have been feeling the same as he whispered, 'I want to kiss you right now.'

I blushed, giggling like a schoolgirl.

'Ditto.' I watched as Nico sniggered.

'What's it mean, ditto?'

'It means same.'

He gave an exaggerated nod, smile spreading to flash his white teeth.

The queue at the bar was getting longer and Nico frowned. 'I better get back, see you later.' He brushed his fingertips against mine, igniting tiny pulses which ran the length of my arms.

I stayed to finish my drink, watching Nico mix cocktails, his biceps bulging as he gripped the shaker. In a few hours, I'd have him all to myself. The swirling in my stomach was such an unusual sensation. Ryan hadn't given me butterflies for years, but I put that down to the longevity of our relationship.

Eventually, I dragged myself off the stool, knowing I'd have to go back to the apartment to dress for dinner. How strained would it be, the four of us tonight? With Bobby's weird comments from earlier, Ryan and Liza's argument and her not knowing anything about her husband's supposed inheritance, it would likely be tense. Perhaps it was time to do a little covert digging of my own to find out what was going on.

21

Ryan seemed relieved to see me when I got back to the room, as though he wasn't sure if I was going to come to dinner or leave him to explain my absence to Liza and Bobby. I ignored him and got ready, not interested in making conversation.

He held my hand on the way to the restaurant, gripping tightly as I squirmed, like a parent leading a toddler.

'Come on, we need to move past this, Kel, work through it.'

'I need to work through you shagging Liza and potentially knocking her up?' I snapped.

He halted, turning to face me in the middle of the paved walkway, the smell of tonight's menu wafting down from the restaurant doors. 'I didn't. I told you. Bobby knows something's up; he keeps asking me why you're so moody.'

'I heard what you said to Liza in the nightclub last night so stop bullshitting me and I'm sorry I'm not thrilled about acting like we're still together while you've been busy ruining our lives.'

'What do you mean acting?' he asked, glossing over the fact I'd caught him out.

'I've told you, Ryan, it's over. Once we're home, I'm leaving and there's nothing you can do to stop me. Debt or no debt, we're finished.' I wrenched my hand from his grip and walked ahead, leaving him trailing behind.

Liza and Bobby were already seated by the window, with drinks for all of us.

'Indian tonight.' Bobby's boyish grin was back, the weirdness from earlier gone, yet it left me unsettled like I'd imagined the whole thing because he was acting completely normal.

'Yes, mate!' Ryan replied, rubbing his hands together like our words outside hadn't penetrated. Perhaps he still hoped I'd change my mind.

As usual, the boys went and got their food while Liza and I remained at the table.

'Do you think Bobby suspects?' I asked, still a little freaked out about his visit to our apartment earlier.

Liza glared at me. 'Oh God, you're like a broken record! There's nothing to suspect, Kelly. I told you, *nothing happened.*'

'Surely you can't still be keeping that up. I saw you!'

'Saw what? A snog? It's hardly the crime of the century.'

My mouth dropped open; how callous could she be.

'When did you turn into such a bitch?'

'It didn't mean anything and I can't help it if your lecherous husband jumped on me when I went outside to get some air.' Liza ran her fingers through her hair and I scoffed.

'Yeah, you tried really hard to fight him off, didn't you?'

'I'm bored of this conversation; I'm going to get something to eat.' Liza got up and sauntered off to the counter to grab a plate.

My appetite evaporated and with it my enthusiasm to play detective. I couldn't believe we used to be friends, it was like she hated me, and for what, because I'd caught them out? How was she still denying what I'd seen with my own eyes – and not just on my wedding day, I'd seen the looks pass between them since then. They were both trying to gaslight me. They were toxic!

Bobby must have clocked my expression when he was the first to return, his plate full of chicken biriyani and rice. 'What's up?' he asked, looking at me, then over his shoulder at Liza, as if sensing something had happened between us.

'Nothing,' I replied, scowling into my drink, unsure if I could trust Bobby either. 'What did you mean earlier when you said I wasn't supposed to get caught up in this mess?'

Bobby didn't even pause, scooping a forkful of curry and shovelling it into his mouth. 'Nothing, just, you know, the surprise of us coming out to the honeymoon.' He wouldn't meet my eye, concentrating solely on his plate, convincing me he was lying.

I wanted to ask about the inheritance, but Ryan came back to the table, his plate stacked high with poppadoms.

'Why aren't you wearing your wedding ring?' Bobby asked, looking at my left hand wrapped around my glass.

'It needs sizing down,' Ryan stepped in. 'Like an idiot, I bought it too big and we didn't want to lose it.' He wrapped his arm around my shoulders, pulling me into his side and kissing my forehead. The lies ran off his tongue like water.

'Yeah, that's it, babe.' I ruffled his hair as he tried to flinch away, knowing how much it annoyed him, before getting up and heading towards the food.

I settled for a couple of samosas and some sag aloo which was delicious and when I returned to the table, Bobby suggested a day trip he'd seen advertised in reception to visit Dikteon Cave tomorrow.

'We should soak up as much of the local history and culture as we can while we're here,' Bobby persuaded, and I wished I'd booked a solo visit to Spinalonga island.

'You're right. It's just such a shame we're going home on Saturday, we should have booked the full week,' Liza sighed, her hand stroking Bobby's thigh. His eye twitched at her touch, an involuntary movement, but I caught it. Perhaps it wasn't all roses between them after all.

'We've still got one full day left and I think we've imposed on Ryan and Kelly's honeymoon long enough, don't you? Plus it'll be good to get back to work, lots of jobs waiting for us.' I hoped he was right. 'Are you missing the dogs, Kel?' Bobby added.

'Yeah, Boycie is such a character, he follows you everywhere.' I thought of the gorgeous French bulldog who would do anything for a treat. He was my favourite and I walked him every day while his owners worked. Most of the dogs were one or two days a week, so Boycie was the one I spent the most time with, although I adored them all.

'We'll get a dog one day, won't we?' Ryan said, although it had never been discussed.

'I'd like to,' I admitted, playing the game and watching Ryan beam at my response. It was all for show, I couldn't imagine any future involving him now.

* * *

'I'll go to the bar,' I offered when we made our way around the pool after dinner. I ordered a cocktail for each of us, virgin for Liza, and some tequila shots. If I was going to sneak off with Nico later, I had to make sure Ryan was drunk enough not to notice.

'I'll bring them over beautiful,' Nico said, giving me a wink.

I watched him interact with another holidaymaker. A tall, skinny blonde who was giggling at something he said, my stomach fizzing with jealousy. I had to remind myself Nico wasn't mine and he never would be, we were passing through each other's lives, although I was certain he'd made more of a mark on mine than I had on his.

After a couple of rounds, we hit the amphitheatre for the first time to watch the evening's cabaret act – a group performing renowned songs from hit musicals. It wasn't Bobby or Ryan's thing, but they enjoyed it due to the amount of tequila consumed. My shots had been lime and water after the first one, courtesy of Nico, and, of course, Liza hadn't been drinking either. As soon as the act was over, we filtered out of the amphitheatre for last orders at the bar.

'Last orders?' Bobby complained as Liza stifled a yawn. 'It's only early!'

'The bar inside reception is open until midnight and the nightclub serves until 2 a.m.' Nico gave us his spiel. I smiled, necking my shot of water.

'Why don't you two head off to the nightclub, I'm ready for bed.' I glanced over Ryan's shoulder to watch Nico serve a long line of thirsty customers queuing to get their last drink of the evening.

'No, come on, Bobby, I'm tired. Let's go back to the room.' Liza tugged on Bobby's arm and I could see him debating, but I knew that look in his eyes. He was grinning at Ryan and Liza had lost him to another night of partying.

I looked on; smug I'd got one over her.

'Fine, don't come back too late and wake me up like you did last time,' she snapped, defeated.

I walked with them back towards reception, as though I was heading to my room.

Ryan kissed me on the cheek, holding on to my hand longer than was necessary. 'I do love you,' he whispered, 'and I know I'm an arse.' It was the understatement of the year.

'Have fun,' I said in reply and trailed a few paces behind Liza until she reached the entrance to her apartment. She didn't bother to say goodnight, just let herself in and closed the door. I couldn't have cared less, I had much more important things on my mind.

With butterflies in my stomach, I waited a beat and turned around, heading back to the bar.

22

Barely anyone was around now the lights of the bar had been turned off. The front shutter was already lowered, signalling it was closed, and the last few holidaymakers had disappeared to the remaining open bars or retired for the evening. Nico loitered at the entrance, checking his phone. He raised his head as I came into his field of vision, a sloping smile appearing on his face.

'Are you here for the heavy petting session? As that started five minutes ago?'

'Heavy petting?' I giggled, stepping forward and wrapping my arms around Nico's middle.

'What? It's on the swimming pool sign.' He frowned at my teasing.

'You are funny, Nico.' I barely managed to get the words out before he pressed his lips against mine, pulling me inside the bar and swinging the door shut, plunging us into darkness. 'It's pitch black,' I squealed as Nico's hands ran all over me. I didn't protest for long and kissing turned into tugging at each other's clothes. We couldn't see anything, but I could hear Nico's breathing, heavy against my neck, senses heightened as his body rubbed against mine. Briefly the question of how many women had been behind the bar, squashed against him in the narrow space, popped into my head, but I forced it away. There was no point in pretending this was more than it was.

'Are you okay?' Nico asked a little while later, pushing open the door a crack to let in some light from the complex as he did up the buttons of his shirt.

'I'm fine,' I said, rearranging my clothes until I looked suitable enough to step back out to the seating area. Behind the bar had been stifling without any fans running and perspiration ran down my back.

'Did you have a bad day?'

'Yep, stuck on a boat with my husband and his mistress, so it wasn't great.' I smiled tightly, not mentioning the fact I'd nearly drowned and I didn't know if it had been on purpose.

'Her?' he said, his eyes wide, referring to Liza.

'Yep, her.'

Nico blew air out through his cheeks, as if realising just how awful my honeymoon had turned out to be. 'You know what we need to do.' Nico's eyes glinted like a child in a sweet shop.

'Haven't we already done it?' I laughed and he tutted, shaking in his head in mock condemnation.

'Let's go for a midnight swim in the ocean.'

'I haven't got my suit.' In truth, I was unsure whether I wanted to go back in the ocean after today's events.

'No clothes.' His eyes sparkled mischievously.

'Skinny dipping?'

'Dipping, yes.' Nico nodded enthusiastically. 'Clear night, the stars are out.'

I pouted, being naked in the sea wasn't making the prospect sound any better.

'Come on, where's your sense of adventure?' Nico tugged me

by the hand, and before I could object, we were on our way to the beach, taking off our shoes and strolling along the sand as the water lapped at our feet. What if Ryan and Bobby had decided to leave the stuffy nightclub for a trip to the beach? The thought of getting caught was nerve-wracking yet exciting at the same time.

We continued walking side by side until we found a stretch that was unoccupied.

'Perfect,' Nico said, already unbuttoning his shirt and dropping it to the sand. He looked beautiful, his muscular bronzed chest and broad shoulders bathed in the moonlight. I wished I could take a photo without him knowing. Something I could cherish when I returned to reality.

'I think I'm going to really miss you when I leave here.' The words escaped from my lips.

Nico had already stripped to his black boxer shorts and he wrapped his arms around me. 'So stay.'

'Sure, I'll just move in with you,' I quipped, wishing for a second life could be that easy. That I didn't have to go back to England and sort out the mess of my marriage.

'You could,' Nico said, an innocence in his eyes which made me melt as much as it infuriated me. Our lives could not have been more different. He didn't have to worry about cheating partners, divorces or relatives in care homes and I envied his carefree wistfulness.

'Are we going in or not?' I asked, sliding the straps of my dress down as Nico looked on, biting his lip. I hoped I looked as appealing in the moonlight as he did.

Seconds later, we ran naked, shrieking as we hit the chilled water, disturbing the calm surface. We played and splashed, kissing until our teeth chattered and our flesh was covered in goosebumps when we finally decided to get out, hurrying back to the pile of discarded clothes and wrestling them on.

'Are you coming back to mine?' Nico asked, shaking out his wet hair.

I retrieved my phone to check the time, but the battery had died.

'What's the time?' I asked.

'A little after midnight.'

'Okay, for a while I will.'

We made love and drank cheap wine out of a box in Nico's fridge as he told me some of the things he'd seen working at Elouda Bay. Some women tipped him heavily before making their move, although it didn't happen as often as I'd thought due to the fact it was mostly couples at the resort.

'Have you not met anyone you want to settle down with?' I asked, curious as Nico was a catch but at the same time unable to quell the bubble of jealousy I felt at my question.

'I want to see the world before I think of all that. I've been putting money by for the trip for years.'

'Do you think your dad will be mad about the family business?'

'He's not ready to retire yet, I've got time.'

'I better get back.' I stifled a yawn and looked around for my dress, but Nico was already handing it to me.

'When do you fly home?'

'Early Wednesday morning.'

'I have Sunday off, could you get away? We could go and see some sights, Knossos Palace maybe, lots of history there.'

'What about Spinalonga island, I'd love to go there.'

'It's a date.' Spending the day with Nico somewhere I'd always wanted to visit would be much more preferable than putting up with Ryan. Perhaps I could feign illness or even tell Ryan the truth. I wasn't bothered about keeping up appearances, until I remembered the sting of his hand slapping my cheek.

The streets were dead, it was nearly three in the morning and I was desperate for sleep. The nightclub closed at two, so Ryan should be passed out drunk when I got back, hopefully on the sofa and not in my bed. He hadn't attempted any kind of intimacy bar the proposition in the shower and for that I was grateful. The thought of him coming anywhere near me now made me nauseas.

'I'll see you tomorrow.' Nico kissed my cheek, 'I'm working at eleven.'

'Okay, thank you for tonight.' We'd stopped at the entrance to the complex to say goodbye before Nico jogged back towards his flat, the sole of his trainers slapping the concrete. All of Elouda Bay was asleep as I crept back towards the apartment.

'Kelly!' A voice carried from the other side of the pool.

I looked up to see Ryan jogging over the bridge, his face ashen and startlingly sober. Had he seen me with Nico? My heart leapt into my mouth.

'Where have you been? We've been trying to call you!'

'My phone died; I couldn't sleep, so I went for a walk.' His words slowly registered. 'Who's been trying to call?'

'Your mum, your sister, me!'

A lump formed in my throat, pulse quickening. It was Dad, it had to be, something had happened. My mouth went dry and I gripped onto the railing for support. 'What's happened?'

'There's been a fire at the house!'

Whose house? Mum's, Ruby's or maybe the care home? I wanted to vomit and clutched my stomach.

'Is everyone okay?' I spluttered, eyes out on stalks. Blood pumped in my ears, invading the quiet of our surroundings.

'What do you mean, of course they are, no one is there,' Ryan snapped, pacing around in circles. He was angry – why was he angry? My brain couldn't connect the dots, but the penny finally dropped.

'Our house?'

'Yes, our house. The fire brigade have managed to put it out, but downstairs is a wreck.'

Ryan's news hit me like a steam train and my legs sagged. All of downstairs? Our lovely home we'd worked so hard for, all the mementoes and photos I had, my laptop and business documents, all gone up in smoke.

'How?' I asked, sinking onto the concrete, my head in my hands. Had Ryan left an appliance on before he came out to Crete? I wouldn't have put it past him.

'The fire brigade reckon someone poured petrol through the letter box.'

23

I struggled to sleep, grief-stricken at the image of our home, charred and blackened with smoke. All of our possessions lost, at least the ones downstairs. Who would do such a thing? Questions swirled around my brain as I listened to Ryan snoring beside me, having flatly refused to spend another night on the sofa. In protestation, I'd made a barrier of pillows between us. It was too late to ring Mum; I sent her a message to let her know I'd call first thing in the morning.

Eventually I dropped off, falling into a fitful sleep. Coming to was like being pulled through the fog. Vaguely aware of a heavy pressure over my face, restricting my breathing. My right arm was pinned to my side by the sheet tucked beneath the mattress and the other flailed, trying to reach the obstruction. I gasped for air, peeling my eyes open yet seeing stars, realising it was my pillow blocking out the light and Ryan's dead weight was upon it.

'Ryan,' I gasped, barely audible. Managing to turn my head away slightly, I shoved at the mound. My chest constricted as I drew in a shallow breath, grateful for the small reprieve. I was stuck beneath his arm and shoulder, which secured the pillow in place, and thrashed my legs as much as the tucked sheet would allow. He grumbled sleepily but didn't move as panic set in. My lungs felt as though they would burst. Finally, my nails found his flesh and I clawed at his skin, trying to rouse him, the tiny air pocket I'd made by turning my head rapidly depleting.

Eventually, he shifted enough for me to heave myself out from under him, grunting with exertion.

'Jesus Christ, Ryan!' I panted, freeing myself from the sheets and scrambling out of bed.

'What?' he mumbled, raising his head to look at me bending over to catch my breath.

'You were laying on me,' I managed, my voice shrill. Had he been asleep or was he doing a good impression?

'Go back to sleep,' he yawned and rolled over, taking back the pillow and propping it underneath his arm.

I stared at him, sunlight peeking through the curtains drawing a golden line across the bed. Trembling in my pyjamas because Ryan had turned the air conditioning too high, I was unable to focus, my brain fuzzy from lack of sleep. Refusing to get back into bed, I slipped out onto the patio and curled up on a lounger in the warmth of the early-morning sun. What if I hadn't woken? Would I just have slipped away, unable to breathe? Was that what Ryan was hoping for, to suffocate me?

My thoughts, now firmly suspicious, flicked back to the boat yesterday. Had it been Ryan and not Bobby who'd pulled me underwater? And what about the fire, had Ryan got someone to do it, a way to claim on the insurance and get us out of debt? He'd refuted that when I put it to him last night, shocked I'd even asked, but he'd been proven a liar, an adulterer; what else had he neglected to tell me?

I checked for available flights home, none today, but it seemed there were some seats on the same flight Bobby and Liza were getting tomorrow. Despite not wanting to travel with them, I wanted to get home, I was no longer safe here with any of them. There wasn't much I could do when I got back, other than salvage what was left, but if I could help with the police investigation, sure there would be one if the fire was deemed intentional, then I wanted to be there. Mum had sent some photos through to Ryan, the fire raging out of the lounge window, smoke curling up the brickwork, flames rising outside to the floor above. The images broke my heart.

I'd have to go to Mum's and Ryan, well, he could sort himself out, go back to his parents. So far this week, I'd lost control of my finances, my marriage was a mess and now my house had been destroyed. It would take forever to get back on track, but it was pointless dwelling in the misery. It wouldn't fix anything and if I let myself be pulled into a hole of despair, I'd never crawl out again.

I called Mum once it turned eight, her voice thick with emotion after barely sleeping a wink either. The family next door had alerted her to the fire late last night, knowing we were away. Living around the corner, she'd rushed straight there, arriving at the same time as the fire brigade, whose quick actions had prevented it spreading further. The thought of dealing with the insurance company when I got back was already stressing me out and I prayed we had enough cover to sort out the mess.

'Oh, Mum, I can't believe it. It's all been a disaster. I can't wait to come home. Do you mind if I stay with you?'

'Of course, both of you can.'

'It'll just be me.' I paused long enough to hear her gasp, ploughing on. 'I don't know what's going to happen and we might have to look at Dad's care home fees but I can't stay with Ryan, not now.'

'Don't worry, we'll sort it out. Getting home and taking care of the house is the main thing and you can stay with me as long as you like. I'm so sorry this has happened, love. I'd give anything to give you a hug right now.'

'Me too.' My chest burned with longing for comfort only a parent can give. 'Thanks for going to the house last night. I'm going to call the holiday company and change our flight back, so hopefully we'll be home tomorrow.'

Mum had enough to cope with, without my drama adding to it, but I knew she'd be there to support me regardless. Our family was tight, our bond grown stronger since Dad's diagnosis, and this was another bump in the road, but we'd overcome it. I said goodbye and got in the shower, the bright sunshine streaming through the window at odds with how dark the thoughts in my head were. Ryan, who'd still been asleep when I'd come in from outside, burst in to use the toilet, and I turned away from him, cursing myself for having forgotten to lock the door.

'I'm starving.' He yawned.

'Is that all you can say. Our house has bloody burnt down, our marriage is a sham and you're hungry!' I yelled, unable to stop the rush of anger. I stepped out of the shower and quickly wrapped a towel around me, my neck mottled with rage.

'It's not been burnt down, you've seen the photos, stop being so dramatic.'

'Dramatic!' I shrieked, incredulous. 'Everything downstairs will be ruined.'

'We'll sort it out when we get home,' he sighed before adding, 'don't forget we're going to the caves today.'

I stormed out of the bathroom and picked up my phone again, unable to believe how laid-back Ryan was being about the whole thing.

'Who are you calling?' he asked, following me out, still drying his hands on a towel.

'I'm getting our flights changed, today if we can get seats.'

Ryan screwed his face up as if the idea didn't appeal to him.

'You're unbelievable! Stay if you want to, but I'm going home to sort out our house.'

'Fine, I'll come,' he conceded with a sigh. As much as I would have been happy to leave without him, it was our house and he should be there to help.

Ten minutes later, I'd changed our flights with the assistance of a lovely lady at the end of the phone, who apologised once I explained our problem because we'd have to pay a small fee. As I'd thought, there weren't any flights available until tomorrow, the same one Liza and Bobby were on, but I didn't care we'd be flying together. I wanted off the island as soon as possible.

Ryan had showered and was getting dressed as I swiftly threw on a top, some shorts and my sunglasses. We walked to breakfast in stony silence; I knew he was sulking about leaving earlier than planned. I wasn't hungry at all, but I was so tired, I craved caffeine, the memory of my wonderful evening with Nico not enough to pull me out of my despair. Our trip to Spinalonga wasn't going to happen now.

'There you are!' Bobby exclaimed when we found them sat at our usual table, their plates empty and on their second cup of coffee.

'There's been problems at home,' Ryan announced as he slid into his seat and began explaining the phone call he'd received from my mum last night. Liza's mouth gaped and Bobby's eyebrows knitted together at the shocking news.

'You've got insurance, haven't you?' Liza asked.

'Of course we have,' I snapped, glad it was one of the direct debits I'd set up, so I knew payments were being made monthly. I got to my feet and headed for the pastry table still scowling. It was going to be a struggle to maintain any pleasantries today.

I stood perusing the selection, opting for an almond croissant to go with a strong coffee, aware of someone stood close behind me, their breath hot on my neck.

'I saw you,' Liza taunted low in my ear.

I turned to face her, frowning.

Liza's dark eyes glistened with delight. 'Who'd have thought, you and the bartender. Aim high, Kelly.' Leaning across me, she grabbed a chocolate twist and added it to her plate, licking the powdered sugar from her fingers.

'Careful, you know eating for two is a myth, don't you?' I shot back, wanting to wipe the smile off her face. 'But I guess you've always had child-bearing hips.'

Had I gone too far? I couldn't help it, every word that came out of Liza's mouth wound me up and I was on the edge as it was. She relished having something over me. Would she tell Ryan and did I care if she did? He could hardly call me out on it when the baby in Liza's stomach could well be his. It all paled into comparison, knowing there'd been a fire at my house last night. And here I was, stuck in Crete, powerless to do anything, investigating a cave all day when all I wanted to do was go home.

When I got back to the table with my coffee, Ryan was already halfway through a full English breakfast, talking shop with Bobby. Liza had eaten half her chocolate twist and left the rest, which boosted my miserable mood for a second.

'We need to be in reception in twenty minutes,' Liza said, twirling her ponytail around her fingers.

'Do you still want to go?' I asked Ryan, watching as a look passed between him and Liza.

I rolled my eyes, catching Bobby watching me, an amused look on his face, although I didn't know what on earth could be funny about our situation.

'Of course, it'll be a good distraction.' Ryan patted my hand as though I was a child. After the pillow *incident*, his touch made me squirm more than usual. I used to feel so safe with Ryan, but not any more.

The memory of last night on the beach with Nico made my heart heavy. Today would be the last time I'd see him, as we were leaving early tomorrow morning. Our holiday fling had been the only thing which had kept me going this week. I wasn't ready to say goodbye, knowing the fun we could have had, the lightness I felt every time we were together. It was infatuation, I knew it, yet I bit back tears at the thought of never seeing him again.

'Shall we go and get our stuff then. Trainers I'm guessing?' Liza stood, looking down at her fluorescent Havana flip-flops, but Bobby's eyes were still boring into me. I flushed. What was his problem?

'Sure,' he said eventually, pushing his chair back.

'We'll meet you there,' Ryan said, finishing his coffee, turning to me once we were alone. 'Where were you last night?'

'I told you, I couldn't sleep so went for a walk, to clear my head.' The lie tripped off my tongue so easily. 'One more day, Ryan, and we're done, I can't keep up this act.'

'I'll make it up to you, Kel. Say it's not over, I love you.'

I snorted, almost spilling my second espresso. *Except for when you're trying to smother me in my sleep.* 'Whatever we had is gone and you have to accept it. Once we're home, I suggest you tell Bobby the truth and try to work out a way to salvage the business. I'll be going to Mum's. We'll patch up the house, then it's going on the market.' All I wanted now was a clean break. The sooner I was done with Ryan the better.

24

We piled onto the half-empty coach. Liza had changed from a cotton dress into beige shorts and a tank top, her hair plaited down one side like she was Lara Croft. We all wore trainers and each carried a backpack with water, sun cream and snacks to keep us going. As we drove, the rep at the front stood swaying with the movement of the vehicle, microphone in hand as she gave a brief history of Dikteon cave, famous due to it being the place where Zeus was born and garnering thousands of visitors a year.

The journey took around an hour and once the tour guide finished, I put in my AirPods to drown out the sound of Liza moaning about her mosquito bites. Ryan sulked as he stared out of the window and I was glad he wasn't spending the journey bending my ear, trying to convince me to stay with him. As the Stereophonics blasted into my ears, I closed my eyes, mentally preparing a list in my head of what I had to do when I got home. Salvage what we could – if the house was safe to enter – pack, go to Mum's and contact the insurance company. All of the documentation was downstairs in a cupboard and I had no idea if it had gone up in smoke. Then Ryan and I could sit down and have a frank discussion about finances, exactly how much he'd screwed us over and what we were going to do about it. It still didn't add up; a huge tax bill and cost of materials increasing meant they'd never factored in any contingency in their budgeting. Either that or they hadn't been paying tax correctly from the outset. It wouldn't surprise me if Ryan had been trying to dodge it. Also, there was the mystery of Bobby's inheritance. Did it exist if Liza knew nothing about it or had he kept it a secret from her to plough straight into the plumbing business? It seemed both of our husbands might be keeping secrets from us.

Sensing the coach coming to a stop, I opened my eyes as Ryan made to stand, ushering me into the aisle.

'We're here.'

I yawned, recoiling as the heat hit me once I descended the steps of the coach.

The rep made payment for our group, telling us she would be waiting with the coach when we came back and we hiked north towards the entrance of the cave. The humidity was stifling and it was slow-going. My muscles ached from lack of sleep and I'd consumed half of my water before we reached the top, T-shirt damp with sweat. Liza moaned the whole way, but it pushed me to stride ahead so I didn't have to listen to her whining.

When we reached the entrance, the steps into the first chamber were steep and there was only a rickety metal rail stopping you from falling into the black abyss. As soon as we descended, it was like entering another world, eerily silent, except for the chattering tourists, and the temperature seemed to plummet after the oppressive heat outside. The sweat on my skin turned cold, sending a chill through me.

'Wow, this is amazing.' Bobby aimed his phone high to take pictures of the wonderland of stalagmites and stalactites hanging above us. Everything had a green hue due to the lighting set up from deep below and it resembled a movie set in the prehistoric era.

'Jesus.' Liza scowled as she momentarily lost her footing, sliding into Ryan, who caught her arm and held her upright. Her hand flying immediately to her stomach.

'These steps are treacherous!' I clung onto the railing, my heart racing as it wobbled.

We slowed our pace as we wound our way towards the bottom, moving into the second chamber, where the air seemed to shift. We gawped, taking in the sights and stepping carefully on the stone. It was a long way down and the route was busy, making some of the narrower pathways difficult to navigate.

'Excuse me,' Liza used her snippy tone to a French couple trying to take a selfie.

A few people bumped past me, the last one knocking my backpack off my shoulder. I scowled and bent to retrieve it, scrabbling on the cold stone for my bottle of water, which had fallen out of the meshed side pocket.

As I reached for the bottle, legs brushed me as they passed, then a sharp nudge in my back propelled me forward. My arm went out from underneath me and I lost my balance, the water bottle slipping from my fingertips and rolling over the edge into the depths of the cavern. Unable to stop, I almost slid over the edge, letting out a shriek and just catching the metal railing, which groaned in protest under my weight as one leg dangled into the abyss.

'Kelly,' Bobby cried out in alarm, grabbing a flailing arm as my grip on the railing loosened, palms clammy. Trying to position my weight to stay on the steps, I was unable to get purchase. Bobby grabbed the waistband of my shorts and hauled me back onto the walkway as onlookers gasped around us. 'Christ, that's a bloody death trap.'

Liza and Ryan were further down the steps, looking back to see what the commotion was. I gripped onto Bobby's arm tight enough to cut off his circulation as he pulled me to my feet. Hyperventilating, I let him hold me up as my legs turned to liquid at how close I had come to plummeting to the depths of the cave below. Imagining my body breaking into pieces on the rocks at the centre of the cavern.

'It's okay, I've got you,' he breathed into my hair as I shook in his grasp.

Someone had pushed me, a knee in the back right at the moment I was unbalanced to send me hurtling off the edge. I looked up at Bobby, his eyes wide – was it him? Was this his second attempt on my life after failing to drown me in the sea?

Untangling myself from him, I paused to catch my breath as Ryan and Liza made their way against the traffic back towards us.

'Did you slip?' Ryan asked, finally reaching us.

Tourists tutted as they made their way around the narrow section of the walkway we were partially blocking.

'I was pushed!' My voice was jittery, as I joined the flow of people moving down the steps, keen to be away from all of them. I was thirsty, mouth dry, but my bottle had been lost. All I could concentre on now was getting out of the cave, back in the daylight and on solid ground where there was no danger.

I could hear Bobby and Ryan talking as they followed, picking out my name. I hadn't imagined it; I'd felt a push. Someone was trying to hurt me on this holiday and there were only three people it could possibly be. It seemed Bobby had been the nearest on both occasions, but it didn't make any sense. What would he gain?

When we finally reached the bottom, I leaned against the

side of the cave, happy to have a solid surface to prop myself up against. After a quick breather, I followed a new set of steps back towards the top. I'd lost the rest of the group and was shivering now, my muscles pumping hard to get me out into the fresh air and cloying heat at the surface.

I reached the exit of the cave before Liza, Bobby or Ryan and plonked myself on a bench in the shade of a large tree, letting the warmth dry the cold sweat that clung to my skin as my terror subsided. I was never going back in a cave again, no matter how beautiful it was.

'That was over quickly,' Liza moaned as she emerged down the slope. 'I thought we were supposed to stop and take photos.' Her dig was directed at me, but they didn't have to follow. I would have gladly sat alone, given myself time to calm down, as it was I was still jittery, breath hitching.

'Do you want a beer?' Ryan called ahead, he and Bobby lagging behind yet already eyeing the hut selling drinks and snacks.

'Just a water, I lost mine.' I kept my head low as I spoke, not wanting to look at any of them, afraid of what I might see in their eyes.

'Have some sugar, it might help.' Bobby retrieved a cereal bar from his backpack and pushed the cold wrapper into my hand before joining Ryan and heading for the hut.

Liza sat beside me, slipping off her trainers and rubbing the soles of her socked feet. We didn't speak, but I was aware of her eyes on me, burning into me. I was exhausted from the shock of my near-death experience, the cortisol in my system retreating, causing me to crash. I didn't want to be around them. It was no joke; I could have died. Was it Liza? Trying to get rid of me so she could have Ryan all to herself, ensuring their secret never got out.

'Well, wasn't that fun.' Her sarcastic tone snapped me back to the present.

I didn't reply, which seemed to infuriate her. Liza didn't like being ignored.

'Some holiday this turned out to be,' she continued, eventually getting a rise out of me.

'It was supposed to be my honeymoon, I never invited you,' I bit back, unable to stop myself. God, she was so self-centred. If anyone had the right to complain, it was me.

'Urgh, lighten up, Kelly! It's no wonder Ryan's got wandering eyes if this is what you're like at home.'

Her words struck like bullets and my face flushed. How could she be so cruel?

'He didn't have wandering eyes until you set your sights on him, prowling around like a dog on heat.'

'I don't need to prowl, Kelly, you know that,' she said, toying with her plait. 'Maybe he's looking for something he can't get at home.'

I wanted to claw that sneer off her face. 'Where do you get off being such a bitch?'

Liza turned her body round to face me, sighing as I gave her the full force of my venom.

'We were perfectly happy until you decided to shag your husband's best mate.'

'I didn't, he came onto me and I told you for the fiftieth bloody time, nothing happened. I'm not interested in your husband.'

'It looks to me like you want whatever you can't have. Is Bobby not keeping you satisfied, is that it?'

Liza scoffed. 'My sex life is fine, thank you. I'm not a bore in the bedroom like some.'

I ignored her insult, letting her catty remarks wash over me. It was the rise she wanted. 'What makes you think I won't tell Bobby everything?'

'You have no proof, because nothing happened. There's nothing to tell.'

'We'll soon see, won't we,' I said, pointing to her stomach, 'because genetics and DNA don't lie and if that baby pops out looking like Ryan, I'd like to see you talk your way out of that one.'

'Bobby and I are happy, we're having a baby, I'm sorry things aren't working out for the two of you, but your jealousy is ruining the vibe of *my* holiday.' Liza turned her attention to slipping on her trainers as my mouth gaped. Her entitlement was off the charts.

I dropped the cereal bar to the ground. Without realising, I'd mushed it in my hand, unable to comprehend Liza was still trying to gaslight me when the image of her in a steamy clinch with Ryan had been burnt into my retinas. It was like even she didn't believe it had happened. Is that why she'd pushed me – was she worried I was going to spill the beans and ruin everything between her and Bobby?

25

I knew Liza could be a little spiky, I'd teased her about it often, but I'd never been on the receiving end before. How hadn't I seen what an utter cow she was? In fact, she was so blasé about what I'd seen, maybe she was right and the kiss in the summer house had been a one-off. Had Ryan drunkenly manhandled her after a bout of flirting? No, I'd seen it with my own eyes here in Crete, Liza bending over in her orange bikini, the charged looks and subtle flirting – there was more to it. Not to mention Ryan's reaction to her pregnancy announcement.

Even if there wasn't anything going on between them now, the fact Ryan could do that on his wedding day had to mean he wasn't invested in the vows he'd made. Yes, I'd been distracted with Dad and wedding plans, Ryan had been working all hours with the business, but surely that was no excuse. Was Liza right, had he become bored of me? We'd been together for ten years, since I was sixteen and he was eighteen, there'd been no time for either of us to sow our wild oats. I hadn't been interested in playing around, preferring commitment to one-night stands, but perhaps Ryan thought he was missing out?

'We got you some water.' Ryan approached with his arm outstretched to hand me a bottle.

I took it, nodding my thanks, but checked the seal was intact before unscrewing the cap and glugging half of it down. Bobby and Ryan held a plastic cup of beer each and a water for Liza.

'I'm ravenous,' Bobby said, looking around for the rep, who appeared from the door of the coach a hundred yards away as if she'd heard his stomach growl.

'I hope you all enjoyed the cave; we have lunch set out under the pergola,' she gestured to our left, where a spread was being laid out on a picnic tables, covered in checkered cloth. Plates of cured meats, olives, humous, flatbreads and cheese were positioned around the edge and a couple of members of staff carried out steaming trays of chicken and lamb skewers to place in the centre.

The rest of our party gathered around and I grabbed a small portion to nibble on before retreating back to the bench in the shade, preferring to be alone while Bobby and Liza mingled, aware that tomorrow I would be trapped in a metal cage thirty thousand feet in the air with all of them.

'Are you okay?' Ryan asked, eventually coming to join me.

'No,' I answered honestly, 'I just want to get out of here.'

'Maybe we should complain about the railings. Someone might have a serious accident.'

'I almost did!' My voice was shrill.

Ryan shrugged like I was overreacting, but, thankfully, thirty minutes later, we were summoned back to the coach. I couldn't wait to get back to Elouda Bay. I wanted to see Nico's smiling face, to feel safe in his company, so declined when Bobby suggested spending the rest of the day on the beach.

'I'm going to start packing,' I said and Liza rolled her eyes before flouncing off to her room to change out of her *Tomb Raider* get-up.

'Are you sure you don't want to come, last chance for a trip to the beach?' Ryan said, not realising I'd already been but with much better company.

'I'm sure.'

* * *

'Boy, am I glad to see you.' I slid onto a stool at the bar once Ryan had departed.

'I am glad too.' Nico smiled, coming around the side of the bar to sit next to me. The bar was quiet and I was relieved Nico had a couple of minutes to spare, although sitting close enough to smell him made me want to tear his clothes off. I wanted to forget about the events at the cave, the fact I was sure one of our party meant me harm, but I knew I had to deliver the news of our departure.

'We've changed our flights. I'm going home tomorrow.'

Nico's face fell, disappointment clouded his eyes, and I was genuinely touched by his reaction. Had I been more than a passing fling?

'Why?'

'Because there was a fire at our house and I have to go home to sort it out.'

'Was anyone hurt?'

I shook my head. 'No, but it's a wreck.'

'I'm sorry.' Nico tilted his head to the side. 'I'm working until eleven, will you be here?'

'I'll make sure I am,' I said, my stomach fluttering as Nico leaned in and kissed the side of my head, not caring who saw us. A second later, he jerked upright off his stool, his back pin straight when a man in a white shirt and black trousers appeared behind the bar.

'What can I get you?' Nico asked me, moving round the bar, his smile fading.

'A piña colada please,' I replied, realising the smartly dressed man worked at the hotel and was possibly Nico's boss.

Nico served my drink as the man barked orders at his colleague in Greek, waving his hands around animatedly. They both seemed to shrink in his presence. Eventually, the man finished ranting and began inspecting the glasses and equipment under the counter.

'There's been a leak at one of the other bars and they've had to shut it. He thinks we'll be busy soon,' Nico confided when he'd gone.

'It's not worth me staying then?' I asked, my buoyant mood evaporating.

'Stay for another at least.' He stroked my forearm across the bar.

'I can't say no to you.' I laughed, draining my glass and holding it out to him.

A few customers came and went and the manager didn't return, so the mood behind the bar relaxed a little. Nico's colleague, Tomas, cranked up the summer playlist and had a little boogie in between customers. I stayed, chatting to them both while Nico and I shared a packet of paprika-flavoured crisps I'd spread open on the bar.

'You must get a proper lunch break on a twelve-hour shift?'

'I do, at four.'

I checked my watch, grimacing, it was half an hour until then.

'Go on, I'll cover for you,' Tomas butted in, winking at the pair of us.

I blushed, but Nico grabbed me by the hand and pulled me towards reception.

'Wait here, I'll be back in a minute.' He stepped inside and, to my horror, I saw Ryan, Liza and Bobby making their way down the path back from the beach already. I retreated into an alcove, partly concealed by a bush, hoping I wouldn't be seen.

'She's probably still packing, miserable cow,' Ryan tutted as he went past, trailing behind Bobby, his eyes searching for me at the bar where I'd been seated moments before.

'Stay out with us and enjoy yourself. It's our last day.' Liza rubbed his back in a circular motion, unseen by her husband at the front of the pack. I gritted my teeth, wanting to wallop the pair of them. They were so brazen and Bobby was being taken for a fool, but at least I hadn't been spotted.

Nico came into view, looking left and right when I wasn't where he'd left me, fearing I'd changed my mind.

'Here!' I called, beckoning him over.

'Why are you hiding?' he asked, a bemused smile on his face.

'Ryan was just here; he's looking for me.'

'Come on, I have a plan.' Nico waved a card momentarily in my face before grabbing my hand again and scuttling in the opposite direction Ryan had walked in. Back inside the main building, he pulled me up two flights of stairs and down a corridor, stifling a giggle.

'Where are we going?'

'Here,' he replied, stopping outside room 72 and sliding the card into the reader. The door popped open and he beckoned me inside.

'How did you wrangle this?' I asked, a laugh escaping as I looked around at the room, my eyes resting on the unmade bed.

'Maria on reception owes me a favour. Housekeeping won't get to this one until later and they've checked out already.'

I wrinkled my nose at the bed, who knew who had slept in those sheets, and if Nico thought he was going to have his wicked way with me in there, then he was going to be disappointed.

'How about a shower?' Nico's eyes sparkled feverishly.

'Okay,' I agreed, leading him by the hand to the bathroom, with its enormous rainforest shower. 'I'm going to miss you so much,' I said, nibbling at his shoulder as we stood naked, pressed together under the warm spray. More relaxed than I'd been the entire day.

'I feel the same.' Nico wrapped his arms around me and lowered his face to mine. 'You're like a breath of fresh air.'

Later, I watched Nico get dressed, mixed emotions flooding through me. I desperately wanted to go home, but I didn't want to leave Crete, and Nico, behind.

'Do you think you will go travelling?' I asked, watching his reflection as he pulled on his trousers.

'Definitely, sooner rather than later.'

'Make sure you look me up when you come to the UK.' I hoped I didn't sound too desperate.

'You couldn't stop me,' he said, coming over to kiss my forehead. 'You are beautiful, Kelly, and I hope you sort everything out when you get home, starting with kicking that *malákas* out.'

'*Malákas?*'

'Asshole,' Nico explained.

'Oh, he's already gone.' I waved my hand as though I was wafting Ryan out of my life. If only it would be as easy as that, but I knew my decision had been made and there was no turning back.

'I need to take the card back to reception,' Nico said.

'That's a shame, but it was fun while it lasted.' I let Nico pull me towards him for one last kiss before we headed out the door and back down the stairs to reception. Shielding our eyes from the bright sunlight and oppressive heat as we exited the main doors after dropping the key card back, Nico's fingers interlaced through mine.

'Make sure to come and say goodbye.' Our arms stretched out, neither one of us wanting to be the first to let go as we walked across the bridge in our own world.

'Get your fucking hands off my wife,' Ryan snarled from one of the tables surrounding the bar. He stood, rolling his shoulders back, as Liza peered over the top of her mocktail in glee.

We jerked apart, Nico's mouth dropping as Ryan stormed towards us, not even having time to brace himself. Ryan's right arm swung, his fist connecting with Nico's jaw, making him stumble backwards, palms raised in surrender.

'Ryan!' I screamed, launching towards him and latching onto his arm, but he pushed me away. I toppled onto my backside, pain ricocheting up my spine and knocking the wind out of me.

'Come on, mate.' Bobby, always calm and collected, was on his feet, but not before Ryan got another swing in, narrowly missing Nico as he leapt backwards, hands out, trying to pacify the oncoming attack.

Other holidaymakers moved towards us, grabbing hold of Ryan to hold him back.

'I don't want any trouble.' Nico rubbed his jaw and flexed it from side to side.

'I'm so sorry,' I said, getting to my feet and standing beside him, willing Ryan to back off. I didn't want him to get Nico in trouble if his boss wasn't far away.

'You've been fucking the barman?' Ryan shouted incredulously once he'd shirked off his restraints.

My insides squirmed as now we were surrounded by a crowd ravenous for the drama. A woman had her phone raised and I turned away, not wanting to become her latest Instagram reel.

Liza giggled darkly, biting at her straw, watching with relish. She hadn't even got out of her chair, too busy enjoying the scene unfolding in front of everyone.

Something ignited in my chest and I shot Ryan a look of pure disgust, unable to hold it in any longer. 'Like you've been fucking Liza, for months?' Firing at my husband as he turned ashen. His temper receded swiftly into panic.

Bobby's brow furrowed, as though my words didn't make sense, yet I had no remorse. It was time for everyone to come clean. Whatever happened, happened, I wasn't going to lie any more. Not for them.

'What?' Bobby's face crumpled like a child who didn't get the joke. He looked so innocent, his wide eyes darting from Liza to Ryan and back again. It was madness to believe Bobby could have been out to hurt me, he didn't have it in him. The look on his face broke my heart.

'It's lies,' Liza cried. Now she was on her feet, gesticulating frantically. Served her right, the cheating little skank, but I wasn't finished, everything I'd seen came spilling out.

'I caught them, on our wedding day in the summer house. Why do you think I left for my honeymoon without him? You might want to get that baby's DNA checked, Bobby.'

I was on a roll, unable to stop until Nico patted my arm, a warning I'd gone too far.

Tomas appeared the other side of him. 'Nico, the manager is on his way.'

Nico looked at me, his eyes conveying a silent apology before he extricated himself from the drama and returned back behind the bar. Ryan hitting Nico was the last straw and I didn't know if, as a result, what was blossoming between us would die or if he would still have a job if his manager discovered he'd been fraternising with the guests.

The fire had left my belly, the truth spilling out extinguishing the flames, and I turned on my heel to go back to our apartment. Bobby, Liza and Ryan could sort the mess out between them.

As I crossed the bridge, a couple of security staff in grey uniforms stormed past me, someone must have called them about the altercation, but I didn't want to hang around to see if they ejected Ryan from the complex. My husband had pushed me as far as I was willing to go.

26

Back at the apartment, I packed most of my things before heading out to dinner. My head throbbed with the events of the day, my near miss at the cave and Ryan and Liza's affair coming out into the open. Getting on the plane tomorrow morning couldn't come soon enough. Our travel representative had put a note under the door of a new collection time. We had to be in reception at three in the morning for the transfer to the airport. More insufferable hours spent in the company of Ryan, Liza and Bobby. Although, after me blurting out Ryan's secret, I doubted any of us would be travelling together.

In the restaurant, I selected a table in the corner, out of the way of the thrum. It was an American grill menu and I selected a cheese burger paired with curly fries, although my appetite was fading. I was only halfway through my meal when Liza plopped into the chair opposite me, her eyes red and swollen from crying.

'How could you?' she cried.

'How could I?' I stared at her, incredulous, a chip halfway to my mouth.

'Think of the baby!' she raised her voice, causing the occupants of the next table to glance over at us.

I gripped her arm with salty fingers. 'Your baby – whether it's Ryan's or Bobby's – is of no concern to me,' I said through gritted teeth. 'You ruined my marriage; I have no sympathy for you, Liza. We were best friends and yet you had no qualms about taking Ryan for yourself, you weren't thinking of me when you were screwing him, were you?'

Her eyes downcast, she looked admonished, those long fake lashes wet with tears.

'Bobby was going to find out eventually,' I added.

'He doesn't believe you anyway,' she sneered, as if trying to convince herself more than me.

I scoffed; Bobby couldn't be that stupid, could he? Surely he'd noticed there was something between them, but, to be fair, I hadn't before what I'd witnessed in the grounds of Gravetye Manor.

'It's done now. Ryan and I are over, you can have him if you want, I don't care anymore.'

'Now you've finally sampled the delights of someone else, you know what you missed out on?' She laughed dryly.

'Rather that than not being able to keep your legs closed from one day to the next,' I shot back.

Liza raised her eyebrows at me in mock horror, a hand planted to her chest like I'd wounded her innocent soul. 'Well, Ryan and Bobby are currently in the bar talking things through. Ryan will deny everything and I've told Bobby it's rubbish, you're just making shit up to cover you sleeping with the hired help.' Liza examined her perfectly painted acrylic nails as my blood boiled.

'You don't really believe that, Liza.'

'Don't I?'

'Why the tears then?' It was obvious she'd been crying; her eyes were still red-rimmed.

'Well, I had to make him believe me, didn't I? You know, pregnancy hormones can come in handy.'

I swallowed down the anger that threatened to spill out. This perfect princess who always got her way, who did what she liked with no consequences. It wasn't fair. I had to hope karma existed and she got her comeuppance, because clearly Bobby was entirely pussy-whipped and couldn't see past the end of his nose.

'Well, I best get started on packing. I'd like to say this has been a holiday of a lifetime, but, to be honest, the company could have been better.' Liza, with her razor-sharp tongue, stood, flicked her black mane over her shoulder and sashayed out of the restaurant.

I pushed my plate away, appetite gone. How had I been friends with such a bitch and hadn't even noticed how self-centred she was? I truly hoped Bobby realised he was being duped. Did she mean to carry on with Ryan as before, all the time being married to Bobby? I pitied the unborn child whose father could be either of them.

It was time to go home and sort out the mess Ryan had caused before getting a quickie divorce and moving on with my life. If Nico had taught me anything, it was I did have a future, the buck didn't stop with Ryan. I was young, I could find someone else and be happy, maybe have a family. The termination of my marriage and the loss of my home wasn't the end of my life, that could have happened in the cave today. But I was still here and I would rebuild.

At a loose end after leaving the restaurant, I sat by the pool back at the apartment, soaking up what would be last of the Crete sun and likely any decent temperatures I'd be seeing for a while. Ryan hadn't returned to pack – had what Liza told me been a lie? Had the security team removed him from the premises? He'd be screwed getting home if he couldn't get his passport. Or was he really in the bar with Bobby, working things out?

I hoped there hadn't been any repercussions for Nico. I'd be mortified if he lost his job because of Ryan's outburst. I was tired and my body ached, but we were getting collected so early in the morning, I wasn't sure it was worth going to bed. I could always snatch a few hours on the flight, if it meant not having to talk to Ryan who I'd automatically seated next to me when I'd changed the flights. It was an oversight but I was on autopilot when I made the call. I should have seated him at the front of the plane near the toilets. Maybe I might have got lucky and he'd have been stuck beside a screaming baby the whole way home. I hoped Liza and Bobby were at the opposite end of the plane. Once we were back home, we could finally go our separate ways because I didn't want to see any of them again.

My phone buzzed and I saw I'd missed messages from Ruby and Mum, checking in to see if I was okay. Mum was letting me know she'd had a visit from the police asking when we were returning. The fire had to have been caused deliberately if they wanted to talk to us. Was it kids messing about or had Ryan had another one of his stupid ideas and had arranged it to get us out of debt? I wasn't sure I believed the denial about his involvement. I responded to Mum and Ruby, giving them my flight details for tomorrow and telling them I was keen to see them both.

I scrolled up to the latest message to find it was from Nico and my heart swelled.

> Hope you're okay. I was thinking, if you're flying home early tomorrow, why don't you stay at mine, bring your suitcase to the bar and I'll give you the keys.

It made perfect sense, the last few hours I could spend with Nico and it would save me having to see Ryan or any of them tonight.

I packed up the last remaining items and double checked I had my passport. Ryan's stuff was everywhere, discarded around the room haphazardly, but I wasn't his mother – or his wife any longer, for that matter. He could pack his own shit.

Glancing around at the beautiful apartment one more time, I wheeled my case out and let the door swing shut behind me.

27

'You got my message,' Nico said as I wheeled my suitcase to the bar. I'd arrived during a lull of customers, relieved to see him still working and not unemployed after Ryan created a scene this afternoon.

'I did and I accept, thank you,' I replied. 'How's the chin?'

'Bruised!' Nico rubbed at his jaw before laughing it off.

'I'm so sorry.'

'It's okay, I've had worse. I've been worried, he's got some temper, huh!'

I nodded, although not even I had witnessed Ryan the way he had been this afternoon.

'Security escorted him off the premises to cool off. Have you seen him?'

I replied I hadn't and took a sip of the drink Nico pushed towards me.

'What are you going to do, when you get home, I mean?' he asked.

'See what's left of my house after the fire, I guess, pack up what I can and move in with my mum while it's repaired.'

'And then...'

I stirred my cocktail, watching the condensation run down the side of the glass. 'And then sell up and file for divorce. It's got to be the shortest marriage on record surely.' I grimaced. What a mess it was, but things were going to change. It was time to find out who I was without Ryan.

'It'll be okay.' Nico leant over and stroked my cheek. The kindness in his eyes sent the butterflies in my stomach crazy. 'Do you want to wait at the bar or go back to mine?' Nico asked, handing me his key.

'I was thinking I might dump my suitcase and go for one final stroll along the beach before it gets dark, then I'll climb into bed and wait for you.' I gave him a wink and Nico grinned.

'That sounds perfect.'

'Thank you,' I held the key up, 'for this. I mean, we hardly know each other, it's very kind of you.'

'I know enough. I'll see you in a bit.'

I wheeled my suitcase to Nico's and headed straight back out to the beach, intent on watching the last sunset in Crete before reality came crashing in tomorrow. It was still busy, kids reluctant to leave their sandcastles despite their parents suggesting they should get going. Couples were snoozing on sun loungers in the sinking sun, seemingly without a care in the world. I plonked myself on the sand, inches away from the retreating tide, and breathed in the scent of the sea.

I was going to miss this beautiful island. The hotel had been amazing and the weather glorious, but Nico had made my week. What could have been a living hell after Ryan, Liza and Bobby had turned up had been made bearable thanks to him. He'd given me an escape more than once and I wished I didn't have to say goodbye. But it could never be more than a holiday romance, and for all I knew, there would be another woman next week only too happy to take my place. However, to me it had been real.

'Kelly!' a voice called and I turned to see Janice striding towards me, a hand raised in greeting. She kicked up sand as she walked barefoot.

Greg stopped a few yards away staring out at the horizon taking photos with a professional-looking camera, the strap straining against his neck.

'Hiya.' She sank onto the sand beside me, brushing grains from her white cut-off trousers.

'I'm going home tomorrow.' All of it coming out in a flood: the fire, our trip to the cave, Ryan's affair, while Janice sat open-mouthed. It was so good to offload and Janice was patient, waving Greg away with a flick of the wrist when he approached as I struggled to hold it together.

'Why didn't you say anything, you could have spent your days with us. I got the impression you and Ryan were happy.'

'That's what he wanted everyone to believe, but now it's all out in the open, and if I'm honest, I don't feel safe around him anymore – in fact, around any of them.'

I lowered my head to my knees, gently rocking them against my chest.

Janice placed a cool palm on my shoulder for comfort, offering what words of wisdom she could muster, but I under-stood it was a lot to take in. I'd splurged all my problems onto a virtual stranger, albeit a kind one.

'What a silly boy, he's got no idea what he's lost.'

I smiled weakly at Janice's comment. 'I hope you're right; I hope he looks back and realises what a twat he's been.'

'I think that's a given. Do you want to come back with us?'

'No, I'm fine,' I replied, adding, 'but if you read about me in the paper, if I suddenly go missing or have an accident, make sure you tell the police what you know.' It seemed outlandish, suggesting I was in danger and maybe I was overreacting, but what if I wasn't?

'Don't say that, I'm sure you'll be fine.' Janice's brow creased. 'Where will you go when you get home?'

'My mum's,' I replied.

'She'll keep you safe, I'm sure.'

We stood and Janice enveloped me in a tight hug.

'Take care of yourself, Kelly,' she said, reluctant to let go.

'You too.'

We swapped numbers and bid our goodbyes as the sun sank beneath the waves, shimmering the sea with gold.

Eventually, I tired of walking the shore and made my way back to Nico's flat. It was already gone nine – only another couple of hours to wait for his return. I made a cup of coffee and sank onto his bed, curling my legs up beneath me. My phone had buzzed non-stop while I was at the beach, Ryan searching for me, so I sent him a text to let him know I would be in the hotel reception just before three to meet the coach and he could check out for the both of us. I'd placed my key card on the bed back at the apartment when I'd left.

Warm and cosy in Nico's duvet, I drifted off, dreaming about plummeting to the bottom of the cave, the fall never ending, before I was woken abruptly by knocking on the door.

'Kelly, it's me, let me in.'

I pulled open the door to see a bright-eyed Nico grinning in the darkness.

'I got off early,' he said, coming in and kissing me on the lips.

'What time is it?' I yawned.

'Half ten. I'm just going to jump in the shower and then how do you fancy a grilled cheese sandwich?'

'Hmmm,' I agreed, still half-asleep and returning to the bed. 'I'll keep this warm for you.'

Ten minutes later, Nico returned wearing only a towel, still dripping.

'God, you're a sight,' I breathed, my eyes wandering over every inch of him.

'So are you,' he said, jumping on top of me.

Later, we sat in his bed munching grilled cheese sandwiches as Nico told me the route he'd been thinking about travelling.

'I thought maybe Seville first, then Paris, then London...'

'Where you'll visit me of course,' I interjected.

'Of course! Then Dublin for a Guinness, then Amsterdam, Prague, then...'

'You'll be gone for months, what will you do for money?'

'Oh I don't know, bar work I guess. Either that or I'll be a gigolo.'

I laughed, swatting his arm as he wiggled his eyebrows. 'Is that how you get your tips?'

We chatted until gone midnight before we made love again, snoozing until the alarm on my phone went off at quarter past two.

'I don't know how I'm going to get through today,' I moaned, running fingers through my tangled hair.

'You will. Come on, I'll walk you back.'

The streets were quiet as Nico chivalrously dragged my suitcase back to the complex, stopping at the entrance like he'd done before. My stomach sank at the thought of saying goodbye.

'Take care of yourself.' He rested his forehead against mine, our noses touching.

'You too.' I kissed his lips and hurried away, not wanting to prolong the goodbye, for Nico to see the tears welling in my eyes. It was stupid to get attached, but it had been unavoidable, I wasn't made of stone. We'd made no promises to keep in touch and I had to accept it would be unlikely I'd see Nico again. After tomorrow he'd forget all about me but I was still glad our lives had crossed paths.

Steeling myself for the long journey, I dragged my suitcase towards reception, counting down the hours until I was back on home soil, safe under my mum's roof.

28

Inside the brightly lit reception, I spotted Ryan at the desk, checking us out of the hotel, and Liza and Bobby on one of the settees, their body language towards one another frosty. Bobby had angled himself away from Liza, who was scrolling her phone, a bored expression on her face.

'Have you been with him?' Ryan asked when he joined me, his lips puckered like he'd tasted something sour. Alcohol seeped from his pores and he smelt less than fresh. Had him and Bobby been drinking all night?

'Let's not do this here. I just want to go home,' I sighed.

'I'm sorry, I'm having a little trouble understanding how you ditched me for a fucking barman,' he fumed, spittle landing on my cheek.

'He's more of a man than you'll ever be,' I snapped.

'Excuse me, your car has arrived,' the receptionist announced as a black Mercedes swung into the complex and around the giant water fountain, coming to a halt at the steps.

'Ryan said you wouldn't mind us jumping in with you,' Bobby said as he sidled up to us, with Liza in tow.

Great, the four of us squashed into a car all the way to airport, I could practically smell the tension from here.

'Hold my bag, I think I'm going to throw up,' Ryan said, dropping his backpack onto the marbled floor and dashing to the toilet.

'Heavy night,' Bobby explained a little sheepishly before I rolled my eyes. So they had been together? How on earth Ryan had wormed his way out of my accusation, I didn't know. I couldn't believe Bobby couldn't see what was right in front of his face.

Liza smiled, her face smug, as she slipped her hand into Bobby's, awarding me a victorious glare.

My lip curled and I left them there, making my way out of the sliding doors and into the car, Ryan's bag still where it had been dropped. My days of looking after him were long gone. It was about time he stood on his own two feet.

'Gutted your little plan didn't work?' Liza's voice tinkled a few paces behind me, having followed me out while Bobby waited in reception for Ryan, relishing in her triumph.

'I didn't have a plan, Liza; I just told the truth. What Bobby does with it is his business, but I'm done with the lot of you.'

'Of course you are,' she chuckled, 'until you're back on home soil and lonely without your bartender with benefits.'

'Lonely?' I scoffed. 'I can't imagine I'll miss a lying, cheating husband and a back-stabbing friend. I'm sure I'll be just fine without either of you.' I handed my suitcase to the driver to place it in the boot before climbing into the front seat so I didn't have to sit in the back with the three of them. Fury coursed through my bloodstream at the injustice of it all. Why did Bobby not believe me? Surely he must have a shred of suspicion, some of what I said had to ring true.

Finally, the boys joined Liza in the back and I gazed out of the window as the car trundled along, watching the blinking lights from the surrounding buildings in the darkness become sparse as we hit the main road towards the airport. I wanted to doze but couldn't get comfortable. Hopefully I'd pop in my AirPods, drown out the noise of the cabin and sleep on the flight.

Thankfully, no one was chatting much due to it being three o'clock in the morning, all of us yawning and trying to nap. When we arrived at Heraklion airport, we waited while the driver retrieved our luggage before making our way inside the terminal, following the crowd towards baggage check-in.

'Hang on,' Ryan said, dropping to his knees and rummaging through his backpack.

Liza, Bobby and I hung back as people moved around us.

'What's up?' Liza asked as Ryan's face paled. He emptied out the contents of his backpack on the floor, upending the bag and shaking it.

'It's not here.'

'Your passport?' I asked, a knot forming in my stomach.

'It's gone!' Ryan stood. 'Let me see if it's in the car.' Leaving his stuff, he ran back outside to try to catch the driver.

'That's why Bobby always looks after mine,' Liza said, bending to put Ryan's things back in his backpack.

A few minutes later, Ryan came back in, his forehead shiny, panting from his short jog. 'It's not in the car, I must have left it at the hotel.'

'There's a coffee stand over there, let's grab a drink,' Bobby suggested, pointing to his right.

'I need to go back and get it; I'll miss my flight!' Ryan's skin was blotchy with oncoming panic.

'You ain't getting that flight, mate. Come on, we need to have a chat.' Bobby turned and strolled towards the coffee stand, not even waiting for us to follow.

'Bobby, I need to find my passport,' Ryan called after him, his hands raised to the heavens. 'What is he on?' Ryan added, flinging his backpack over his shoulder and glaring at Liza.

'I have no idea.' Liza shook her head, yet they both followed.

I was torn between pushing on through baggage drop-off and leaving them to it, but curiosity got the better of me and I trailed after them.

Bobby bought a round of lattes, despite not asking if we wanted one, and we gathered around a tall circular table near the floor to ceiling window. I watched as Ryan stood perplexed, scratching at his arm, keen to sort out his missing passport and not waste time. I had the tiniest slither of guilt about not double checking but quickly forced it away. He was a grown man; he could look after himself.

'Here's the thing, Ryan.' Bobby pulled some papers from his backpack and placed them face down between the coffees. He let out a theatrical sigh and grimaced, his forehead wrinkling. 'I've been waiting for the perfect moment, but we've had such a great holiday, I kind of didn't want to ruin it – our last hurrah, so to speak.'

Ryan shook his head, eyes darting to Liza, who shrugged, looking as puzzled as he did.

My neck prickled with unease. Something about Bobby's tone was too staged, like he'd rehearsed what he was about to say, and I had the urge to intervene. 'Bobby, what are you talking about? We've got a plane to catch.'

Bobby raised a hand to silence me, his eyes never leaving Ryan's. 'I know you've been screwing my wife. I've known for months.'

I bristled, every tiny hair standing to attention, but Bobby was calm, complacent almost.

'It's not true, I told you she's lying!' Liza insisted, pointing at me and turning on the waterworks with startling efficiency.

'Shut the fuck up, Liza. Oh and where's your passport?'

'You've got it?' Her face fell as Bobby smirked.

'Have I? I'm not sure I have, love.'

Liza grabbed Bobby's backpack from his shoulder and began rooting inside as he pulled his own passport from the rear pocket of his jeans.

'This is the only passport I've got.' His lip curled upwards in a menacing smile and my blood ran cold.

29

Out of instinct, I immediately checked my passport was where I'd put it, in the zipped compartment of my backpack. Relief flooded through me as my fingers closed around the familiar leather-bound book, pulling it out to check it was my name printed inside.

'What have you done?' Ryan asked, his face now grey.

My palms began to sweat, the tension around the table was palpable. What was going on?

'Here's the thing,' Bobby began, scratching at his day-old stubble with the palm of his hand before continuing. 'You've screwed my wife – hell, you might even be that little thing's father.' Bobby pointed to Liza's stomach. 'You've screwed the business too, we're at rock bottom, about to fold because you haven't been able to pull your head out of your arse and sort the finances. In fact, you've pretty much fucked everything I care about.'

Liza wiped away her tears, rounding on Bobby. 'Where's my passport?' she shrieked, gaining attention from passing travellers.

Bobby peeled his eyes away from Ryan to look at his hysterical wife. 'It's back at the hotel, with Ryan's,' he told her matter-of-factly before turning back to him. 'You shouldn't have left me to look after your bag, mate.'

For a second, it looked as though Ryan was going to swing for Bobby, who was chuckling to himself, but Ryan's shoulders sank and he rubbed at his bloodshot eyes.

Bobby had us all rapt and my stomach churned as we waited for some sort of explanation. All holiday I'd been the one play-acting – albeit poorly – yet Bobby had pulled off an Oscar-winning performance. Since they'd arrived, I had no idea anything was amiss between him and Liza.

'Neither of you will be catching this flight,' he continued, looking pointedly at Ryan, then at Liza. 'But it'll give you a chance to read through these.' He placed a palm over the pages he'd pulled from his bag, before turning them the right side up. They were typed documents secured with paperclips, and he handed one lot to Ryan and the other to Liza.

'Divorce papers!' Liza's hand flew to her mouth and she began to sob, her entire body trembling as tears spilled down her face. It was the most genuine reaction I'd seen from her all holiday; her bravado had disappeared. By rights I should have felt satisfied by this turn of events, Liza finally getting some karma, but my stomach was knotted so tight I felt sick.

'Yep. Surprise!' Bobby snarked. 'Oh, and don't worry, if the baby is mine, I'll take care of it, but I'm going to be needing a DNA test once you've popped it out.'

I cringed at his flippancy. I hadn't wanted him to be made a fool of but the savagery of what was unfolding shocked me to the core.

'What's this?' Ryan asked, waving the paper as if he couldn't make head nor tail of it. I craned my neck to see what it was, catching some legal jargon.

'You're signing the business fully over to me. From now on, you have no rights to it – the name, the shipping container or any of the stock we have left. Nada,' Bobby explained.

Ryan scoffed and chucked the pile back on the table derisively. 'As if I'd do that.'

'I'd think long and hard about it if I were you, mate. I mean, those people you borrowed money from are a nasty bunch, but I'm sure I could help them locate you once you're back on home soil. You might get away with a kneecapping, but it's not looking good. They've already tried to burn down your house.'

'What!' I choked, saliva rushing into my mouth.

'It... it was an accident,' Ryan stammered.

'Unlikely, mate. I mean, you were supposed to give them half the money before you got married – how much was it again, twenty grand?'

My eyes were huge orbs as I stared at Ryan, who seemed to shrink into himself, refusing to meet my gaze. 'I thought you borrowed from the bank?' I said, looking from Bobby to Ryan.

'Oh, this is on top of that loan, Kelly. Your husband has got himself in a whole world of shit.' Despite Bobby's directness, there was no malice in his tone.

'I can't listen to any more.' My cheeks burned. How could Ryan have jeopardised our home, our safety, borrowing money from someone other than a bank? Someone who had no qualms about setting fire to our house when they didn't get paid. 'I'm getting on the plane,' I added, walking away and leaving the three of them standing around the table.

'I'll catch up with you airside,' Bobby called, but I didn't turn around. He'd known what Ryan had done, the danger he'd put us in. What if we'd been in the house, asleep in our beds, we could have been killed!

Anxiety clamped around my lungs like they were in a vice,

cinching ever tighter until I struggled for breath. Going through the motions, I queued to check in my baggage and then again through security, still reeling from Bobby's revelation. The whole honeymoon had been a farce, a platform for Bobby's stupid ruse. A way to watch them together while he planned his next move and now it was checkmate. Ryan and Liza wouldn't get back from the hotel in time to make their flight, so who knew when they'd get home. It seemed Bobby cared as little as I did. We'd both been duped, but he'd been the smart one, waiting until the pair of them believed they'd gotten away with it before outing them in a spectacular fashion. He'd fooled me, but I'd gotten used to being blindsided now. It seemed everyone was hiding something. If I was lucky, I wouldn't see Bobby for the rest of the journey.

My head spun, but I tried to focus. I purchased another coffee, having left the one Bobby bought, and found a bench just vacated in the corner of the waiting area, keeping an eye on the electronic board for the announcement of which gate the plane was at. I considered texting Mum and Ruby with the development, but it was the middle of the night back in the UK and would be easier to explain in person. In a matter of hours, I would be back home, sitting at my mum's dining table, nursing a cup of tea. She'd offered to pick me up from the airport but it was just as easy to get a taxi.

'There you are.'

I groaned inwardly as Bobby sank down next to me and unwrapped a breakfast burrito.

'Here, I got one for you too. Come on, you need to eat.'

Reluctantly I unwrapped it, the smell of freshly fried bacon and egg making me salivate.

Bobby turned to me. 'I'm sorry, I really am. I didn't mean to drag this out any longer than I had to.'

'So why did you? Why did you let me marry him?' I asked stiffly, wiping my mouth with a napkin Bobby handed me.

'Because I had to be sure it was Ryan she was sleeping with. It didn't take long for Liza to give the game away; you know, I actually caught them kissing.'

I swung my head around so fast I almost gave myself whiplash. 'When?'

'The day of the catamaran trip. They thought I was far enough away in the sea, underwater,' he scoffed. 'I mean, I've seen the messages on her phone, she'd saved his number under the name Rachel. I'd known she was lying to me, but I didn't want to believe it was Ryan she was fucking behind my back.'

'Our backs,' I corrected. 'I should have told you when I caught them, but I was so upset I fled.' I sighed, resting my burrito in my lap, taking a sip of coffee and putting it back down by my feet.

'We're a right pair, aren't we.' Bobby stared into the distance, chewing rhythmically.

'I don't understand what you've got to gain with the business though, Bobby, with all the debt attached to it. How did you let it get so bad?'

'Unexpected tax bill, then a fine for submitting late – owed suppliers, backdated invoices, rent on the lock-up. The list goes on. Ryan decided from the outset he'd deal with the finances, that he was better with figures than I was, and stupidly I let him. I didn't bother looking at the accounts, I trusted him when he told me everything was fine – business was booming, he'd said. It wasn't until I started digging through some papers he'd left out that I saw we were in the red. I won't make that mistake again.'

'So why do you want the company if it's in ruins?'

'Because I can pull it out. All the money Ryan borrowed to prop up the business was in secret. I didn't know about it at first, he hoped I'd never find out, so it's in his name, not the company's.' The corners of Bobby's mouth turned upwards in a smug grin, which I didn't reciprocate. He might be sitting pretty, but I wasn't.

'The debt's in my name too – at least what he borrowed against the house is. I didn't sign anything, so he's done it illegally. What a complete bastard.'

'I'm sorry, I didn't know he'd done that until you mentioned it. You need to get in touch with a solicitor, tell them it was fraudulent.'

'If you knew he'd borrowed money elsewhere, why didn't you tell me?'

'At the time, I thought it wasn't any of my business and I wasn't going to go behind his back, we were mates.'

'Until he slept with your wife.' A cheap shot, but I was fed up being kept in the dark.

Bobby didn't defend himself and we sat in silence, finishing our breakfasts. What did life look like for me now? I'd spend the next five to ten years digging myself out of the debt Ryan had got us into with nothing to show for it. Surely whatever we'd made on the house would get swallowed up and Ryan would likely have to declare bankruptcy, which meant I'd likely have to do the same. My credit rating would be zilch and any landlord would be reluctant to take me on as a tenant. It made my blood boil that at twenty-six I was going to have to start again back at ground zero, relying on my mum.

'Ryan said something about you putting in some inheritance?'

'We had a grant to help with the business, but that was ages ago, he's talking shit. He lied about money a lot; we were doing fine until we weren't because of his poor management. If he'd just come to me to begin with after the tax bill, we could have worked through it together, but he was so secretive and things started to slip.'

More lies, it was like Ryan didn't even know what the truth was any more. Constantly lying to cover his tracks and hide the fact the business was falling around him.

'Are you going to move back in with your mum?' Bobby asked, breaking into my thoughts.

'Looks like I'll have to. I'm just hoping our insurance allows us to fix the fire damage, then we'll have to sell, pay off the debt against the house with the equity, if there's enough.'

'I'm sorry, Kel, what can I say, he's a twat. He screwed us both.'

I considered Bobby's words for a minute, there was little point in feeling sorry for myself when he too had been a victim of Ryan and Liza's betrayal. He might still have his home, but he was going to have to go through a divorce and I couldn't imagine Liza rolling over and giving him whatever he demanded. 'I'm sorry about Liza, I had no idea. I never thought she'd cheat on you for a second.'

'Things haven't been great for a while now. Even when she's there, she's not present. Probably thinking about her next hook up with Ryan.' Bobby rubbed at his forehead and screwed up the wrapper of the burrito, shooting it into the bin with perfect precision.

'Is that why you kissed me in the hotel room, to get one over on Ryan?'

Bobby blushed and nodded. 'Yeah, stupid macho bullshit, I'm sorry.'

'What did you do with their passports?' I asked, watching Bobby's face lift.

'I slipped Ryan's out of his bag when he went to the toilet before we left,' he chuckled, 'and I hid them both in the plant pot in reception. Petty, but my last little fuck you to the pair of them. When I left, they were trying to get a cab back to the hotel.'

I laughed along with Bobby. It served them right and might take Liza down a peg or two. They'd likely miss their flight, unable to get to the hotel and back before the plane departed, which meant more money spent on another ticket. At least our credit cards weren't jointly owned. Anything Ryan spent on getting home would add to his tally, not mine.

30

'Mind if I sit in Ryan's seat?' Bobby asked as he followed me onboard. The plane had arrived at gate 18 and we'd queued to have our tickets and passports checked again before boarding. I had hoped for the extra space and peace during the four-hour flight to gather my thoughts. I was constantly spinning from one disaster to the next and the stress was starting to catch up with me, not to mention the fact I was running on about an hour's sleep but I could hardly say no after what had just gone down.

'Sure.' I smiled weakly and moved my bag under my seat.

Thankfully, our row of three ended up with us having a spare seat and Bobby plugged his headphones in as soon as we took off.

I took a quick glance out of the window, wishing my trip to Crete had been the dream honeymoon it was supposed to be. The last time I'd sat on a plane a week ago, I'd been crushed and utterly heartbroken. On the return journey, steely determination was at the forefront of my mind, an urge to put the past behind me and move on. I closed my eyes and drifted off, the events of the past few hours catching up with me.

Bobby nudged my arm awake and I jolted upright, pulling my AirPods out.

'Seat belt sign is on, they just made an announcement, they're starting their descent.'

I nodded, wiping the sleep from my eyes. My skin was dry and papery and I glugged from a bottle of water Bobby passed to me.

'You slept through the turbulence,' he chuckled, stretching out his legs as much as his tall frame would allow.

'I'm shattered,' I admitted, cricking my neck from side to side. 'I wonder if they'll manage to get another flight today?'

'Who knows. I just bloody hope she signs those divorce papers.'

'I think you may have a battle on your hands there.'

'I got her banged to rights; I took screenshots of all the messages.'

'So you're kicking her out?' I asked.

'Damn right I am, I'm packing all her shit up as soon as I get home and leaving it in the porch. I've already booked the lock-smith in for this afternoon. I'm not messing.' Bobby scowled at his phone, itching to use it despite having no connection yet.

It was almost seven in the morning local time, the whole day ahead of us, but I wanted to crawl under my duvet and sleep it away.

Within ten minutes, we'd touched down and everyone stood, rummaging through the overhead compartments to retrieve their things.

'Want to share a cab or are you getting picked up?' Bobby asked.

I nodded, suggesting a taxi, and we shuffled off the plane as soon as the walkway had been fitted and the doors opened.

Passport control was smooth and we were quickly through to

collect our baggage, waiting as the conveyor belt moved on a loop, devoid of suitcases.

'Why are they always so slow,' Bobby grumbled.

I checked my phone, I'd had a couple of messages from Ryan, begging me to wait for him, but that ship had already sailed. He must have been mental to think I'd miss my flight. Apparently he'd made it back to the airport with his passport but was now waiting for an available seat on the next flight. At least he'd get to spend some quality time with Liza.

Finally, our bags came through and Bobby called a local taxi firm to pick us up. Cheaper than using one of the airport taxis.

'The Glades please,' I instructed the driver as I climbed into the back after a short wait on the chilly concourse.

Bobby refused any money from me when we stopped outside Mum's, who had been watching out for me and was at the gate before the driver had turned off the engine. I was itching to see the state of our house and if it was at all habitable, what out of our precious belongings could be salvaged, but I didn't want to do it alone, knowing I'd need Mum's morale support.

'Take care of yourself okay.' I patted Bobby's arm before climbing out, a rush of emotion hitting me as I fell into my mum's warm embrace.

'Oh, Kelly, I've missed you.' She held me at arm's length, taking in every inch of me as if I'd been away to a war zone instead of a luxury hotel. 'I take it Ryan's not with you?' she asked, looking over my shoulder at the empty pavement.

I shook my head. 'How are you? How's Dad?'

'You know, good days and bad. Yesterday he wasn't so great, but he might brighten if you visit him later, if you're not too tired of course.'

I nodded and dragged my suitcase up the path and inside my

childhood home, the smell of Mum's baking bringing back fond memories.

'I was awake early tracking your flight, so I made some short-bread. Let's have a nice cup of tea and you can tell me about your week.'

'Okay, but then we go round to the house.' My voice was firm, knowing Mum would likely want to protect me from the sight, but I'd have to deal with it at some point.

Mum's eyes were like orbs by the time I'd told her everything, from the second I stepped into the grounds the evening of our wedding where I saw Ryan and Liza in the summer house, losing the plot and deciding to honeymoon alone, to how awkward it had been when the three of them had turned up in Crete. I also told her how Ryan had got himself in debt, although I didn't go into details.

'So Liza's baby could be Ryan's?' Mum's mouth hung open; she'd loved Ryan like a son for the past ten years. My betrayal was hers too.

'Hello,' Ruby's booming voice accompanied the slamming of the front door as she'd let herself in.

'We're in here,' Mum called back, a reprieve from my miserable tale.

Ruby appeared in the door of the kitchen, rushing forward to fling her arms around me. We argued like any other siblings, bickering about our parents, clothes I'd borrowed and not returned and whose turn it was to pay for lunch when we went out, but I knew she always had my back when I needed her.

Mum made more tea and I finished the summary of my time in Crete, leaving out details on Nico. Now I was back on home soil, he felt like more of a dream than ever.

'Well, it sounds like Bobby certainly got his own back,' Ruby chuckled when I told them what had happened once we'd got to Heraklion airport.

'I just don't know why he waited so long to confront her. Why did he let me marry Ryan if he suspected what was going on between them?'

Ruby looked away, gnawing at her lip. 'I guess only he can answer that.'

'It would have saved me a lot of hassle and expense if he'd spoken up.' I shook my head and Ruby put her hand on my arm.

'I'm sure Bobby's hurting too.'

'Oh he is, and he's pretty much forcing Ryan to sign over the business. He's going to be left with nothing.'

'It's what he deserves! I can't believe he's got you involved in his mess; I mean, loan sharks... what was he thinking?' Ruby was hard-faced, her lips turned up into a snarl.

'I have no idea.' I was still unable to get my head around the chaos Ryan had caused.

'You have to tell the police. What if you'd been inside the house when they set it on fire?'

'It doesn't bear thinking about,' Mum added, closing her eyes and shaking her head.

'Speaking of which, can we go and see the damage now? I need to pack some things anyway.'

'Let's put the washing machine on first. Empty your suitcase and we can wheel it round there for you to load it up again.'

I threw as much in the machine as would fit, leaving my toiletries, sun cream and make-up on the kitchen side before the three of us embarked on the five-minute walk to my house. It was a walk I'd done many times before but for the first time I was filled with trepidation at what awaited me.

'Christ, I can smell it from here,' I said as we turned into Saxon Road. Old, stale smoke hung in the air. It was sunny but also breezy, carrying the scent of burnt timber along the road. At least my dog walking van was still in one piece, parked a few houses down where I'd left it while we'd been in Crete. We were still paying off the loan we'd borrowed to buy it. I couldn't say the same about our home though.

As I approached our small, terraced house, my heart sank. A piece of plywood had been nailed to what remained of the door frame. Black smoke stained the brickwork above and there was another piece of wood where the lounge window had once been. Dark swirls of ash tarnished every surface, a trail of it on the window ledge, doorstep and patio.

'Oh God,' I whimpered, my hand over my mouth as I stifled a sob. Our lovely home, although not a pile of rubble as I'd imagined, was still a shock to see. It was a nightmare but it could have been so much worse. If we'd been asleep inside at the time of the fire, we may not have survived it.

31

'We'll have to go in around the back,' Mum said gently. 'The fire brigade had to kick in what was left of the front door.' She went along the garden path, whereas my feet remained planted on the pavement, reluctant to move. I wasn't sure I wanted to see any more, the outside was heartbreaking enough.

'I'm sure it's not that bad inside,' Ruby offered, and I scoffed, eventually following Mum, who had unlocked the side gate and was making her way around the house.

Thankfully, at first glance through the glass back door, the kitchen looked untouched. The fire hadn't managed to spread its way to the rear of the house and I hoped it had been contained in the hallway and the lounge.

As soon as Mum unlocked the door, taking control as I couldn't get my legs to move, the smell hit me. The acrid odour of smoke wafted out and Ruby held her hand in front of her nose.

'We need to open some windows. I came in yesterday to check it was safe and tried to air it but didn't want to leave anything unlocked just in case.' Mum's voice had a forced joviality. She stepped inside, leaving the door open and pushed the kitchen window as wide as it would go. 'Careful, the tiles are slippery,' she added as I crossed the threshold, leaving my suitcase by the back door.

The still-damp floor squeaked under my trainers and I gingerly walked towards the front door, where what remained of the hallway carpet was sodden. Blackened wallpaper peeled away from the plaster and excess surface water dripped occasionally from the ceiling, but at least it had held.

In the front room, there was smoke and water damage. The television screen had cracked and the fireplace blackened. The cushions I'd purchased after waiting an age for them to be on sale were scorched, along with the sofas which had been a house-warming gift from Mum and Dad. All of it ruined.

I sighed, hands on hips, surveying the damage, my eyes resting on the photo of me and Ryan on the mantelpiece, a large crack dividing us.

We'd need to redecorate, fit a new carpet and replace furnishings before we could sell, but I'd expected the place to be uninhabitable. Ryan would be able to stay when he flew back, if he could put up with the stink, but I was still going back with Mum. It would be too painful to stay, too many ghosts and constant reminders of what we'd had, what Ryan had thrown away.

'It's fixable, love.' Mum put her arm around me as I sniffed but it wasn't just the house I was mourning, it was the loss of everything.

The worst of all the damage was by the front door, a circular-shaped black hole where the carpet had disintegrated right down to the floorboards, the rest which was intact squelched under foot. Someone had poured something flammable through our letter box, it was the only explanation. The fire had started in the hallway, but thankfully hadn't got very far before the firemen arrived and saved our home.

'I best get cleaning,' I said stiffly, moving to the kitchen and pulling on pink rubber gloves.

'I mopped it up as best I could,' Mum followed, indicating to the variety of towels hanging on the line, 'but there was so much water.'

'Thank you, I'm sorry you had to deal with this.' I imagined the firemen with their hoses, firing gallons into my home to control the blaze. It must have been horrific for her to watch, knowing there was nothing she could do and we were thousands of miles away.

'We'll help.' Ruby had already started to roll up her sleeves.

'No, no, go and see Dad, make sure he's okay. Tell him I'll be over this afternoon. I'll make a start here, then pack a suitcase. I've got my keys.'

They didn't look convinced, but I wanted to be alone, to absorb the devastation, because although I was trying to put on a brave face for Mum and Ruby, the sight of my beloved home in disrepair made me want to cry. Partly due to the damage from the fire but also because of the memories of my relationship with Ryan I'd be leaving behind.

Ruby stood by the back door, reluctant to leave. 'Are you sure?'

'Go, you'll only get under my feet,' I chuckled, trying to mask my misery.

Eventually, Mum and Ruby left and I scrubbed every inch of the kitchen, even the walls, until bleach permeated the air, despite knowing Mum would have already done it. It was therapeutic, getting my stress out on the dirty surfaces yet still, some of the cloths came away grey with smoke. It latched onto everything, even the kitchen would need a new coat of paint. The downstairs would take weeks to sort out before we could put it up for sale.

I soon found out washing the hallway was pointless, I was swirling black stains further around the walls, so eventually I gave up and moved on to the lounge with a bin bag, putting in anything that was soggy, soiled or broken. The room was practically bare by the time I'd finished, but it looked like I'd hardly made a dent.

Thankfully, the cupboard where all of our household documentation was stored was situated in the furthest corner away from the door. Although charred, the thick wood hadn't been penetrated by the fire. I pulled out the untouched folder and flicked through to find our insurance policy.

I'd have to speak to the police before I made a claim, which, despite having had little sleep, I'd need to do today. Deflated, I squelched up the soggy stairs, carrying my suitcase, relieved to find the spare bedroom and bathroom untouched. The smell would take a while to leave and I opened all the windows to get air circulating.

I intended to pack enough clothes to keep me going for a week, but when I got to our bedroom, it looked like it had been burgled. Drawers had been left open, clothes strewn everywhere, bedside tables both ransacked, but I knew it had been Ryan desperately searching for his missing passport the day after our wedding. He hadn't even bothered to make the bed. I stared at the rumpled sheets, not wanting to touch them. Had he been in there with Liza? Had she slipped in while I'd been out walking the dogs, shagging my fiancé? What a fool they must have taken me for. Good, dependable Kelly, completely clueless. The lump in my throat grew and suddenly the house became oppressive.

I threw some clothes, toiletries and underwear into the suitcase and headed downstairs and out of the back door, desperate to leave. Pausing for a second to fill my lungs, I lugged the heavy case back along the garden path and around the side of the house, where I discovered a burly man peering over the front hedge.

'Ryan about?' he asked gruffly.

I stared at him, taking in his dark crew cut and sculpted beard that he'd looked to have grown to hide the pockmarks on his face. He was about six feet tall and heavy-set, with what looked like a star tattoo poking out above the collar of his shirt as he lifted his chin, waiting for me to answer.

'No.' I hurried past.

'That's a shame, Kelly. Tell him we'll be waiting,' he called after me, omitting a dark chuckle which made the hairs on the back of my neck stand on end.

I froze, slowly turning around. 'How do you know my name?'

He smirked, closing the distance I'd put between us in a few large strides. 'Oh, we know all our clients intimately.'

'I'm not one of your clients,' I said stiffly, 'and Ryan is still in Crete. Who are you?'

The man slipped his hand into the pocket of his trousers, retrieved a wallet and prised out a business card. He held it out, looking me up and down as though I was a piece of meat. I took the card from him with trembling fingers. It had barely any text on it, just the words DAR Lending, with a mobile number printed underneath.

'Tell him we can come to an arrangement, there's other ways he can work off his loan.'

Saliva rushed into my mouth as he licked his lips, sizing me up.

'Ryan and I are getting divorced. I have nothing to do with the money he's borrowed.'

'Shame that, such a pretty face would gain a high price.' He clicked his tongue against the roof of his mouth as nausea washed over me.

'I have to go.' My voice was shaky as I dashed away as fast as the heavy case would allow.

Counting to ten, I glanced around and swiftly raised my phone to snap a photo of the man's retreating back, then another of the black Audi he climbed into, although the numberplate was partially obscured. Was that who had set fire to my house? The man who Bobby said might break Ryan's kneecaps if he didn't pay up? My extremities went cold despite the warmth of the sun.

I kept walking, dragging my suitcase behind me, glancing over my shoulder every few seconds to make sure he wasn't following me towards my van, that me and my family were safe, but thankfully he'd driven in the opposite direction. Did Ryan have any idea what he'd got himself into?

Back at Mum's, I took advantage of the empty house and showered, desperate to wash that man's eyes from me. I put on clean clothes, sure I could still smell smoke on my skin, although it may have been in my head. Passing Ruby's old bedroom, I spied a pile of wedding gifts that had been stacked in the corner, beautifully wrapped in gold and white glittery paper with bows and ribbons. I couldn't bear to touch them, the thought of telling everyone Ryan and I were splitting up made me shrink. Tears welled up in my eyes for all they symbolised, the hope of a new life together as husband and wife, one that had ended before it had begun. I'd have to return them, but I couldn't deal with it right now, not when there were more pressing issues.

Ever practical, Mum had left the telephone number of the police officer who had called round to speak to me on the kitchen side by the kettle. Steeling myself, I dialled.

'Hello, my name is Kelly Quinn, I want to talk to someone about the fire on Saxon Road.'

32

'So, Ms Quinn,' the police officer across the desk from me cleared his throat before continuing. 'We believe from the investigation that an accelerant was poured through the letter box of your property late on Thursday the twenty-fifth of July. A rag was then pushed partially through and set on fire.'

I nodded grimly. After my call, I'd been invited to the police station to make a statement and headed straight there, keen to get the insurance process started but also wanting answers.

'Both you and your husband were in Crete on your honeymoon at the time, yes?'

'That's correct, yes.'

'It appears to be a targeted attack. Do you know of anyone who might want to cause damage to your house?'

'My husband is due to fly back today or tomorrow; he's been delayed, but I've recently found out he borrowed a large sum of money from a loan company.' I slid the business card of DAR Lending across the table.

The police officer steepled his fingers as he looked down at it, his eyebrows knitting together.

'A man was at the house this morning, at about ten o'clock. I went back to get some things and he was hanging around. He asked after Ryan and gave me his business card.'

'Did he threaten you?'

'No, but he was intimidating. He knew my name. I'm guessing it might be connected, maybe a warning for Ryan to pay up, but I had no idea he'd borrowed any money. I only found out just before I flew home.' Tears obscured my vision, but I blinked them away.

The police officer looked at me kindly, his lined face strangely soothing, although I shuffled uncomfortably in the plastic seat. The room was stuffy and perspiration dampened the underarms of my T-shirt. 'We'll look into it, thank you.' He took the business card and put it on top of his notepad. 'These people can be dangerous, do you have somewhere else to stay?'

'Yes, I'm staying with my mum at the moment.'

'That's good. Would you mind jotting down the address and telephone number?'

I did as I was asked and he smiled gratefully.

'We'll be in touch with any new information and, of course, if this man approaches you again, please call us straight away.'

'I don't suppose you can give me a crime reference number?' I asked. 'So I can call my insurers?'

He flicked through his report and wrote the number on a page of his notebook, tearing it out for me. 'We've been inside and assessed the damage, taken photos and the fire investigation team has been in, so you can go ahead and start to repair.'

It hadn't even crossed my mind I shouldn't have gone inside my own property. There was no crime scene tape or any deterrents, apart from the boards put up to secure the front door.

As I left the police station, I was overwhelmed by all I had to do. I needed to contact the insurance company to get the ball rolling now I had a crime reference number and notify the mortgage company too before any repairs could be started. Although Ryan had been the catalyst behind all this, his absence was as much of a frustration. He should be sharing the load; it shouldn't all be on my shoulders. I hadn't heard if he'd managed to get on a plane. Perhaps there were no seats available today and he couldn't get home.

It was only approaching lunchtime, yet tiredness washed over me. My limbs ached and I wanted to find a corner, to curl up and sleep, but I still needed to visit Dad. I climbed into the liveried van, a huge smiling French Bulldog on the side with my logo, Walkies, arched over his cute cartoon head. It would be good to get back to work, I'd missed my dogs and the endorphins from the exercise, regularly doing around eight miles a day over three group walks. Despite having Michelle booked in to cover my regulars until Thursday, I was keen to get back to normality. Every penny would come in handy now, especially as Dad's care home fees might be hanging in the balance. Another burden I'd have to shoulder alone.

The care home, or rather, assisted living complex, was set in a quiet area of Crawley surrounded by well-kept lawns and plenty of colourful outside spaces, with benches dotted around for residents to get some fresh air and enjoy the weather. Inside, the accommodation was bright and airy, calming green and blue tones with furniture that was comfy yet easy for residents to get out of. Everything had been modified to provide easy access and mobility for the residents, but it was the staff who'd sealed the deal for us when we'd visited. Everyone who worked at Parkgate went out of their way to be nice and not just when they were being watched.

A care worker called Hazel was Dad's favourite, she helped him with jigsaws and read the football results to him, occasionally bringing him in one of his favourite chocolate bars if he was a bit low. Mum had bonded with her, the pair of them being about the same age, and Hazel brightened her day too, understanding the weight which sat on Mum's shoulders.

That's where I found Mum after I signed in, giggling in the kitchen with Hazel as she helped prepare lunch for my dad.

'Hey, I thought I heard your voice? Is Ruby with Dad?'

'Yes, he's pretty lucid today and she's making the most of it. I think they are playing checkers.'

'He's beaten me twice already this morning!' Hazel grinned.

I smiled and rolled my eyes. 'That's because he cheats,' I replied, causing Mum to give me a playful whack on the arm. I repositioned my bag on my shoulder and left the kitchen for my dad's room, which was on the ground floor, along a corridor to the left.

A porter wheeled a trolley past me, the smell of cottage pie wafted beneath my nose, causing me to salivate.

'Smells good,' I said, and the porter chuckled.

'It's a popular choice,' she replied.

As I approached Dad's room, excitement bubbled in my chest, I couldn't wait to see him. Since his diagnosis, I'd not gone more than a few days without visiting, convinced our presence and love alone would bring him back to the man we adored. It hadn't of course but I never lost hope.

'It's just I feel so bad for keeping it to myself. I could have changed things.'

I frowned at the sound of Ruby's voice, floating from the room. Her words made me pause in the hallway. What was she talking about?

The shrill sound of my phone emerged from my bag,

announcing my presence. I fumbled for it, seeing Ryan's name on the caller display. Had he managed to get back?

'Are you going to answer that?' Ruby scowled from the doorway, making me jump. I declined the call.

'What were you talking to Dad about?'

'I wasn't, I was on the phone.' My sister's face paled and her eyes narrowed, yet still she scowled.

I folded my arms across my chest, sure there was something she didn't want to say.

'Are you coming in? Dad's looking forward to seeing you.' Mum appeared behind me, cajoling me into the room.

Dad was sat in his chair, perusing the checkers board, halfway through the game. The seat opposite had a Ruby-shaped dent in the cushion and I bypassed it, sliding my arms around him.

'Hey, Dad,' I said, kissing his cheek.

'Kelly.' He patted my arm with his weak hand, fingers curved inwards. He'd had his nails recently clipped and they were razor sharp.

'You need a shave.' I laughed as he nuzzled his cheek against my face.

'I'll help you with your razor later, Brian,' Mum offered, removing the checkers board and placing the cottage pie on the table. I moved out of the way as she brought round the chair to help feed him.

My insides shrank. Even after all this time, I couldn't get used to watching the man who had cared for us now being able to do so little for himself.

'I've got to go,' Ruby hovered. 'I need to do some shopping.' She bent and gave Dad a kiss before moving towards the door.

'Ruby, wait,' I called after her.

She paused and turned back at me, a strange look on her

face, not able to meet my eyes. 'We'll talk later.' She hurried out of the door as my stomach curled in on itself. I knew my sister better than anyone and something was going on with her. Was it serious, should I be concerned? With so much having happened recently, my addled brain was frazzled and there was a possibility it was nothing. Was I overthinking it?

33

I stayed with Dad for an hour, recounting fake stories of my amazing honeymoon. It didn't seem right to tell him the truth. What was the point, why upset him when he didn't need to know about Ryan's betrayal? I was happier for him to live in his bubble where everything was perfect. Mum's eyes viewed me with pity as I talked, but I refused to look at her. I couldn't burden my dad with the fire at the house, how I was going to be back living with Mum until my annulment came through, if I could even get one.

When I'd worn my mask as long as I could bear, I said I had to go, explaining that Ryan was waiting for me. Dad bid me goodbye with a one-armed hug and Mum stroked my face before I left the room, my throat thick. My mind was working overtime. Ruby knew something, she'd said as much to whoever she was talking to on the phone, but what was it? I'd had about enough secrets as I could take.

Back in the van, I listened to the voicemail from Ryan, which he'd left whilst at Heraklion airport, about to board a flight to come home. I guessed Liza was with him, although he had the grace not to mention her. Did he expect me to be waiting with open arms? Though, as much as I hated him, he needed to be warned about the guy the loan shark sent, what he might do if Ryan didn't give them their money back. I had little faith in the police finding them before they found Ryan. If he had any sense, he'd lay low and I tapped out a text to tell him as much.

> A man has been looking for you at the house. I've told the police. Go to your mum's, it's not safe.

I hoped he'd stay away until the police had a chance to investigate, but he might think I was exaggerating, making excuses so I wouldn't have to tolerate his presence. No matter what he'd done, I didn't want him physically hurt.

I drove past my blackened house, a blizzard erupting in my chest when I saw the Audi was back and parked directly outside. I kept my eyes front as I passed, not wanting to attract attention from the stocky man in the driving seat. How long was he going to sit there – until Ryan showed up?

When I got back to Mum's, I locked the door behind me and went upstairs to my old room, feeling unsettled and unable to shake the notion of being watched. Could they be keeping tabs on me too? I kept peering out of the curtains to see if anyone was loitering, checking for the Audi, but the street was quiet.

Ryan would be back at Gatwick in a matter of hours but I'd warned him, what more could I do? I had a headache brewing from lack of sleep and curled up on my teenage bed, the iron frame creaking beneath my weight. Pulling a blanket over me, I closed my eyes.

* * *

'Kelly.' A warm hand patted my leg and I woke to find the sun sinking beneath the tree outside the window. Sitting up, I rubbed my eyes, Ruby knelt beside me, her face level with mine.

'How long was I asleep for?'

'It's seven. Mum's going to order a takeaway. She's been with Dad all day.' Ruby rose to her feet and padded to the door.

'Tell me what you were talking about earlier.'

She slowly turned around, chin wobbling and looked away, shrugging. 'What do you mean?' Her act wasn't convincing.

'You said you felt bad about keeping something to yourself, I overheard you. Who were you on the phone to?'

Ruby's eyes misted and she wrapped her arms around her middle.

'What is it?' I pressed, my veins filling with ice. Why was my sister acting so weird? Normally nothing was off the table, we could talk about anything without it being awkward. Ruby was the blunt one of us two, every conversation was no-holds barred, but something was clearly bothering her.

'I didn't know, I swear. I didn't know about the baby.' She shook her head, eyes sinking to the carpet. I'd never seen Ruby look so guilty; it didn't make sense. It was like she was trying to make herself as small as a mouse.

'Liza's baby?'

'Bobby had no proof, just suspicion. He knew something had been going on for months, and that day, he went to your house, looking to confide in you, but when you weren't there, he came here. He was upset, we ended up chatting... and it sort of grew from there.'

'Ruby,' I snapped impatiently, getting to my feet, 'what are you going on about?'

She sighed, running her fingers through her long blonde hair. 'Bobby. I've been seeing Bobby.'

I gasped, taking a step backwards, resting my hands on the windowsill, trying to take in her revelation. Bobby and Ruby?

'How long for?'

'A few months, he knew Liza was having an affair, but he couldn't prove it. I'd had that doctor's appointment and left work early, so I'd popped in here to see Mum and, well, he was just so broken and sweet...'

'Jesus, Ruby!' I sighed, rubbing the back of my aching neck. The headache had left but was already threatening its return. I paced the length of my bedroom as Ruby chewed her lip. They were as bad as Liza and Ryan, carrying on in secret.

'Nothing happened before he was already sure she was seeing someone else,' Ruby said, as if that made it all better.

'So you were part of the charade, you knew what Bobby planned to do when he flew out to us?'

'No, not really, he wanted to keep things normal until he could catch Liza in the act, but I really like him, Kel. He was who I was on the phone to when I was with Dad.'

Something stirred in the pit of my stomach as my disjointed thoughts connected together. 'Bobby told you he thought Liza was sleeping with Ryan?' I demanded, my voice growing louder with every word.

Ruby backed away from me towards the door. 'He suspected, but I told him it wasn't possible, Ryan loved you, he wouldn't do that. I had no idea I was wrong, Kel, I promise. I'm as in shock as you are.' Her words came out in a rushed stream, hands gesticulating wildly.

'You let me marry him!' I shouted, forcing my fingers into my hair and pulling at my scalp, unable to believe my sister could let me tie myself to Ryan despite Bobby believing he was having an affair with Liza. How could she not have said something or even casted some doubt on our nuptials? I might not have acted, but I would have listened.

'I'm sorry,' Ruby moaned, holding her hands out to me as I glared at her.

'How could you?' My face burned red; neck mottled with mortification. Ruby, my flesh and blood, my big sister, the one I'd always looked up to and depended on, had betrayed me. Had the pair of them been laughing behind my back? The pit of my stomach bubbled with a rage I was struggling to contain.

'What's going on?' Mum burst through the door, summoned by the shouting, a tea towel over her shoulder and hands wet.

'Ask her!' I spat, pointing at Ruby, whose bottom lip quivered, but she remained mute. Fine, I'd spill the beans for her! 'She's been seeing Bobby, and they knew about Ryan and Liza, yet they let me marry him anyway.'

Mum bit her lip and stared at Ruby, whose shoulders were shaking. She raced from the room, unable to bear the guilt any longer.

'Ruby?' Mum shouted down the stairs after her, but the front door slammed. Seconds later, I heard her Kia start up and pull away. She always said I was the one who ran away from my problems, yet she'd fled as soon as the spotlight had been turned on her.

I paced the room, anger coursing through my bloodstream, bypassing the pain of her betrayal that I knew would hit later. Could we ever be sisters again after this?

My phone vibrated and I snatched it up, expecting it to be Ruby calling from her car, begging for forgiveness. But the screen bared Ryan's name and I answered it.

'What?'

'I'm at the house,' he said, stifling a yawn.

'Didn't you get my text message?'

'There's no one here, Kel. Can you come round so we can talk?'

Before I answered, I heard banging on a window in the background, a man's muffled voice shouting something I couldn't understand.

'Don't let him in!' I shrieked, the phone burning like a flaming stake in my hand, but Ryan was no longer on the line.

34

Ruby's revelation was catapulted to the back of my mind as I raced out of the door and sprinted along the pavement, ignoring Mum hollering behind me. I'd left my keys behind, it would be quicker to run than drive. The sun had set and the street lights illuminated the gloom as I reached the end of the road, almost slamming straight into a man carrying his shopping.

'Oi,' he said, dropping one of his bags, clipping my ankle, but I didn't feel anything, neglecting to apologise as I raced past. Acid burned in my thighs and sweat pooled at my waistband; phone gripped tightly in a sweaty palm. I'd never run so fast in my life, not since Boycie had legged it after a squirrel through Buchan Park, his lead trailing behind him.

I reached Saxon Road in a couple of minutes, spotting the Audi outside the house, but it wasn't until I reached the gate that I heard the shouts, followed by an almighty crash. I fumbled with my phone, dialling 999, the battery dying as the call handler answered.

'Shit!' I hissed, looking back at the street, then towards the house. It sounded like the place was being torn apart and Ryan was in there getting beaten to a pulp, what choice did I have but to help?

The side gate was open and I flew through it, round the back, to find the door hanging off its hinges, glass shattered and footprints visible on the PVC edge where it had been kicked in. My trainers crunched over broken shards as I stepped over the threshold.

'It's simple really. You've got two choices, Ryan, you either pay up or you don't walk again.'

I crept towards the voice coming from the lounge, the damp odour of burnt wood filling my nostrils.

'I... I don't have it...' Ryan cried, his voice phlegmy before the sound of skin hitting skin rang out, making me wince.

'What about that pretty little wife of yours, she not got any money tucked away? She runs her own dog walking business, must be lucrative.'

My breath caught; how did he know so much about us?

I peered around the corner, heart leaping into my throat at the sight of Ryan cowering in one of the kitchen chairs which had been dragged through into the charred lounge. My husband's face was bloody from a split lip and I watched as the burly man rolled up his sleeves, perspiration drenching his forehead, before picking up a rusty crowbar from the ground.

'The thing is, you owe Deano twenty grand, payment terms were half paid by last Friday. He was feeling generous, what with your wedding and all, but then to find out you flew out of the country without so much as a word, looks like you were running, mate.'

'It was my honeymoon!' Ryan spluttered, spitting blood onto the filthy carpet.

The man raised the crowbar high in the air and I held my

breath, legs threatening to give out underneath me. I leaned heavily on the wall, the only thing keeping me upright.

'Wait, I can give you some money today, please, please don't hurt me,' Ryan begged.

'How much?'

'Five hundred.'

The man bellowed with laughter, bending to catch his breath, his palms on his knees before straightening and raising the iron bar again.

'Stop!' I burst into the room, my stomach knotting as the man's lip curled, eyes glinting at my arrival.

'Ah, we have company. Kelly, lovely to see you again. I don't suppose you're here to pay Ryan's debt, are you?'

'I've called the police,' I lied, but as soon as the words were out of my mouth, he swept across the room like a tornado, gripping my throat and pinning me against the door frame, slamming my back into the wood. Shooting pains radiated up my spine and I gasped for breath. He wrenched me upwards, toes grazing the carpet, scratching around for purchase. I clawed at his hand, large and unyielding, as it squeezed and my eyes bulged as I choked for air. His sour cigarette breath hit my face, but I couldn't recoil. Up close, I saw the pockmarked skin as though he'd suffered with bad acne as a teenager. When I thought I was going to pass out, he released me and I slumped to the floor coughing, rolling onto all fours and crawling on my hands and knees out of the room until I was dragged back, arms flying out in front of me. My chin came down hard on the exposed wooden floorboards and I yelped.

'Not so fast, Kelly, you're not going to want to miss the show.'

I scooted back against the wall, cupping my face, chin searing.

'I'm so sorry,' Ryan said, his eyes damp before the man kicked out his foot at the chair and he toppled onto his side with a thud, howling in pain.

'Are you two getting the picture yet?' he shouted, glaring at both of us and wiping his brow with the back of his hand. He paced, nostrils flaring, kicking out again at the already shattered television, knocking it off the scorched wooden unit. I winced at the crash, hoping someone would hear us, a passer-by maybe. One of our neighbours, Maud, was elderly, she wore hearing aids, when she remembered to put them in. On the other side was a family of three, but they were often out at the weekend.

'Let's start this again,' he said.

Ryan lay crumpled on the floor, whimpering. His shoulder looked strange; it wasn't sitting right.

'You've got one week. Deano wants his money, all of it. You've got until Friday, otherwise I'll be paying you another visit.' He kicked Ryan in the stomach for good measure before stepping over him and out of the room, rolling down his shirtsleeves as he went.

A surreal silence descended over the space where Ryan and I lay shell-shocked until he emitted a low groan and made to stand. I moved my jaw from side to side, the bones clicking, the whack to the chin was making my muscles pulsate.

'I need to go to a hospital,' Ryan stood over me, 'can you drive me?'

'Can I drive you?' I clambered up, heat rushing to my face. 'We need to call the police!'

'No police, it'll just make things worse.'

'I already told them about him, this morning at the station. I gave them the card he gave me when he was looking for you.'

Yet still my sorrowful husband shook his head. 'You shouldn't have done that.'

'Ryan, it's not safe! Jesus, he could have killed you; he could have killed us both.'

'He wants his money, that's all.' Ryan winced, holding on to his arm. We moved slowly through the house, both of us battered and bruised. Ryan was stooped from the kick to the stomach and my jaw clicked every time I opened my mouth.

Outside I boarded the back door up as best I could with some plywood found in the shed, propping the door back into the space and covering the holes. It wasn't particularly secure, but it would do. As we left, I locked the side gate, not that I imagined it would be much of a deterrent for the thug we'd just encountered.

Ryan and I hobbled back to mum's house to get the keys for the van and the pair of us drove to the hospital in silence. I was too furious at my husband's stupidity to speak. What kind of people had he borrowed money from? The worst kind. Were they gangsters or bailiffs maybe? Able to rough someone up at the drop of a hat, no questions asked. No moral compass and no qualms at hurting a woman. My chin throbbed where it had bashed the floor and for those few minutes I'd never been more terrified in my life. The man we'd encountered was a monster and he needed to be locked up, but Ryan was too scared to go to the police.

I dropped him off at accident and emergency while I searched for a parking space. It would be easier to stick around than have to pick Ryan up again, plus I wanted to try and talk some sense into him about going to the police. Once inside the hospital, I took a detour to the ladies' to check my chin in the mirror. It was red and would bruise, but the skin hadn't broken. No visible marks had been left around my neck either. I shuddered at coming into contact with that monster again. What would happen when he came back?

It didn't take long for them to pop Ryan's dislocated shoulder back into the socket, give him some painkillers and put a strip over his busted lip. I waited outside in the sunshine, turning my face upwards to soak up the rays. I closed my eyes, trying to ignore the traffic sounds, imagining I was back in Crete, laying on the beach next to Nico. A million miles away from this mess, until Ryan finally emerged from the entrance.

'So,' Ryan began as he eased himself into the passenger seat of the van, 'can I stay at your mum's until I sort this mess out?'

35

I didn't want Ryan near me or my mum, but when I found out his parents had taken an impromptu trip to Cornwall after the wedding to visit his ailing grandmother, I didn't have much choice. He had no keys to get in their house and he'd burnt his bridges with Bobby, so he couldn't stay there. He had other mates but no one close enough he could turn up on their doorstep and ask to sleep on their sofa for a few days.

'One night, that's it, okay. Then you've got to sort something else out.'

'Jesus, Kelly, you're my wife, can't you find a little compassion.' He hit out at the plastic dashboard, making me jump and swerve momentarily into the oncoming lane of traffic. Jaw flexing, he was like a bomb waiting to go off. I'd never seen him so rattled. He gnawed at his fingernails, blinking rapidly as I gripped the steering wheel tighter. I had to keep him calm and level-headed, even if it meant biting my tongue.

Mum was sour-faced when I returned with Ryan in tow, making it obvious that she wasn't overly impressed with our guest. He had the good grace to look sheepish, speaking only when spoken to, which wasn't a lot. Claiming he'd tripped when Mum enquired about his injuries, his arm in a sling, as he ate the reheated Chinese with his good hand. Mum's eyes dampened when I asked if Ruby had been back and she shook her head.

'I wish you two wouldn't fight, you're sisters, you have to be there for each other.'

I declined to comment in Ryan's company when he asked what we'd been fighting about. The fact Ruby and Bobby were seemingly in a relationship was none of his business. Liza had to be back now too. Evicted from her own house, I guessed she'd gone to her parents; it was a shame they couldn't take Ryan in too.

When we were finished, I cleared away the plates and Mum made her excuses to go upstairs, saying she had some ironing to be getting on with.

'What are you going to do?' I asked Ryan once we were alone.

'I don't know, maybe go and see Bobby, beg him for a loan.'

I sniggered.

'What?' he snapped.

'Well, it's like robbing Peter to pay Paul, isn't it?'

'Got any better fucking suggestions?' I'd never known Ryan to be so aggressive, not when he was sober, but he clearly felt backed into a corner. 'I'm going out, can I have a key?' He stood, palm outstretched.

'Where are you going?'

'The pub.'

I sighed, taking the spare off the hook by the kettle and handing it over, glad he'd be getting out of my hair for a few hours.

'I'll make up the sofa for when you get back.' I held firm despite his derisive look and eventually he slunk from the kitchen like a disgruntled teenager.

Where was Liza in all this? Was Ryan planning to meet with her?

You don't care, the voice in my head persisted and it was true, I didn't. The only thing that mattered right at this moment was getting those people their money back. Out of the whole list of problems facing me, that was the one which needing dealing with first, otherwise I feared I wouldn't have a house left to sell or a husband to divorce.

What little takeaway I'd eaten was sitting in my stomach like a rock. I was itching to call the police, to tell them what had happened at the house, but Ryan was more on edge than I'd ever seen him and it wouldn't take much for him to lose it completely. I had little sympathy; the stupid arse had brought it all on himself, but whether I liked it or not, my connection to him remained.

Upstairs, I said goodnight to Mum, who was still ironing in her bedroom while watching her small television. I could tell by the look on her face she had things she wanted to say, but thankfully she spared me a lecture about having Ryan stay. I knew it wasn't great circumstances, but my hands were tied.

After a fitful sleep, nightmares of the pockmarked man cutting off Ryan's fingers one by one, I woke to sunlight peeking through the curtains and a throbbing headache. My mouth was like sandpaper, as if I'd spent a night on the sauce. Groaning, I heaved myself out of bed and checked the time; it was eight o'clock on Sunday morning. From not having enough, perhaps now I'd had too much sleep. Was I coming down with something? Even my glands were a little swollen. Opening the window for some fresh air, a breeze blew in, disturbing the nets, and it was only then I noticed the smell.

My bedroom door was open despite me shutting it on purpose last night, concerned Ryan was going to come back drunk, decide he didn't want to bed down on the sofa and would much prefer to climb into bed with me.

Out in the hallway, the smell was stronger and I wrinkled my nose.

'Mum?' I called out, her bedroom door was open too, which was strange, she always shut it. Inside, I spied the unmoving lump under the duvet. Eight o'clock was a lay-in for her, usually she was up and about, getting the morning paper or rustling up a batch of Dad's favourite cookies to take to him for a weekend treat.

I frowned, padding down the stairs, where the air became thick. Coughing, I lifted my crumpled T-shirt over my nose and moved faster, all at once recognising the smell and the faint hiss coming from the kitchen.

The gas hob was on, all four rings dispersing toxic fumes into the air.

'Fuck!' I turned them all off and opened the kitchen door, grabbing whatever I could to waft out the gas. Rushing to the front door, I opened that too, so a steady flow of air could move through the house. 'Ryan?' I called through coughing, but the front room was empty. The duvet and pillow rolled on the sofa where I'd left them last night. It looked like he hadn't been home.

I moved through the house, opening every window and shaking Mum awake, terrified she'd been poisoned in her sleep. Her eyes slowly unfolded in a haze; the master bedroom closer to the stairs than mine.

'Mum, did you leave the gas on?'

'What?' she mumbled. 'Why is the window open?' She frowned at the curtains billowing in the breeze.

'The gas was on; I'm trying to air the house out. Are you okay?'

'I've got a headache.' She lifted a limp hand to her brow and licked her dry lips.

'I'll bring you some water, stay here.'

I closed the bedroom door and ran downstairs, the smell already fading in the summer breeze. Thank God for the British weather. Filling a glass of water, I returned to my mother, who was sitting up in bed. She sipped it slowly, but I was reluctant to stay upstairs too long, knowing the front door was wide open.

'Don't get up until you're ready, I'll make some tea in a bit.' My voice was too high, pretending everything was fine when, in reality, we both could have easily died last night.

Downstairs, I shivered in my short pyjamas, the wind had a biting edge to it as I waited for the house to be cleansed of gas. I didn't even want to switch the kettle on, what if there was some unseen spark, the whole house could go up? It was the sort of thing Dad might have done when he still lived at home, sometimes getting forgetful and leaving taps running or the oven on with a cremated meal inside. It was what drove Mum to seek help. My heart sank, was she going the same way? No, surely not, but what was the alternative? Someone had been in the house last night while we slept and tried to poison us.

36

'Why didn't the carbon monoxide alarm go off?' Mum asked when we were seated around the table with a cup of tea a while later, our hoodies on with all of the windows still open. I was too nervous to close any of them.

'Because they don't react to gas, Mum, that's not how it works. Are you sure you didn't leave the hob on?'

'No! I wasn't even cooking anything, we had takeaway remember, and even if I did, I wouldn't have used all four rings.'

She was right, it made no sense. It wasn't like her to be forgetful, but sometimes with all the plates she had spinning I did worry she had too much on her mind. But if it wasn't her, then who was it? My skin prickled with unease at the thought.

'Where's Ryan?'

'No idea, I haven't seen him. I don't think he slept here last night. I better text him,' I said, grabbing my phone and seeing I had a message from Nico.

'You don't think he did it, do you?' Mum's voice had an edge to it which grabbed my attention.

I narrowed my eyes. What if she was right? What if he'd come back and turned on all the rings to cook something, too drunk to realise what he'd done? But if he had, then where were the leftovers and the mess? I'd seen him trying to make a toastie when he was half-cut and the devastation left behind all over the kitchen worktops. If it had been Ryan, then it wasn't an accident.

Mum reached over and rested her hand on mine, her eyes imploring. 'What happened to your chin?'

'Oh nothing, I fell up the step and knocked it on the wall.' The lie slid off my tongue like syrup.

Mum looked at me like she didn't believe a word I said.

'You need to get the key back, he's not welcome here anymore.'

'It's not as easy as that,' I said, knowing full well she believed he was the one who'd hurt me. Maybe she thought I'd given as good as I'd got when she saw Ryan's split lip and arm in a sling.

'He owes money, doesn't he?'

'What are you getting at?'

'You have life insurance, you're his wife.'

I laughed, cranking my neck back. The idea was ludicrous. 'You're not serious?' But she was.

Mum's face seemed to deflate in front of me and she gripped my hand. 'Get that key back, Kelly, today.'

I swallowed hard at the seriousness of her tone, but the idea he'd tried to hurt us was abhorrent. Flashbacks of my near drowning in Crete, being pushed in the cave and the weight of Ryan's pillow over my face played out like a film reel behind my eyes. Was my death Ryan's solution to his money worries?

I stood from the table, shaking my head. 'No, Mum, he wouldn't.' I didn't want to believe it.

Her face softened at my pained expression. 'I'm not saying he did, love; I'm just saying he's not welcome here.' She wrapped her hands around her mug, avoiding my eye. Waiting for me to figure it out by myself as was her way, but giving me a little nudge in the right direction.

'I need a shower.'

I escaped upstairs, my head all over the place, and sat on the toilet seat with my phone. I sent a message to Ryan, asking where he'd been last night before finally reading the message Nico had sent late last night.

> Missed you at closing time tonight, hope you got home safely. N x

To be held in Nico's warm arms was what I wanted, although it already felt like I hadn't seen him for weeks. I'd come home to a whole stack of problems and the memory of my trip to Crete was fading faster than my lacklustre tan.

I remained on the toilet seat with the bathroom door locked to text Nico back before googling how to annul a marriage. Apparently you could do it via the government website by completing a form. It would cost five hundred pounds, but I could live with that if it freed me from Ryan. I just had to make him see reason. If he fought it, it would cost us both more money, which neither of us had. We were better off apart; what we'd once had couldn't be salvaged, no matter how much he protested. It wasn't only about the cheating now, but all the lies and the danger he'd put us in.

After a quick shower, I felt more human. Mum would be spending her Sunday with Dad as she did every week and I spent my morning completing an online claim form with the insurance company. Around lunchtime when I'd finally got the admin under control and was making headway, I heard from Ryan.

> We need to talk, meet me in the County Mall Car Park, top level at two pm.

His message was abrupt and sounded ominous. Where had he spent the night? Had he come back here at some point and left the gas on or had he been hiding out with Liza because he was he worried he was being followed? It was the only reason he could want to meet in a car park of all places. I considered suggesting a coffee shop or local pub, but perhaps he was trying to lie low so I sent a message back agreeing before going downstairs to grab a sandwich.

Gas no longer permeated the air and my headache had faded, but how close had we come to being poisoned or going up in a fireball if someone had lit a candle or come too close with a cigarette? I couldn't ignore that someone had deliberately tried to hurt us, leaving the gas on and opening our bedroom doors in the hope we wouldn't wake up. The idea didn't bear thinking about and I was glad Mum was safely at Parkgate with Dad.

What if that man had followed me here and broken in whilst we were asleep, was it another warning of how serious they were if Ryan didn't pay up? How would they have got in, though, when there was no forced entry to any of the doors or windows?

The only people who had a key last night other than us were Ryan and Ruby and no matter what was going on between us there was no way Ruby would do anything to cause me or mum physical harm.

My sister hadn't materialised since our spat. I didn't expect her to contact me, she was hiding with her tail between her legs. I still seethed about the torment she could have saved me from, how my own sister could have followed me down the aisle, concealing what she knew, even if she didn't have all the facts and it was just an inkling. Her not telling me was hateful.

Trying to push Ruby's betrayal aside, I jumped in the van and stopped off for petrol, filling it ready for Monday, remembering I'd have to ring Michelle to let her know I was home to pick up

my rounds. I'd grab her some flowers to say thank you for covering, but I was keen to get as back to normal as I could. Some
stability in my life would be a good thing right now when everything else was chaotic.

As the County Mall car park loomed ahead of me, I queued
at the traffic lights waiting to enter. The mall itself was a huge
grey-brick building over three floors smack in the middle of
Crawley where you could park undercover, shop and eat in one
place. As I drove around and up through the levels, I wasn't
surprised to find it busy. Most people who came shopping in the
town centre parked there and weekends automatically meant
more shoppers. When it rained you'd be lucky to get a space, but
the late July weather was fine and when I reached the roof of the
car park, Ryan's van was easy to spot alone in the corner.

He stood by the barrier basking in the sun as I approached,
stopping a few spaces away. Most of the shoppers parked as close
to the stairs as they could, so the far end of the car park where
Ryan waited was empty.

'This is very cloak-and-dagger,' I called, stepping out of the
Walkies van, the breeze taking my hair.

Ryan looked like he hadn't slept, dark circles had taken up
residence beneath his eyes and his clothes from yesterday were
rumpled. His sling had been abandoned. Had he even gone to
bed last night and if not what had he been up to? Was there a
chance he'd been the one to come back and leave the gas on?

'I wanted to make sure we were alone. I'm being followed.'

His sentence made me stop where I was, a few strides away
from him as the sun disappeared behind a cloud.

'Come here, I want to show you something.' Ryan's brow
creased, his hands on his hips as he measured the distance
between us, and my mind flew back to the morning, waking
amidst the fog of gas.

I stared at my husband, the two of us alone on the roof of the multistorey, Mum's words charging through my head at a rate of knots. An icy finger caressed my back as the warmth rescinded and the breeze picked up. My breathing shallowed, stopping altogether when he tilted his head to the side and took two steps towards me.

37

'Stay there.' I held my arms out and he halted, a dry laugh escaping his lips.

'Kel, what's the matter? I was just going to show you the view while we're up here, that's all, I've not noticed it before.' He turned towards the edge, holding his hand out across the skyline. 'It's amazing, you can see for miles.'

My throat was thick and goosebumps sprang up on my bare arms. Was I being foolish, overreacting? Regardless, I didn't want to be here any longer than I needed to.

'Why are we here?' I sounded shaky. Mum couldn't possibly be right, could she? Either way, there was no chance I was going anywhere near the ledge where it wouldn't take much for Ryan to overpower me if that was his plan.

'Well, I wanted to talk, obviously, somewhere private. I've been followed, there were two of them at the pub last night, I had to slip out the back after last orders.'

'Where did you sleep?'

'In the van, I didn't want to lead them back to your mum's.'

'So you didn't come back to ours and leave the gas on?'

Ryan shook his head. 'No, why would I do that?'

He looked genuinely perplexed, but I hadn't forgotten he'd been lying to me successfully for months, pulling the wool over my eyes with ease.

'Because someone did, they came into the house, turned the gas on and opened mine and Mum's bedroom doors.' My voice choked when I mentioned Mum, I'd put her in danger.

'Holy shit,' he replied, but his reaction seemed staged.

We stared at each other for a second before I cleared my throat and spoke.

'I'm going to get our marriage annulled, we can fill out a form if we both agree and split what's left equally, if anything, once the house is sold. I've filed a claim with the insurers this morning and requested they assess for repairs as soon as possible.'

Ryan's jaw flexed and I could tell he was grinding his teeth, but I ploughed on.

'This is happening, Ryan, the sooner you come to terms with it, the better. If we drag it out, it's going to cost more money in the long run.'

'I'm not signing.' Ryan crossed his arms petulantly.

'You don't have a choice. I don't want to be forced to tell the police or the mortgage company you falsified my signature.' I used the only leverage I had left.

'Bitch,' Ryan spat, turning away from me, balling his hands into fists.

I took a tentative step back, closer to my van, keys at the ready, but he spun around, dropping to his knees. With his hands covering his face, he started to sob.

'I'm sorry, Kel, I know I fucked it all up.'

I sighed, he looked pitiful. Where had the man I'd fallen in love with all those years ago gone? The one I was still in love with just over a week ago. It was crazy what could happen in such a short space of time. I softened at the state of him, what he'd been reduced to.

'It'll be okay.' I moved closer until I could rest a hand on his shoulder.

He wrapped his arms around my middle, still on his knees, burying his head, seeking comfort I couldn't provide.

'Have you asked your parents to lend you the money?'

'No,' he sniffed, 'they're still away. Nan's sick and they don't have it anyway.' He looked up, wide-eyed and expectant. 'Could you ask your mum? What if she got a loan out against the house?'

'No way, Ryan.' I tried to wriggle out of his grasp, but his arms locked, squeezing me tighter, refusing to let go.

'Please, I'm desperate. They'll kill me!' His knees dragged along the concrete as I shuffled backwards.

'Then go to the police! You should have done that in the first place.' I heaved him off me, nearly losing my balance.

His mood flipped again, eyes flashing black. 'You don't fucking get it, do you? I'm in it up to here,' he shouted, levelling his hand to his neck. 'What about Bobby, you could ask him for me?'

'After what you did? You are joking? I didn't think there were any funds in the business left.'

'I'm sure he's squirrelled some away somewhere, he's bound to have.' His tone was bitter. 'Please, Kel,' he begged.

'I'll ask,' I eventually conceded, 'if you give me the key back.' Using it as a bargaining chip, knowing I'd feel safer if it was no longer in his possession.

Ryan fumbled in his pocket and tossed it over to me. There was a chance he could have had another one cut; I wouldn't have put it past him but right now I wasn't going to question him, I just wanted to get out of here.

I backed towards the van as Ryan got to his feet, not willing to lose sight of him in case he sprang forward and tried to accost me.

'Don't come back to the house,' I said over my shoulder as I climbed in the van and started the engine, reversing quickly out of the space and speeding along the concourse towards the exit.

* * *

Bobby's house was not so dissimilar from mine, a small red-bricked mid terrace with a black painted fence and a gate which squeaked as I pushed it open and made my way towards the front door. I knocked, taking a step back to look up in time to see the curtain twitch on the first floor. Heavy thudding of footsteps on the stairs sounded before the front door swung open.

'Kelly.' Bobby filled the doorway in a dazzling white T-shirt and jeans.

'Hi, Bobby, sorry to disturb your Sunday.' I waited a beat as he considered inviting me in. Eventually politeness won and he stepped back, waving me over the threshold and heading towards the white gloss kitchen.

'You looking for your sister?' he asked at the same time as an overhead floorboard creaked. Of course she'd be here. Although how, knowing Liza was pregnant and there was still the possibility Bobby could be the father, was beyond me. What was she getting herself into?

'No, I came to see you. Have you heard from Ryan?'

Bobby shook his head, his dark mop of curls bouncing. 'Nope, not that I want to, mind.'

I nodded, understanding where he was coming from. I shuffled awkwardly from foot to foot.

Bobby in comparison seemed at ease, leaning against the marbled worktop. He glanced at the kettle. 'Tea?'

'I'm all right, thanks. Umm, he sent me round. To be honest, he's desperate.' We both were. I wanted to pay and make the problem go away because I didn't feel safe knowing that man was out there and Ryan owed him. Who knew what he'd do next.

Bobby let out a hearty laugh. 'For money? Well, you can tell him to jog on, Kelly, he's not getting a penny out of me. What are you doing running around for him anyway, I thought you two were finished.'

'We are, but he's terrified. I don't know what he's going to do. Things have been... scary.' I explained the visit from the loan shark's muscle, wanting Bobby to know the danger we were in, yet I couldn't blame him for not caring.

'You need to kick him to the curb, you're better off without, he's only going to drag you down with him.'

'It's not as easy as that,' I replied. It seemed to be my stock answer to everything involving Ryan recently, but maybe Bobby was right. What was I doing turning up at his door, the husband of the woman Ryan had been sleeping with behind our backs, asking for financial help on his behalf? 'Have you heard from Liza?'

Another floorboard squeaked and I visualised Ruby loitering upstairs eavesdropping on our conversation.

'There was a bit of a showdown when she came home and found her things all packed waiting for her to collect.' A slow smile spread across his face.

'I bet! Did she sign the papers?'

'They both did.' I raised my eyebrows, surprised Ryan had conceded so easily. 'So that's one thing less to worry about.'

'Do you know where she's gone?'

'No clue, I assumed she was with Ryan?'

'Not unless she's sleeping in his van,' I said. 'Anyway, you've replaced her pretty quickly.' The words slipped out and I immediately regretted them as Bobby's face darkened and he folded his arms across his chest.

'I know you're upset, but Ruby didn't know about Ryan and Liza.'

'Sure,' I replied, my voice dripping with sarcasm. I'd assumed she'd run straight to Bobby to tell him about our argument and I wasn't wrong. She was hiding out here and even with us in the same house, she didn't want to face me. I suspected that was because they both knew more than what they were willing to divulge. Not that it mattered, what was done was done, but it proved to me I couldn't trust anyone, not even my sister.

'It's true,' Bobby protested.

'If you suspected it was him, then you must have shared it with her! I'm not the fool everyone takes me for,' I snapped, letting my frustration out on Bobby.

He looked away; the silence broken by footfalls on the stairs.

'He mentioned Ryan as a possibility, but I told you, I dismissed it, I couldn't believe it was him.' Ruby's voice carried through from the hallway and she entered the kitchen in her loungewear.

I faced her, a snarl erupting from my lips. 'Well, perhaps if you'd told me, I wouldn't be in this mess now. We've got a loan shark after us demanding money and I don't know how to fix it.' I fought back angry tears, but the stress was all-encompassing.

'It's not down to you to fix it, Kel, it's his problem,' Bobby said, his exasperation evident, but I carried on regardless, on a roll now.

'You know someone left the gas on at the house last night, Mum and I could have died.'

'Who? Mum?' Ruby grimaced.

'No, I think it could have been Ryan as it didn't look like anyone broke in. He had a key, but he says it wasn't him.'

'Fuck!' Bobby rubbed at back of his neck, yet still I sensed these were my problems to fix. Bobby had hung Ryan out to dry and me with him.

'And you believe him?' Ruby's face was one of outrage.

'No, I don't,' I replied, although saying it out loud terrified me. I had no idea who my husband was any more or the lengths he'd go to. Just how dangerous was he?

38

The clock kept ticking, Friday and the debt collection loomed over me with each day that passed. The nightmares persisted and I never felt truly rested when I woke, although I tried to carry on as normal. I called round to Michelle on Sunday night, taking with me a bunch of flowers to thank her for covering the walks with my dogs. It was lovely to have a catch-up with her and let her in on the truth of my disastrous honeymoon. Once I'd divulged Ryan was a cheating bastard, I wanted to change the subject before emotion overtook me.

Michelle was happy to discuss a different topic and we soon got to talking about business and the possibility of merging, employing more walkers and taking on more dogs, how we could potentially offer a franchise and extend the opportunity to other dog walkers in the area whilst taking a percentage. Michelle also had the idea of opening a grooming parlour too, although she was yet to do a qualification like I had. It was a service in demand with the popularity of cockapoos and similar breeds. On top of that, there was holiday sitting or even opening a doggie hotel.

Before I knew it, we'd been chewing the fat for a couple of hours and decided to meet for a drink next week to discuss further and make a start on a business plan. It felt like a glimmer of hope in the cesspit that my life had become in the past two weeks.

My thoughts of the future turned back to the present once I'd left Michelle's, the anxiety creeping up with every hour, inching closer to Friday. I'd barely seen Ryan and I had no idea if he was still sleeping rough in his van. I'd sent him a message to let him know Bobby had flatly refused to help, but I was sure it didn't come as a surprise. In fact, I felt like an idiot even asking. I'd embarrassed myself, but the need to offload was too much.

Ruby had stayed away from Mum's, deliberately avoiding me, although Mum said she'd been in touch, checking to make sure we were both okay. She'd been shaken by the gas incident as much as we had.

At home, Mum and I had become more vigilant. On my way home from Bobby's on Sunday, I'd stopped by a hardware store and bought some deadbolts for the front and back doors. Now we checked every night before bed that everything was off and the doors and windows remained locked even when we were home, but it still didn't help either of us sleep. Every floorboard creak or pipe rumbling made me start, believing someone was trying to gain entry. At least we knew Ryan didn't have access to the house, but it was like a cloud had descended over our family and none of us could truly relax.

I was struggling to get back into the swing and spent every spare minute thinking about Nico back in Crete, despite having enough to concern myself with here. We'd been messaging back and forth most days and I was pleased to know he hadn't forgotten about me yet, although our lives had to go on.

In between dog walking shifts, I'd been back to our wreck of a house numerous times, at first to let in the assessor from the insurance company. Thankfully, arson was covered in our policy and they were happy to proceed once they'd received the crime report from the police confirming we were out of the country at the time. Things moved quickly from there, starting with a visit from a salvage company to pull up the carpets and take the damaged door, scorched furniture and broken television away. The glaziers had been back to install new front and back doors, plus the window, and next were the industrial cleaners, who filled me with hope when they said they'd tackled much worse.

The main issue was drying the place out from all the water that had been pumped in. I'd moved everything of value out, so was happy to give them a key while they got on with it, moving in portable heaters which meant they were working in sweltering conditions. Apparently it worked faster than waiting for the summer heat to do its job. It had been busy, but I was cracking on with it as Ryan hadn't offered to help. I guessed he was too preoccupied.

Because I hadn't seen the pockmarked man loitering around, occasionally I was able to forget about Ryan's debt. My main concern, other than my husband being maimed if he didn't come up with a way to pay, was that our house, which I was repairing without any input from him, would be a victim of his actions again. I'd told the cleaners explicitly not to give the key to anyone or even answer the door if someone other than us came knocking. They'd been a little taken aback at the level of my security consciousness, until I'd explained the devastation they were fixing had been the result of a targeted attack.

By Wednesday, they'd made significant progress and after I dropped the gorgeous Boycie back to his elderly owners, I popped in at their request. Everything downstairs had been cleaned, even the kitchen gleamed. The black smoke stains on the walls and ceilings had been heavily reduced, ready for the decorators to come in and work their magic.

'Your husband came by yesterday,' Chris, the owner of the cleaning business, informed me, wiping his hands on his overalls.

'Did he?' I'd mentioned we were separated but warned Chris that Ryan might stop by. I'd kept Ryan updated by text but received no response. It seemed my husband wasn't interested in getting the house sorted ready for sale. I refused to let it get to me, having to handle everything myself, instead focusing on the end goal, which was putting the house on the market and getting rid of it as soon as possible. It wasn't the same house we'd fallen in love with. I didn't even know if the memories there were real, everything had been tarnished with his infidelity.

'Yeah, he packed up some stuff. I think he was drunk, if I'm honest.' Chris grimaced.

I shook my head, unable to hide my disgust. It didn't surprise me. Ryan had no idea how he was going to fix his problem so instead had hit the bottle to block everything out. 'I'm sorry, I hope he wasn't rude to you?'

'No, he didn't really speak, he was only here for half an hour and left with a couple of bags. I wasn't sure if I should mention it?'

'I'm glad you did, thank you.'

'Anyway, we're all done here, ready for the decorators. I'll liaise with the insurers, but it's been a pleasure working with you.' He offered his hand to shake, which I accepted gratefully. He'd done a sterling job and I wouldn't hesitate to recommend him. Once the place had a fresh lick of paint and new carpets, it would be good to go. At least it no longer smelt like a bonfire had been put out in the lounge; now, the only lingering scent was bleach.

I said goodbye to Chris and locked the door behind him. I hated being in the house on my own now, but had a quick check upstairs to find Ryan had almost emptied the place of his belongings. Perhaps his parents had returned from Cornwall and he'd taken his stuff there. I saw my jewellery box had been riffled through and some of my dad's old records taken. I'd forgotten some of the older ones were worth a bit of money and I imagined Ryan in his desperation had torn through the house appraising everything he thought he could sell, although it wouldn't amount to nearly enough.

Anger surged through me, how dare he steal my things, precious items of sentimental value I'd wanted to keep. That bastard. In a fleeting moment of rage, I hoped the loan shark would arrange a hiding he wouldn't forget. I regretted it as soon as it entered my mind, but I never wanted to see Ryan again.

Knowing how I couldn't wait to be free of my marriage, Mum had given me the money to pay for the annulment and I'd left the form on the kitchen table for Ryan to sign in case he came back. Surprisingly, it was still there but now with his signature on it. No doubt a guilty gesture of goodwill after taking my dad's records. I'd expected him to put up more of a fight, but maybe he'd come to the conclusion, as had I, that our marriage was a lost cause. I tapped the completed form against my chin, if it was posted today, it wouldn't be long before I'd officially be Kelly Quinn again. Kelly Carbon would be dead and buried.

Without wanting to hang around any longer, I locked up and went home to get out of my dog walking clothes, which were covered in muddy paw prints and hair. I often took them to Grattons Park where there was a small stream with stepping stones to cross and, no matter what the weather, some of the pack would always go in for a swim. Eventually when they'd emerge racing over for a treat, I'd get smothered in smelly water and silt. So when I arrived back at Mum's looking forward to a hot shower and found her sitting at the table drinking tea with Ryan, my heart sank.

39

'What are you doing here?' I slung my keys on the kitchen side with a clatter. The real question I wanted to ask was why had Mum let him in? On the side, I saw two bunches of supermarket-bought white roses.

Ryan followed my gaze and jumped up to hold one out to me. 'I brought these round, for you and your mum, to apologise.'

At least he looked sober, beard trimmed with fresh clothes on and not slurring his words. Perhaps he'd finished his drunken wallowing and was deciding to confront his problems head on. Although how, I had no idea. Perhaps he thought if he'd signed the annulment form, then I'd no longer see him as a threat.

'Thank you,' I replied stiffly.

Mum gave me a pointed look before getting to her feet. 'I'll give you two a bit of space.' She left the room and I heard her footsteps padding up the stairs.

'Did you get the form?' Ryan lifted the mug to his lips, draining his tea.

'I did, thank you.'

'You don't have to post it. That's why I'm here.'

I gave a slow nod, realisation hitting, he was trying to worm his way back in.

'We don't have to end things, we can move on, sell the house, buy somewhere new. What's to stop us? What if we went to counselling, started over? I can make it up to you, Kel, I know I can.' He was like a broken record. I was sure he'd accepted we were over, but here he was with his last-ditch attempt to save our marriage.

'And what about when Liza's baby arrives, what then? I mean, does she even know you're here?'

'We're not together, I haven't seen her.'

I laughed mirthlessly. So poor Liza had been abandoned by both prospective fathers of her baby. I had no doubt Ryan was hedging his bets. As soon as he knew there was no moving forward with me, he'd crawl back to her declaring his undying love. Well she was welcome to him, in fact they deserved each other. 'I don't trust a single word coming out of your mouth, Ryan. I'm sending that form today; the sooner we're divorced, the better, and we can both move on with our lives.' It was a lie; I'd probably missed the last post of the day unless I went into town, but I wanted Ryan to know how serious I was.

He slumped down in his seat like a petulant child. 'You're making a terrible mistake.'

'You made that when you slept with Liza,' I shot back. 'Now please leave.'

Silence stretched out between us, but he made no move to get up.

'Your mum said she might be able to help, she has some savings.'

My jaw twitched, teething grinding together. 'That's why you really came, isn't it, still trying to dig yourself out of the pit you're in. Get out!' I screamed at Ryan, pulling him out of the seat and shoving him towards the door.

In a flash, he turned, pushing me backwards onto the table. 'Get the fuck off me.' Rearranging his shirt where I'd bunched it up, he walked towards the door.

'Arsehole,' I shouted, throwing the empty mug towards him and watching it bounce on the carpet and split in two before it reached its intended target.

By the time Mum descended the stairs, her mouth agape, Ryan had gone, the front door swinging open. 'What happened?'

'Why did you let him in? God, Mum, he gives you his sob story and you just roll over. You're not giving him a bloody penny!'

'I know, I'm sorry.' She collected the mug fragments and closed the front door. 'He's my son-in-law too.'

'He's trying to take advantage of you.' I slumped forwards, elbows on the kitchen table, my head in my hands.

'I'm sorry, love.' Mum was at my side in an instant.

'I'm scared, what if they come back and destroy the house, or worse, they find him? They aren't messing around.'

'Haven't the police found the arsonists?'

'No.' Mum didn't know about the assault at the house and I wanted to keep it that way. It was idiotic not going to the police and she'd tell me so. That guy had hurt us, my chin still bore the bruise and Ryan's shoulder had been dislocated. He'd needed hospital treatment, but it could have been so much worse. Who knew what lengths the pockmarked man would go to come Friday.

'What about the bank?'

I laughed at mum's suggestion. 'They won't lend him any more, we're already up to our eyes in debt.'

'*We?*' Mum asked, her eyebrows shooting to her hairline.

'He borrowed against the house and forged my signature.' I sighed, it was another piece of information I hadn't disclosed to Mum and her expression said it all.

Wordlessly, she moved to the kettle to make some tea. I could see her chewing the inside of her cheek, seething for me and the havoc her son-in-law had caused. Had she known, I doubted she would have invited him in.

His visit had unsettled me and not even a hot shower or late-evening call from Nico made me any calmer. Now I'd burdened my mum too when she already had enough going on. Namely how we'd pay for Dad's care without Ryan's help. The police hadn't been in touch and I doubted they'd done more than call the number on the business card, but then they had no idea how much danger Ryan was in and that it could extend to me too. He had one more day to make the payment before they came looking for him and there was no way he was going to raise the money in time. Despite that, I had no choice but to keep going; I'd been told the decorators would arrive on Friday, the carpet laid early next week and I had a business to run.

On Thursday morning, I got up at seven, showered and put on my dog walking clothes before jumping in the van with a thermos of coffee to start my rounds. I had four dogs to collect for their eight-thirty walk and the weather was dry but early for it to be cool enough for them to have a good run so. Once I'd collected Bessie the chocolate Labrador, Beau the Maltese terrier, Snoopy the beagle and Arthur the pug, I made my way to Tilgate Park for a walk around the lake. All of the dogs were well behaved and remained by my side, helped by a pot of diced cocktail sausages I kept in my pocket, stopping every so often to call them back for a treat.

The sun shimmered off the lake and it was quiet at that time of the morning, with the exception of joggers and other dog walkers. I bumped into Michelle halfway round and stopped for a quick chat while my dogs played happily with her group.

'How's the house coming along?' she asked.

'Not bad actually, the decorators are coming tomorrow, so I just need a new carpet. Once that's done, then we're ready for sale.'

'That's great, and the annulment?'

'It's signed and ready to post this afternoon when I get off work.' Only now did I remember I'd left it on Mum's kitchen worktop.

Michelle rubbed my arm, her face a picture of sympathy, at a loss for words.

'Don't worry, I'll be okay. I'm excited to get started on our new venture once the house is sorted.' Ever the optimist, I had to cling on to believing I'd get through it.

'Where are you doing your eleven o'clock?' Michelle asked, referring to the next walk of the day.

'Grattons Park, it's going to be a warm one and I'm sure they'll want a dip in the stream.'

'Sounds like a good idea, I might see you there.'

We said our goodbyes and headed off in different directions, me back to the van to take the dogs home and Michelle continuing her walk. Once I'd dropped the dogs off, I stopped to get some petrol, my skin prickling as a black Audi pulled in at the pump behind me. I stayed in the van as a familiar figure got out and walked past straight into the shop without getting any petrol. Shit! Frozen rigid, I couldn't move until I regained control of my body and scooted lower in my seat ensuring I was barely visible through the window. Was it him or just another burly man in a black Audi?

My heart raced yet I remained motionless until he came out carrying a can of Monster and a packet of cigarettes and then I was certain it was the man who'd attacked Ryan. Had he followed me here or was he just making himself known? A subtle reminder that payment was due. I waited for a tap on the window, my mouth devoid of moisture but he headed straight back to the car, getting in and driving around me without so much as a glance in my direction.

40

When I could finally move, I got out and filled the van with shaking hands, fumbling with my phone to pay at the till, keeping one eye on the forecourt in case he came back. It had to be a coincidence he was there; payment wasn't due until tomorrow and it wasn't as if I knew where Ryan was any more than he did.

Ten minutes later when I left the petrol station, I didn't spot the Audi despite looking in all my mirrors every few seconds for the familiar black car. Paranoia wove its way through my skin, leaving me ice cold until I reached Boycie's house for my next collection.

Before I'd even swung my legs out of the open van door, a shadow loomed large, blocking out the sun. A meaty hand lurched forwards, gripping beneath my armpit, and yanking me swiftly from the car and onto the kerb in one fluid movement. I tried to let out a scream, my knees buckling when I recognised the cultivated beard and pockmarked skin, but before I could, a palm clamped heavily across my nose and mouth. My chest erupted in a volcano of utter panic.

Pressed tightly against him, my back hard against his chest, he dragged me the few steps from my van with ease, as though we were one body moving together. I glared at each window at Boycie's house, despite knowing no one was home to witness the assault, no one to call the police. I had to pray a neighbour in the quiet cul-de-sac might at least have heard a scuffle. Ignoring my struggling, the man emitted a raspy chuckle, his even breath ruffling my hair as though I was as much of a threat as a toddler in the midst of a tantrum. I kicked my legs out, vying for purchase on the concrete, but his grip tightened still, a vice against my ribs. Easily twice the size of me, I was no physical match for him. My brain fired with useless self-defence moves I couldn't execute.

In a split second, I was roughly deposited in the boot of the Audi and cloaked in darkness as soon as the lid slammed down. Terror pelted my body, my worst nightmare become a reality. I was trapped, at the mercy of a monster, and no one knew where I was. My phone was still in the cab of the van and I had nothing in my pockets except for cocktail sausages and poo bags. None of which would help me escape.

The engine started and I thumped the metal coffin, screaming at the top of my lungs until loud rap music flooded the car, drowning me out. Bass reverberated through my body as he threw the car around every corner, tossing me around the tiny space. I bore the brunt of each bump and pothole, reaching out to try to feel around for anything I could use as a weapon. By the time he stopped, my body was battered and bruised and my hands empty.

Sunlight assaulted my eyes when the boot was raised and I barely had time to inhale as the man I'd had nightmares about for days wrenched me out onto the concrete. I landed hard on my side at his feet as dust and grit flew into my eyes. Before I could react, he was already pulling me upright, a tight smile stretched across his lips.

'Hello again, Kelly,' he whispered low into my ear as he marched me forward. My feet dragged behind as though I was a rag doll.

It took a few seconds to get my bearings, for my eyes to adjust. I was disorientated, initially not recognising where he'd taken me until we passed through familiar gates onto a wide concourse housing rows of shipping containers. He'd brought me to the edge of Crawley, where residential areas made way for industrial units leading towards the airport.

When Ryan and Bobby had started their business, they'd rented a container to use as storage as it worked out cheaper than the warehouse space they'd looked at. Bobby had set up a desk at the far end with the intention to create a makeshift office, but there was no electricity. The last time I'd visited, it was a mess of paperwork, invoices and orders yet to be filed, so I could well believe Bobby's claims the admin side of the business was a mess. The rest of the space was a dumping ground, a collection of copper pipes, tools and a variety of cisterns, basins and even a lone bathtub that had been removed during a refit but was too good to dump.

Their container was the third in on the second row and had seen better days. Originally painted a navy blue, it was now chipped, exposing spots of rust with a variety of dents along one side. As the loan shark dragged me towards it, I tried to shrug out of his grip, planning to make a run for it as he stopped at the door. With his free hand, he used a crowbar to force the large padlock securing the entrance, but as I tried to twist away, he tightened his hold on me, fingers digging into the muscles of my arm until I howled. No one was around to hear my cries; the Audi had been the only car I'd seen on site. The lot was empty, but that was no surprise, it was the wrong time of day for people to be using their lock-ups.

I held on to a slither of hope, surely Bobby would be by at some point, to drop off tools or empty his van once he'd finished work, although that could be hours yet. It wouldn't be long before I had calls from dog owners wanting to know why I hadn't collected their babies to take them out for their daily walk. Would Michelle get in touch if she didn't see me as planned? If she knew I hadn't picked the dogs up she'd certainly raise the alarm, although no one would guess I was here.

Once the door was open, he shoved me inside the dark container, the entrance left ajar for light.

'Where's Ryan?' I asked, turning towards him, his huge bulk blocking the only exit. Surely this was about my husband, not me.

'Plenty of time to worry about him. Let's have a little fun first, just us.'

My breath caught in my throat. The kidnapping was only the start, this was where the real nightmare began. Free from his vice-like grip, I lurched towards a wrench discarded on the floor, but he was too quick, grabbing a fistful of hair and jerking me backwards. I screamed as the hair tore from my scalp, but he slammed me into an upturned cistern. I crawled on my hands and knees, winded, gasping for air, glancing up only to see an oncoming fist.

I wasn't sure how long I was out for, but when I came to, the room was dark, with only a faint outline of light around the metal door. My cheek was on fire and a metallic taste lingered in my mouth. I ran my tongue over my teeth, checking they were still there as warm liquid pooled on my tongue. My wrists and ankles were bound to a dilapidated chair on which I'd been sat facing the door and I groaned as pain thundered up my back, kidneys bruised from landing awkwardly on the porcelain. It hurt to breathe and silence hung in the musty air. Where had he gone? Had he left me here to rot? I had visions of being found days later, rats nibbling at my dehydrated carcass. Maybe that would be preferable to him coming back. I had to get out of here! I cast my eyes around the gloom, looking for anything that might help me escape my prison.

Every part of my body began to shake, even my teeth chattered as adrenaline took hold, pulse accelerating as the door swung open and the shape of my kidnapper blocked the sweet daylight. He carried a long bag, much like Ryan had for his tools, and sweat glinted on his forehead. Panic overwhelmed me and I began to hyperventilate.

'Please,' I begged, as the man stepped inside and took a photo of me with his phone.

'I thought Ryan could do with a little incentive, but I'll save that for later.'

What was he going to do to me? I struggled against my restraints and tried to stand with the chair but couldn't leverage my weight enough to lift it off the ground.

'Help,' I screamed as loud as I could, hoping someone would hear. It lasted barely a second before the man slapped me so hard I saw stars. Roughly tying a dirty rag around my face which wrenched my lips apart and pulled at the flesh of my cheeks, the smell of oil or grease was overpowering and I tried hard not to vomit.

'All that screaming isn't going to help.' His voice was hard and carried no emotion as though he was totally detached from the situation.

With my ears ringing, I watched as he retrieved a small lantern from his bag, winding the lever around at speed until it flickered on, illuminating the room in harsh clinical light before he closed the door to my escape, trapping us both inside. I knew the level of violence this man was capable of; he didn't hesitate to strike out even when not provoked and I shuddered at what his intentions were.

'Now, let's send some messages.' Holding my phone out to my face I briefly saw the screen unlock, the wallpaper of me and Ryan in happier days before he whisked it away and began tapping.

So he had taken my phone from the van. It gave me a glimmer of hope until he spoke.

'I'm staying at the Saxon Road tonight to sort some things with Ryan. See you tomorrow. Love Kelly,' the man said slowly as he typed out each word, like he was announcing a telegram. 'That's for your mum. Shall I send the same to your sister? We wouldn't want anyone disturbing us.'

My mind whirled. How did he know who my sister was and how did he know I wasn't living at the house?

A sneer lifted his scarred face as he read my expression. 'I've been watching you, and Ryan. I know where you live, that your sister is called Ruby and that your dad is wasting away in a care home your mum stuck him in.'

I shook my head furiously at the mention of my dad, pulling against the cable ties and rocking the chair, but all the man did was laugh at my pitiful efforts. Trying to shout was fruitless, the noise was garbled, but still I continued, spluttering onto the rag.

'Let's switch this off.' He put my phone on the table behind me, just out of reach. The hairs on the back of my neck stood to attention as he moved around the chair, resting a large hand on each of my shoulders, massaging gently. 'Ryan is a silly boy to let a prize like you go.' He licked his lips beside my ear and my insides shrivelled. The loan shark stroked his fingers over my hair, leaning down to inhale deeply, rubbing strands between his fingers.

I whimpered, unable to contain the terror rising within me, unsure how long I could hold my bladder.

'It's okay, darlin', we've got plenty of time to get to know each other first.'

41

As he stretched the neck of my T-shirt over my shoulder, the seams ripping to expose my bra strap, I was saved by the sound of his phone ringing in his back pocket. He removed his hands from my skin, a short reprieve from his slimy touch, and fumbled for the phone.

'Yeah,' he answered gruffly, pausing to listen. 'I've got her.' Those three words made my stomach sink.

While he was distracted, I looked around the container for anything that might help me escape, although I was limited, unable to reach anything with my hands tied. He could do whatever he wanted to me and I couldn't defend myself. The thought had me paralysed.

I had to pray someone had seen him take me and report it, but the cul-de-sac where I collected Boycie was quiet, I rarely saw anyone when I picked him up. Everyone was at work, plus it had all happened in seconds and I didn't even get a chance to scream.

'He's where? Okay, I'll be right there.' He disconnected and I snapped back to the present.

He who?

'Don't go anywhere, okay.' He laughed at his own joke, pocketed his phone and retrieved his car keys from his jeans before pushing open the container door.

I tried to shout for help, but it was useless with the rag in my mouth. The door swung shut and the latch was put across. Even if I could get to the door, I wouldn't be able to open it. From afar, I heard an engine start and rumble away, then the only sound was my heart thudding against my chest. I was alone again.

A temporary wave of relief washed over me that, despite my bruises, of which I knew there were plenty, I'd been relatively unharmed. I had to grab the opportunity to escape while he was gone. My phone lay less than three feet away from me and I fruitlessly struggled against the cable ties, but they were too tight. Instead I concentrated on trying to shuffle the chair, gaining purchase on the ground and inching it backwards, one little jump at a time. It seemed to take forever, but finally I bumped against the table. Perspiration massed in the small of my back, the shipping container like a sweatbox in the sun with no flow-through of air. Pausing to conserve my energy, I focused on shifting the chair around one hundred and eighty degrees until finally I had eyes on my phone.

Leaning forwards, I craned my neck to drag it towards the edge of the table with my chin. The bastard had put it face down and even without the gag, no amount of summoning Siri would wake it. How on earth was I supposed to turn it over or switch it on with no hands?

I strained at the gag, trying to push it out of my mouth with my tongue but made little headway, it had been tied too tight. Exhausted and beaten, I slumped forwards and cried with frustration, letting it all out until the gag was sodden with tears and saliva. Time ticked on, although I had no idea how much had passed or when my captor would be back. All my efforts had been fruitless, was it better to give in and accept my fate?

A headache rumbled at my temples and I knew it was dehydration. The container was like a sauna and my T-shirt was now soaked in sweat, but I couldn't give up. I had to use the time I'd been given; it would be senseless not to.

Scanning the desk for something that would help, I scowled at the piles of invoices that would be no use to me. On second glance, I spotted the table leg had metal edging running up it. Part of it had come away from the wood and about five centimetres stuck out at a slight angle. It had to be worth a shot.

Using the last of my energy to turn the chair again, I tried to contort my arm to raise the tie high enough to make contact. The muscles in my shoulder screamed at me, but I persevered until, with a jolt, the cable tie caught on the metal. It flicked off straight away, but if I could get the angle right, it might be sharp enough to cut the plastic.

It took five attempts and three small lacerations to my wrist before the plastic gave and one hand was free. I scrabbled for my phone, but it slid from my grasp, blood and sweat making my hand slick. I let out a howl, silently praying to the lord above that luck was on my side. I'd been struggling for ages and the loan shark could be back any minute. I had no idea where he'd gone, although deep in my gut I knew it was about Ryan.

The phone had fallen out of reach on the floor, but before I could get to it, I had to free my ankles. It was either that or try to tip the chair over.

Engine noise from outside stopped me dead and I froze, listening. He was back. No, it was too soon. Tears clouded my vision and my chest heaved with panic. There was no time, I bounced the chair back to where it had originally been and positioned my wrist to look like it was still tied. If nothing else, I had the element of surprise and when the loan shark was least expecting it, I'd strike. I'd scratch his goddamn eyes out before I'd let him touch me again. I counted the seconds in my head until the latch was pulled and the door swung open.

'It's hotter than the devil's ball sack in here.'

I trembled as he stepped over the threshold, gratefully accepting the breeze the open door swept in. My free hand quivered as I tried to keep it still, to look like it was tied.

'Well, the good news is we've got Ryan. The bad news is he still hasn't raised the funds. Even me showing him the lovely photo I took of you didn't spark any bright ideas.'

I lowered my head. We were going to die, our lives worth a measly twenty grand when it came down to it.

'Unless, that is, you can get it?'

I swallowed the lump in my throat, not bothering to raise my eyes to him. Where could I get it from? I couldn't involve my mum, not that she had it anyway, and no bank would lend it to me.

'That's a shame.'

I heard him walking around, perusing the container, likely to see if there was anything worth taking. Beads of sweat ran down my brow, willing him to come closer so I could lash out but terrified at the prospect.

'So what am I going to do with you?' He sounded like he was talking to a child, yet his tone was still menacing.

I lifted my head, shaking it slightly, begging with my eyes. He bit his lip and knelt in front of me, running his hands up my thighs. Every muscle in my body tensed the higher he went, stopping an inch away from my crotch. His touch me made me want to vomit, but I couldn't avert my eyes, waiting for my chance.

'I don't think we need these anymore.' He clipped at the two ties securing my ankles.

Now was my chance. If he was going to cut at the ties of my wrist next, he might go for the one that was free first, then the element of surprise was gone. His hands held my calves, massaging, looking up at me with those hollow eyes before his gaze travelled down my body in a way that made me want to wash myself in bleach. Reaching the floor, he caught a glimpse of the phone that had moved from the table to the floor, his brow furrowing. It was now or never.

Curling my fingers into a fist, I swung my free hand up, connecting with his jaw. It was enough to unbalance him, but I only managed a step towards the door, dragging the chair with me, before he was on me, throwing me back towards the desk until I was straddled over it, the chair on its side.

'You'll pay for that,' he breathed down my neck, ripping the waistband of my leggings, exposing my underwear before kicking my ankles apart. He forced my face down onto the cool wood and paper glued itself to my cheek. I closed my eyes, waiting for what was to come. What I'd known was going to happen as soon as he'd brought me here. Every woman's worst nightmare. When the chink of his belt loosening sounded, fear took over and urine ran down my leg, puddling at my foot.

42

'Fucking pig,' he yelled, stepping backwards, no longer pressed against me, but still holding me down over the table. Not wanting to get any urine on him, the disgust was evident in his voice.

Momentarily, I was released, but I couldn't bring myself to stand or move, except to reach around and tug my soaking leggings up to cover my modesty. It hadn't been on purpose, my bladder releasing, more a visceral reaction, yet it seemed my bodily function had ruined the moment and for that I'd be eternally grateful. Grabbing my shoulder, he righted the chair and pushed me back onto it.

'Stay,' he barked, as he retrieved more cable ties from his bag, holding them loosely in his hand. His eyes were no longer playful and wolfish, the sneer entirely gone. All of the fun he was having playing with me had stopped, now he appeared like stone.

He paused to light a cigarette, plumes of smoke wafted above our heads as he glared at me, drawing deeply. My heart was beating so fast I was sure, it would burst from the cavity, knowing what punishment was coming would be horrific. He fastened his belt and I saw his mind working, planning what he was going to do, but then both of us were disturbed by a fumbling outside the door. The latch squeaking as it slid across, followed by a clatter onto the ground. Was that the padlock?

A voice I recognised swore before the door swung open.

'Holy fuck!' Bobby was as motionless as a statue halfway over the threshold.

I raised my free hand and pulled the gag out of my mouth. Relief hitting me like a tsunami. 'Help me,' I cried.

'Al, what the fuck are you doing?' he said, his voice quivering as he gestured to me.

My eyes darted from the loan shark back to Bobby, the initial shroud of confusion lifting. 'No, no, no,' I mumbled, but they both ignored me.

'Jesus, I didn't think it was going to go this far.' Bobby put his hands behind his head and blew air out through his cheeks, turning to look at the mess Al had made.

'Deano's gotta be paid, man,' Al replied with a shrug. His nonchalance sent a chill through me. He was so desensitised to the violence he'd committed.

I still didn't know if it was over or if Bobby was in on it. The thought made me shrink back in the chair. There was no way I'd be able to fight off two of them.

Bobby's face paled. 'For fuck's sake, I'll pay!' Already, he was pulling his phone from the back pocket of his dirty work jeans with trembling hands. 'This has to stop.'

I kept my eyes fixed on Bobby as he tapped at his phone, opening his banking app and inputting the details to make a transfer. So he did have the money after all.

'You know him?' I didn't want to believe it. Not Bobby, not our friend. 'You fucking know him?' I yelled, no longer able to control the eruption.

'The Bobster?' Al slapped Bobby on the shoulder in a friendly yet still intimidating gesture. 'Course I do.'

The weight of Al's admission dawned on me; Ryan had been set up from the start.

'He suggested us to Ryan,' Al said, rolling down his shirt-sleeves like he'd finished his shift for the day, 'because he knows we're good lenders, no questions asked. The only rule is you pay when you're due. Something your husband failed to do.'

I closed my eyes, head whirling. When I opened them, Bobby was looking straight at me, eyes pleading.

'I didn't know this would happen.'

'What *did* you think would happen?' I retorted, anger bubbling in my chest, temporarily distracting me from the pain and humiliation radiating through every inch of my flesh. 'Where is Ryan?' I asked. All my fear had evaporated now. Had it all been a ruse?

Al's eyes glinted and he tapped his nose like it was a secret he couldn't divulge. Unease flooded my chest.

'Don't hurt him,' I pleaded. 'Bobby paid his debt, it's over.'

'I say when it's over and I wouldn't give him too much of your pity. When I checked in on him earlier in the week, his solution was to bump you off and claim the life insurance.'

Nausea hit me like a gut punch. Almost drowning in the sea, clinging on to the edge inside the cave, the pillow over my face and the gas leak. Had that all been part of Ryan's plan? If I'd been closer in the car park, would he have pushed me over the railing?

'The problem now is you. If I let you go, are you going to go back home like a good little girl and forget all this ever happened?'

My eyes blurred with vengeful tears, but I nodded to pacify him. I'd do no such thing. As soon as I was free, I was calling the police.

'I'm not so sure,' Al emitted a low growl.

'She will,' Bobby assured on my behalf.

'If you say so, pal, and you better hope she does.' Al patted Bobby's shoulder. 'Pleasure doing business with you.'

Without another word, he left and a sob erupted from my lips.

43

'You can't call anyone, Kel; you don't know these people. They're ruthless.' Bobby strode towards me with a small saw he grabbed from the floor.

'Look at me, Bobby, look what he did to me.' Another sob burst out of me and I crumpled onto the floor as soon as my remaining wrist was cut free.

'I'm sorry, I'm so sorry. I didn't know he'd do this. You weren't supposed to get involved, Kelly,' Bobby's eyes darkened, 'and if Ryan had paid on time, then he wouldn't have come for you. This is his fault.'

'You recommended them!' I snapped. 'And how was he supposed to pay them, with what? Where was he supposed to magic the money from, Bobby?' I added, but he shrugged.

'He said he wanted money to pay the supplier and couldn't borrow any more from the bank.' Bobby scowled. 'Perhaps if he wasn't screwing my wife behind my back, I might have thought twice. I knew they were a bit shady, but I had no idea they would go to this extreme!'

'But you had money, you just paid him.' I stuck out my hand as if Al was still inside the container.

'Yeah, my money. I was saving to buy Ryan out of the business. I told you, he's a liability.'

'Until you found out he was shagging Liza and thought you'd get him to sign over the business for nothing.'

'He practically ran it into the ground, Kelly. Another few months and we would have gone into administration. Save your sympathy for someone else, Al just said he was planning to kill you!' Bobby's face was incredulous, his frustration mounting.

'Al said they had him.' I picked my phone up from the floor and impatiently waited for it to turn on, calling Ryan as soon as it did. The call went straight to voicemail. I urged Ryan to call me as soon as he got my message.

My legs were like jelly and I shrugged out of Bobby's grip as he helped me stand, holding on to the table for support. I was too angry to accept any support from him. My damp leggings clung to me like glue and I was filthy with sweat, dirt and humiliation.

'We've got to call the police.'

The bright mid-afternoon sun was acid to my eyes as we left the container, my prison for what seemed like hours. Cortisol which had been surging around my system left me exhausted with its withdrawal, but the nightmare wasn't over. The mess Ryan had caused spread out so much further than our marriage and I feared he was about to pay the ultimate price. I wanted more than anything to get on a plane back to Crete, to run away, back into the safe, warm arms of Nico.

It was a shock to look at my reflection in the sun visor mirror, my face smudged with blood and dirt. Cheek red and swollen, with welts at the corners of my mouth from the gag.

'We have to call the police,' I repeated as we both sat motionless in the front of Bobby's van, my seat covered in a plastic bag to save the upholstery. The last thing I'd wanted to do was get in. I could no longer trust Bobby but there was no other choice and I left the door open in case I needed a quick getaway. My skin was covered in grime and I wanted a shower more than anything, but Ryan's life could be hanging in the balance.

'They'll come for you if you do.' Bobby's voice was quiet, resigned, as though he knew no amount of arguing would change my mind.

'I'll take my chances,' I said, tapping 999 into my phone and making the call.

* * *

We stayed until the police arrived. Despite my protestation, an ambulance was called to assess my injuries. A portly paramedic with dyed orange hair applied a bandage to my wrist and cleaned my face. Most of my injuries were superficial, although she warned I'd likely be a lovely shade of purple by the morning. I felt like I'd been involved in a car crash, every part of my body tender to touch. I was embarrassed, paranoid I smelt of urine, but no one passed comment. Uniformed officers took our statements while the shipping container was cordoned off. I refused to go to the police station despite numerous requests but emphasised Ryan Carbon had to be found and fast.

Bobby barely gave the police any information. Al was a man he'd come across in the pub, he knew nothing about him other than he worked for a loan shark. He didn't know why Ryan had got involved with him, that he must have been desperate for cash to pay suppliers. He added he'd only come back to the shipping container to drop off his tools and found me there. I didn't care Bobby was saying as little as possible to try to save his own skin, despite Al's revelation, I wanted to make sure Ryan was found in one piece.

I'd given the police everything, his mobile number, photos and all of the relevant addresses I could think of. Plus the photo of the black Audi with partially obscured numberplate. When they finally let us leave the scene, I gave Bobby directions to the location of my van. I was desperate to go home, wanting nothing more than to shower and crawl into bed, the curtains closed, with a packet of ibuprofen and a bottle of wine.

'I never want to see you again,' I said when Bobby parked outside Boycie's house. It was the first time we'd spoken since he'd started driving. I didn't wait for a reply, getting out of his van and into mine, the keys still in the ignition and the familiar doggy smell a comfort.

I locked my doors and drove back to Mum's, knowing the house would be empty. She would have finished her shift at the chemist and gone straight to Parkgate to give dad his dinner. I stood in the shower for a while, watching the tray fill with dirt and blood, gingerly washing my skin where the bruises would flourish. Once out, I popped some painkillers and sat in my towel, dialling Ryan's number on repeat. I must have called over twenty times, but each time it went to voicemail.

Frustrated at being unable to get hold of him, I called all the dog owners I'd failed to walk that day, explaining I'd had a family emergency before apologising profusely and offering their next walk for free. Being unreliable was bad for business and I couldn't afford to lose any clients. Most of them were under-standing and I promised it wouldn't happen again. Michelle had messaged too, checking in after not seeing me at Grattons Park, and I gave her the same explanation and she offered to take on my walks for the next few days. I readily agreed.

Alone in the house, I stood naked in front of the mirror in my old bedroom, assessing the damage. My back was already starting to colour and my face didn't look so hot either, although the swelling was going down thanks to the ibuprofen. My wrists were sore from being bound and the rest of my body felt like I'd been hit by a train, so I took time to douse myself in arnica cream and Savlon.

Pulling on clean pyjamas, I drew the curtains and crawled into bed, dialling Ryan again to no avail and glugging Sauvignon Blanc straight from the bottle until my head was even more fuzzy. Al's revelation had shaken me to the core, but I knew in my gut it was true. Was Ryan so desperate for money that ending my life was the only option, his only way out? Was it a case of self-preservation: me or him?

I cried into the bottle, holding my phone until a text came through from Ruby containing only question marks. I realised she was responding to the message Al had sent from my phone, likely wondering why I'd bother to send her a text with my plans when we weren't speaking. I didn't reply. How much would Bobby tell her of what happened today? It didn't matter, I wanted nothing more to do with either of them. Mum had replied with a thumbs up emoji to Al's message so I knew she wouldn't rush home if she didn't think I'd be here. It would give me a few hours to rest and pray the police found Al before he did something to Ryan that couldn't be undone.

Ryan's bloated lifeless body was found at five o'clock on Friday morning, fully clothed and face down in the lake I'd walked around the morning of my abduction. Tilgate Park was a picturesque nature reserve where locals flocked in the summer months and I pitied the jogger out on her morning run who would forever be haunted by her discovery of his translucent skin and empty staring eyes after she'd tried to roll him out of the water. Tarnished by violence, it would never be the same place for her again, or for me either.

Apparently, initial reports were that there was barely a mark on Ryan and they assumed it was a drowning. That he'd somehow stumbled into the lake and got into difficulty. Even if it was drowning, I knew Al had been behind it. Had Ryan been forced to crumple into the tiny boot of the Audi like I'd been? Were we only yards apart when Al came back to the container or was he already dead by then? I'd never know.

A detective visited to break the news, waking the whole house up. Mum didn't even know I'd returned home, the bottle of wine combined with the exhaustion meant I'd been wiped out, sleeping straight through until the doorbell had rung. She was shocked at the sight of me emerging down the stairs, believing Al's text that I'd stayed at Saxon Road, horrified to learn of the trauma I'd suffered and wounded I hadn't sought her help. Overnight, my cheek had turned a watery purple, as had my back. The skin around my mouth was sore and inflamed, giving the Joker a good run for his money.

The detective told me they were still trying to locate Al and the Audi when I told them I was positive he was responsible for Ryan's demise. He'd had his wallet on him with his driving licence inside when he went into the water so they were quick to identify him on extraction. Mum and I sat, fingers curled around cups of tea neither of us could stomach, trying to take it in. My husband had lost his life because he owed money to some bad people and they were still out there. Al knew so much about me, my family, where Ryan and I lived, I wasn't sure I'd ever feel safe again. Despite the danger he'd put us in, my heart broke all over again. My husband, my childhood sweetheart, the man I'd adored once, was dead and never coming back.

Telling Dad was hard, he knew nothing about what had been going on, so Mum suggested we maintained it was an accident and my injuries were caused by a crash in the van. Guilt ate at me for lying to him, but it was important not to upset him too much.

Visiting Ryan's parents that same day to deliver the news would haunt me forever, with him being their only child, they fell apart. I told them the truth, that Ryan had borrowed some money from some dubious people and I believed they'd caught up with him. My injuries appalled them and they found my account hard to take in, but I promised to keep them updated with any further developments in the case, assuring them I'd be pushing the police to do their job and bring Al to justice.

A flurry of activity followed in the coming days. I had to

provide another statement: when I'd last seen Ryan and my movements the night he died. The fact I was home alone with no alibi didn't worry me. I was the victim of a crime, not the perpetrator of one. Shortly after my interview, I was assigned a sketch artist to comprise a likeness of Al, then asked to look through mugshots of possible suspects, but none matched the pockmarked face I saw every time I closed my eyes.

The Audi had been found on the edge of a council estate, burnt out with fake plates attached. It was no surprise to learn DAR Lending had no record at Companies House, the number on the business card I'd been given was no longer in service. Al and Deano, who I believed ran the business, had disappeared into thin air, but I couldn't deny I wasn't glad they had. Bobby's warning replayed often in my mind, they'd come after me if I contacted the police and I prayed they wouldn't take the risk. Perhaps that's why they had got rid of Ryan, maybe he knew too much?

Mum had found out via Ruby that Bobby had been questioned at length but had stuck to his story of not knowing Al except in passing. He didn't even know what Al stood for – Alan, Alex, Alfred, it could be anything – and he couldn't supply a last name. Apparently Ruby had moved back to her own flat, their relationship broken down since Bobby's involvement had been revealed. I had no desire to see either of them, despite Mum's pleading. Even our trips to visit Dad were carefully scheduled so we wouldn't bump into each other.

The form for the annulment sat redundant on the kitchen worktop by the kettle. I'd never got around to posting it so I became a widow, which meant Ryan's debts, the official ones, were now mine to pay. Ryan's death had left me in more of a mess than his dodgy dealings in life. I had no idea if his life insurance would cover it.

Even so, I mourned him, whatever his choices had been the last few months of his life. I couldn't understand how the man I'd loved had been willing to kill me to save his own skin, if what Al had said was true. Even if it was, he didn't deserve his fate and Bobby had blood on his hands. Everything had got out of control since his cheating had been discovered, events had spiralled and it reminded me how much darkness there was in the world.

A phone call from the detective looking after my case came a week later to let me know Ryan's death had been ruled accidental. He'd had a high volume of alcohol in his system and the official cause was drowning. Al had taken care not to inflict any obvious injuries and I could tell the police believed he might have taken his own life due to the amount of debt he'd racked up, despite my protestations. They assured me they'd keep searching for Al and Deano, but I held out little hope they'd find them. I often had visions of Al pouring vodka down Ryan's throat, forcing him to drink until he passed out. They wouldn't have even had to hold him under, he would have been at their mercy.

With the help of Ryan's parents, I arranged his funeral as soon as the body was released. Bobby and Ruby came to the service separately, both seated as far away from me and each other as possible. It boiled my blood that Bobby had come, knowing he was partly responsible, but not as much as when Liza strode in, wearing a skintight black dress which accentuated her growing bump. I hadn't given her a second thought this past week and guessed she'd seen the article about Ryan's death and subsequent funeral in the local paper but I wasn't going to cause a scene.

I clung to Mum like a shield, refusing to speak to any of them until Liza cornered me at the wake. Mascara stained her cheeks and her tan from Crete was now nothing but a memory. She looked washed out, hardly glowing in her second trimester. I expected to be hit by the wrath of her venomous tongue, but instead she was contrite.

'I'm sorry... about everything.'

I didn't know how to respond – was there any point in saying it was a little bit late to apologise? Instead I mumbled a thank you and turned to leave, but she gripped my forearm to stop me and I frowned down at her red talons digging into my skin.

'Wait, I wanted to tell you...' She paused, pulling in a long breath. 'Ryan and I only slept together a few times, always when he was drunk, and every time he regretted it straight away. I pursued him and blackmailed him when he rejected me, I told him I'd tell you we'd been at it for months if he didn't continue our affair.'

I gasped, causing the surrounding guests to stare in our direction.

Liza pulled me closer, whispering in my ear, her voice catching, 'I thought you should know the truth. You were right, I just wanted something I couldn't have, it was exciting, dangerous even, but I regret it all now.'

'When did it start?' I asked, the question had been burning a hole in my brain since their affair was uncovered.

'About seven months ago. We'd had that games night at ours, you'd passed out on the sofa and Bobby went to buy more alcohol... it just kind of happened.'

I sucked in air through my teeth. Even with Ryan gone, the stab of betrayal was painful to hear yet it saddened me that in a way he'd been a victim of Liza's persistent game of chase. He'd not solicited her affections.

'Is that why you came out to our honeymoon?'

'It's why I came, but it's not why Ryan invited us. He did that when he booked the trip months before that night, he thought it would be fun to bring us out just for a few days, a surprise for you. He'd never cheated on you before, what you had was real, and I was jealous. I flew out to try to rekindle the spark, to let him know it wasn't over for me.'

'But you had Bobby, he adored you,' I said, trying to make sense of it.

'Bobby loved the idea of me but not the reality. We hadn't been good for a while.'

'And the baby?' I asked, my voice splintering.

'I'm sure it's Bobby's.'

I took a step back, taking in Liza's black dress and blood-red lipstick, she was a viper in the nest. 'You deserve to be alone.' I shook my head in disgust before hitting the bar for a large glass of wine, plastering a polite smile on my face as well-wishers paid their respects. It infuriated me that if Liza hadn't been so jealous of what Ryan and I had, things could have been so different.

'We're going to head off now, love, thank you organising such a lovely service,' Linda, Ryan's mum, pulled me into an embrace a short time later. At least she was free from the knowledge of what her son had been up to. I'd not told her anything about the affair, although she'd been understandably upset when Ryan's death had been ruled an accident, knowing she wasn't going to get justice for her son. She didn't believe he'd committed suicide any more than I did. However, at least she could remember him as he'd always been, her cheeky boy who'd worked hard and married his childhood sweetheart. If only I had the same option.

I took a step back once she'd released me, addressing her and her husband Carl. 'Thank you, I hope I've given him a good send-off. It's lovely to see so many of his friends here.' I clasped my hands together, the wedding ring I'd put back on for the funeral felt alien on my finger.

'I can't believe I've lost my mum and my son in a matter of weeks,' Linda said, raising a tissue to dab her crinkled eyes.

'I'm so sorry for your loss,' I replied automatically as Carl wrapped his hand around Linda's shoulder.

'We need to speak to you about that. Linda's mum left Ryan her house in Cornwall, what with him being the only grandchild, so I guess it's yours now. We'll get the deeds sent over to you once we've emptied it.' Carl cleared his throat.

'Her house?' My jaw dropped. 'I couldn't, Carl. Please, you two should have it,' I stammered, it was too much. Worse still they had no idea how much our relationship had broken down before he died. I already felt like a fraud playing the heartbroken widow.

'It's what she wanted and I'm sure it's what Ryan would have wanted too. Keep it if you want a change of scene or sell it, it's entirely up to you.' Linda squeezed my hand and pulled me in for a final hug.

'Don't be a stranger, love.' Carl leaned in to kiss my cheek before guiding Linda towards the door.

EPILOGUE

'I'm confident it'll be off the market within a week, such a good location and the redecoration has been lovely.' The estate agent shook my hand, his palm clammy due to the extraordinary heat of late August, yet he was still trussed up in a shirt and tie.

'I hope so, preferably to a first-time buyer or someone with no chain,' I replied, keeping my fingers crossed that any sale would go through quickly.

'I have plenty of first-time buyers who'd snap my arm off for this place. I'll get straight on the phone as soon as I'm back.'

Bidding goodbye to the estate agent on the pavement, I took in the property Ryan and I had been so happy in, or so I'd thought. It had only been six weeks since our honeymoon, yet my whole world had turned on its axis. I was now a widow, up to my eyes in debt and ineligible for Ryan's life insurance because he'd missed some payments. It turned out he was a mess with finances at home as well as at work. Even once the property had sold, there would barely be any equity left once the bank had taken back what we – well, Ryan – had borrowed against the house. Plus, the additional loan for the wedding and my van would clear me out.

Mum had suggested I get a solicitor for the fraudulent paperwork Ryan had submitted with my faked signature on it, but I didn't want to drag it out for months, especially if it would delay the sale. It was important to me to keep Ryan's reputation intact, at least outside of our inner circle. It was hardly worth dragging him through the mud now, something which would cause his parents pain.

Although it would take a while to get back on my feet again, at least my slate would be clean and my credit rating improved. Once the house Ryan's nan had left him in Cornwall was sold, I'd be able to buy somewhere new. Living with Mum for the past six weeks had been both a comfort during the dark days but also a struggle. She hated letting me out of her sight, paranoid Al would seek revenge for me telling the police once I'd opened up about everything. I was grateful she'd taken such good care of me, but it was time to move out and get my life back.

At least I was back to being Miss Kelly Quinn and no longer Mrs Kelly Carbon. The name change helped me feel more like myself and I was ready to move on and put that tumultuous period of my life behind me, as much as I could. It had been hard to heal from the violence and the terror Al had bestowed even after the bruises had faded, knowing he'd taken Ryan's life, the husband who I'd loved but had betrayed me. I'd lost my best friend and my sister due to their selfish actions and it would take time for me to trust anyone past my parents again.

Dad was still at the care home, his condition unchanged, and we were grateful he wasn't in a decline. In a surprise turn of events, Mum received a call to let her know they'd had an anonymous donation of six months' worth of fees for his care. It may have been anonymous, but I knew Bobby was behind it, something to ease his guilt. I hadn't seen him since the funeral, unless you counted spotting his liveried van around town, but he'd tried to get in touch numerous times. I wasn't interested in his explanations or him seeking forgiveness, nothing would change what he did. Introducing Ryan to Al had unleashed a tragic chain of events which had resulted in him losing his life. Whether he liked it or not, he had blood on his hands.

I'd heard from Mum, via Ruby, that Liza had paid a fortune for a paternity test which I didn't even realise you could do before a baby was born. All they needed was a DNA sample from the prospective father, for which Bobby obliged, and a blood test from the mother. It turned out Liza had been right, her baby was Bobby's, not Ryan's, and despite planning to divorce, they intended to co-parent their child amicably. I was pleased Ruby had got shot of him and wasn't having to take on that baggage.

Mum had decided to downsize, accepting Dad was never going to return home and knowing in six months' time she'd have to find the fees to carry on with his care, admitting it hadn't been fair to rely on her daughters to help out. It made sense financially. It would be a new start for both of us. She was looking at a smaller house within walking distance to Parkgate so perhaps Dad could stay over occasionally. It meant she'd be able to give up one of her jobs, freeing up more time to spend with him.

Walkies was booming and I'd taken on more dogs since returning to work after Ryan's death, helping out Michelle, who had been overflowing with bookings. We regularly hired a secure field for our pups to run around in while we caught up on each other's lives. She was fast becoming my best friend, filling the void Liza and Ruby had left behind although I wasn't sure I'd ever fully let my guard down again. With a takeaway coffee in hand, we'd watch the dogs while firming plans to merge our businesses, something which had taken a back seat since Ryan's death. I was hoping to inject some money from the Cornwall house into opening a grooming parlour too, having been online to scope out possible premises in the area.

I'd heard from Janice too, a couple of long phone calls where I'd updated her on the events of the past six weeks while she listened in stunned silence. We'd planned to meet up in September for a shopping trip to London and I was looking forward to it. She would forever be the connection I'd made in Crete, the lovely lady who'd taken me under her wing when I'd needed it most – much like Nico had been my saviour that week too. He'd been the one good thing to come out of the chaos of the past couple of months.

I took one last look at the house and checked my watch. Nico's flight was landing in ten minutes, which gave me plenty of time to head to the airport and park before he got through passport control and baggage reclaim. Butterflies swarmed in my chest; I couldn't wait to see him. We'd stayed in contact, face-timing often, and he'd taken the leap and booked his ticket to backpack around Europe for a few months. I was thrilled to learn he was going to make England his first and last stop, so we could spend some time together. I didn't know if our holiday romance would translate to this part of the world, but I was excited to find out.

The sun streamed through the window as I got into the stifling van, switching the air conditioning on full blast as soon as I started the engine. It looked like we'd be having an Indian summer, which would in part make up for the soggy spring. At least Nico would be arriving on a day he'd be accustomed to the climate. I checked my reflection in the sun visor mirror, having made extra effort with my appearance knowing I was going to see him. Mum had made a show of making up the spare bedroom, but I was sure we'd squeeze into my single teenage bed just fine. She was looking forward to meeting the man who had given me a lifeline in what had been the darkest days of my life and I couldn't wait to wrap my arms around his neck and inhale him.

With a smile on my face, I put the van into gear and indicated to pull out of the parking space, leaving Saxon Road lighter than I had in weeks. Life was for living and I wasn't going to waste one more second. Not even the glimpse of a lone man parked on the opposite side of the street staring at me through his windshield would sour my good mood. Al and Deano were long gone, weren't they?

ACKNOWLEDGEMENTS

Firstly, a massive thank you to my readers. Without you these books wouldn't exist and it's such a privilege to share what I love doing most in the world with you. I appreciate every single message, every tweet and every mention on social media you take the time to write. It means more to me than you'll ever know.

To my wonderful husband who never complains about how many hours I spend locked away on my laptop, thank you for everything and especially giving me the time to write whilst picking up the slack at home. My beautiful teenage daughters who've both had a pretty tough year, your tenacity makes me so proud. I'm honoured to be your mum.

A huge mention to the fantastic team at Boldwood Books who have changed my life since their birth of publishing reimagined in 2019, I will forever be your loudest champion. Thank you for all that you do, especially my lovely editor Caroline Ridding, who is always there when I need her. Jade Craddock, my eagle-eyed copy editor, I cannot express how grateful I am for your help in shaping each book into the best it can be.

Last but by no means least, thanks Mum for being my first reader and number one fan. The new book will be coming soon, I promise.

ABOUT THE AUTHOR

Gemma Rogers was inspired to write gritty thrillers by a traumatic event in her past. Her debut novel Stalker, released in 2019, marked the beginning of her writing career. Gemma lives in West Sussex with her husband and two daughters.

Sign up to Gemma Rogers's newsletter to read the first chapter of her upcoming thriller!

Follow Gemma on social media:

facebook.com/GemmaRogersAuthor
x.com/gemmarogers79
bookbub.com/authors/gemma-rogers
instagram.com/gemmarogersauthor
tiktok.com/@gemmarogersauthor

ALSO BY GEMMA ROGERS

Stalker

The Secret

The Teacher

The Mistake

The Babysitter

The Feud

The Neighbour

The Flatmate

The Good Wife

The Honeymoon

THE

Murder

LIST

THE MURDER LIST IS A NEWSLETTER DEDICATED TO SPINE-CHILLING FICTION AND GRIPPING PAGE-TURNERS!

SIGN UP TO MAKE SURE YOU'RE ON OUR HIT LIST FOR EXCLUSIVE DEALS, AUTHOR CONTENT, AND COMPETITIONS.

SIGN UP TO OUR NEWSLETTER

BIT.LY/THEMURDERLISTNEWS

Boldwood

Boldwood Books is an award-winning fiction publishing company seeking out the best stories from around the world.

Find out more at www.boldwoodbooks.com

Join our reader community for brilliant books, competitions and offers!

Follow us
@BoldwoodBooks
@TheBoldBookClub

Sign up to our weekly deals newsletter

https://bit.ly/BoldwoodBNewsletter